P9-CAO-588

PENGUIN CRIME FICTION

DEATH OF THE OFFICE WITCH

Marlys Millhiser, a former regional vice-president
of the Mystery Writers of America, lives in Boulder,
Colorado. She has written seven other novels including *Murder at Moot Point*, in which Charlie and
Libby Greene were first introduced.

DEATH
OF THE
OFFICE
WITCH

Marlys Millhiser

PENGUIN BOOKS

PENGUIN BOOKS
Published by the Penguin Group
Penguin Books USA Inc., 375 Hudson Street, New York, New York 10014, U.S.A.
Penguin Books Ltd, 27 Wrights Lane, London W8 5TZ, England
Penguin Books Australia Ltd, Ringwood, Victoria, Australia
Penguin Books Canada Ltd, 10 Alcorn Avenue, Toronto, Ontario, Canada M4V 3B2
Penguin Books (N.Z.) Ltd, 182–190 Wairau Road, Auckland 10, New Zealand

Penguin Books Ltd, Registered Offices: Harmondsworth, Middlesex, England

First published in the United States of America by Otto Penzler Books in
association with Macmillan Publishing Company 1993
Published in Penguin Books 1995

3   5   7   9   10   8   6   4   2

PUBLISHER'S NOTE
This is a work of fiction. Names, characters, places, and incidents either are the
product of the author's imagination or are used fictitiously, and any resemblance to
actual persons, living or dead, events, or locales is entirely coincidental.

THE LIBRARY OF CONGRESS HAS CATALOGUED THE HARDCOVER AS
FOLLOWS:
Millhiser, Marlys.
Death of the Office Witch/by Marlys Millhiser.
p.   cm.
ISBN 1-883402-02-6 (hc.)
ISBN 0 14 02.4340 2 (pbk.)
1. Literary agents—California—Los Angeles—Fiction.   I. Title.
PS3563.I4225D4   1993
813'54—dc20   93–19365

Printed in the United States of America
Set in Janson

For Irene Webb
May she never have Charlie's problems.

Acknowledgments

I would like to thank Mae Woods, Irene Webb, Margaret Armen, Wendy Hornsby, Jim Stinson, and Carol and Bob Verhoef for their patience and assistance in preparing this story. Any errors or misinterpretations are mine and not theirs. And David Millhiser for maintaining his sense of humor while driving me all over the L.A. freeway system.

Death of the Office Witch

1

Charlie Greene turned off the engine and rolled down the car window. When her eyes began to water from the fumes, she rolled the damned thing back up again.

Palm fronds peeking out from an expensive neighborhood on the other side of a privacy fence were drooping in the freeway air, too. Orangy-red roofs of new clay tile showed between the fronds in slices. They relieved the bleakness of a rush hour morning with slashes of color.

Charlie punched the office on her car phone and tried hard not to think of two-hundred-dollar Rollerblades. She tapped on the gray Toyota's gray steering wheel.

Five lanes of traffic sat idling poisons into the air on Charlie's side of the road, while all the cars in the opposing lanes zoomed by unobstructed. She'd left the fog behind shortly after leaving Long Beach, now it was just the usual haze clouding the air. But the sun was beginning to heat up the car through it, causing Charlie's pantyhose to start sticking uncomfortably.

"Congdon and Morse Representation, Inc.," Gloria's New Jersey twang finally came over the line, and Charlie could hear the relentless soft click of the keyboard continue without hesitation. Anybody else would have left off the Inc., but not Gloria. Precise was Gloria.

"This is Charlie. I'm stuck in a grid on the 405 and won't

make the Universal breakfast on time. Can Richard cover for me?"

"He left already to do that, Charlie, swearingeh under his breath. Is it really gridlock, or just Libby?" Gloria's conceit at being unencumbered by children was only one of her irritating traits. Nothing encumbered Gloria but her fingernails. Long, fire-engine red, with different tiny fake jewels set into each one, they were Gloria's glory. "Or did something odd and unexplainable happen to you like I've been saying? I'm tellingeh you, Charlie, it can't be long now. I can feel it."

The only odd thing happening to me is Gloria Tuschman. "Is Larry in yet?"

Charlie dared to turn on the engine and the air conditioning, knowing she shouldn't keep throwing pollutants into the smog. But she needed to look good today.

"Everybody coming in this morning is in except you," Gloria pointed out ominously. "And everybody but me has left again on some errand or other." Larry, Charlie's assistant, had gone across the street to the Chevron to buy Gloria and himself Hostess Ding Dongs for their coffee break.

As soon as the receptionist started detailing the whereabouts of every last person at the office, Charlie cut her off. "I'll do my New York calling now and be in as soon as I can."

New York was three hours ahead of time, and it was a nightmare to reach everyone before they went home. Of course, Charlie had found it equally difficult getting hold of the West Coast when she'd worked in New York.

Charlie Greene was the literary agent for Congdon and Morse. She handled screenwriters for the agency and served as contact with East Coast book publishers. She managed to complete calls now to a literary agency and a New York producer, and leave a message at McMullins Publishing before the gridlock suddenly opened up as mysteriously as it had closed in. As usual, she didn't pass a wreck or a tow truck or any sign of road construction to account for the traffic holdup. And, as usual, she wasn't as fresh as she would like to have been when she reached the office.

A talent agency on Wilshire Boulevard in Beverly Hills, Congdon and Morse Representation, Inc. wasn't one of the best-known or more prestigious, but it had a few older stars on its roster, along with a fair number of up-and-comers. Although many more powerful agencies maintained their own imposing buildings, Congdon and Morse shared the fifth floor of the First Federal United Central Wilshire Bank of the Pacific building, a seven-story white stucco structure with black windows. Fortunately, tall palm tree stalks, sticking out of the sidewalk in front of it, didn't produce any small poofs of fronds until reaching the level of that fifth floor. The FFUCWB of P sat on a corner facing Wilshire with its drive-through banking across the side street, a paved alley running along the other side, its first floor halved in size to provide covered parking in back and two levels of parking under-neath.

Charlie waved away the parking valet, swooped the Toyota down into its own stall on the first level, took the elevators up to the fifth, followed the carpeted hall until she came to a dis-creetly marked door, and buzzed the intercom. There was an even more discreet rear entrance that Richard Morse shared with a shrink at the back of the building's fifth floor, but the help had to use the front door.

"What do you want?" Charlie heard Larry's harried-sounding voice instead of Gloria's familiar insulting one. Gloria's voice could discourage more wannabes than a math teacher's.

"It's me, Charlie." She had her own little card that would slide into the metal box next to the intercom and allow her entrance, but it was simply easier to buzz Gloria. She noted only two manila envelopes lying up against the door.

"Where is she?" she demanded as soon as Larry had let her in.

"Phone's driving me crazy. Our Gloria has disappeared on me." Larry was petulant, California bronze, and big. Charlie often had to stop herself from hugging him. "She did it on purpose, the witch."

"She didn't go far, her car's still down in the barn. Did she leave any Ding Dongs?" It was too late to even try to make the Universal breakfast.

"When I got back with them she was gone. More and more I like Richard's idea of installing voice mail," Larry said, returning to the phones. The last time Gloria left on vacation, the temp had somehow shut down the system, and Richard (the Morse in Congdon and Morse) had threatened to replace the receptionist with voice mail.

Charlie grabbed a gooey cake and headed for the staff bathrooms down the private hall. There was no sign of Gloria in the ladies. It wasn't like her to leave her desk that long. When she took her lunch break she even turned the phones over to an answering service.

The hall was long, narrow, and dimly lit. At its end were the stairs to the VIP exit and a tinted window. Charlie peered into the stairwell, wondering briefly if Gloria had felt ill and had a sudden need for air. She couldn't imagine Gloria choosing anything but the public elevator, no matter how awful she felt. The spike heels she wore were bone crunchers. Charlie called down into the stairwell. Her voice echoed back to her from the floors above as well as those below.

Though the window looked dark from outside, she could see clearly into the alley that ran along the side of the building, the white tiered business buildings running along the other side to Charleville Boulevard, and the off-alley parking spots for the residences incongruously snuggled in behind the bank. A high concrete brick wall painted white with tall flowering bushes hanging over it ran parallel to the bank's rear and separated two parking spaces from the next residence. Just beyond it was the rusty-red of old tiles on a garage roof. A breeze set the leaves to fluttering on the wall, shadow-dappling the concrete below. Something in the bushes caught the sun in tiny glints before the breeze moved on across the alley to play with a discarded food wrapper.

A woman dressed for the office stepped out of a gate and walked toward the garage. She stopped partway there and picked up something red, looked around her, shrugged, and then stuck it in one of the huge garbage cans that lined the alley all the way to Charleville Boulevard.

Charlie turned back to the agency offices, catching herself on the metal railing that lined the stairwell as her heels slid on the gloss of the newly waxed floor. She stopped at a whisper behind her, but when she looked there was no one.

"Someone call me?" It had really been more like a sigh than a whisper. It almost sounded like someone had whisper-sighed, "trash can." Charlie had extra-sensitive hearing, and often heard sounds that weren't there. She hated it.

She expected to find Gloria back at her desk, but Larry, still looking harried, motioned to her with a "we've got trouble" expression on his face.

Larry was one of the best-looking men Charlie had ever seen, with butterscotch-blond hair that kept flopping over onto his forehead and huge watery blue eyes that compelled unquestioning sympathy. He also had a lean, lithe body with muscles built up in all the right places. So far he'd failed in his quest to become a star, although he'd appeared in some very appealing commercials and bit parts on TV. Growing tired of waiting tables and parking cars, he'd found steadier employment at Congdon and Morse. When Charlie had taken her job and moved out from New York a couple of years ago, Larry had come with the office.

Now he held one of the phones above his head, letting lights flash on the other lines. "It's the boss for you. You find her?"

"Not yet. Richard, hi. Sorry I was late this morning. It was the freeway this time, honest, and not Libby." Charlie seemed to be in trouble about every other day around the office, and it was no joke. She had car payments, a killer mortgage, and a kid to raise. "How'd the meeting go?"

"I have no time for excuses, Charlie, and where the hell is Gloria?" It was his dangerous, ever-so-patient-and-put-upon voice. "I am a busy man. I cannot stay in the office every minute to manage it. That is why, Charlie, I spend good money to hire people to help me."

"She must have stepped out, but her car's still downstairs. I've been running around looking for her, and poor Larry's answering the phones." The door buzzer was about as subtle as a smoke alarm, and both she and Larry started when it went off. He pressed a button under Gloria's desk and released the lock for Dorian Black. "Here's Dorian now. He can help us look for Gloria."

Everybody had their special office nickname. Gloria was the Witch, Larry was Larry the Kid, and Charlie was fast becoming Mother of Libby. This was Dorian the Dapper. Dorian did not dress for success, he dressed to kill. Never mismatched, colorful yet tasteful, always the perfect tones and textures. He did not wrinkle. His hair and nails and even his shoes were perfection. Yet somehow Dorian Black still managed to come off with all the grace of a used-car salesman. Charlie would never figure out how he did it. And he would never forgive Charlie for having her own assistant. He had to share one with Luella. Where *was* everybody?

"Dorian can help Larry. Fuck Gloria." Richard Morse crashed back into Charlie's thoughts. "You've got exactly fifteen minutes to get you and your tush over to the Polo. All I could get you was a table on the patio. Monroe and Leffler are at it again, and, Charlie, do I need to tell you about ruffled feathers ruining the stew?"

"Ruffled feathers ruining the stew . . . "

"Do not repeat what I say. That's my schtick. Put Dapper Dorian on the line and hie your tail. I am *counting* on you, Charlie."

Charlie grinned at Dorian and handed him the phone, raced back to the ladies to check her smile for traces of Ding Dong. She'd eaten only half of it, and so far it had been her entire sustenance for the day. The egg and lobster salad at the Polo Lounge was worth the wait, and she knew she could handle Keegan Monroe. But from what Monroe said, nobody could handle Leffler. And "ruin the stew" was a euphemism for queering the deal, which was really serious. Then again, Richard Morse inflated everything but her wages.

Her eyes were still a little tense from her normal morning fight with Libby. Her hair, still a little wilted from sitting in traffic, suffered further as she raced the Toyota up to the Beverly Hills Hotel. But her spirits were rising by the minute. She reassured herself that she was too important to Congdon and Morse for them to blow her off simply because of repeated commuter and family problems.

When Richard Morse had discovered she'd taken a house in Long Beach instead of one closer to work, he'd warned her she was asking for trouble. But a friend of a friend had learned of a semidetached condo for sale in a charming old neighborhood, within walking distance of a high school and the ocean, far from any freeway noise. Since it was under two hundred and fifty thousand—Charlie had gone ahead and sunk every penny she'd ever saved, even selling some stock inherited from her father, to make the down payment. All that for four rooms and a bath, a tiny yard, and a patio. But after a minuscule sublet in Manhattan, it had seemed like the perfect place to raise Libby.

Charlie's mother, who had a whole house to herself now in Boulder, having bought it centuries ago for twenty thousand, was almost too stunned to criticize the purchase. Almost.

However, as Charlie's problems were growing with a growing teen, her boss and mother were growing depressingly more knowledgeable by the day. She and Libby both loved the Belmont Shore area of Long Beach, but it really was a hell of a long way to Wilshire Boulevard. And there was no money left over for things like two-hundred-dollar Rollerblades.

Charlie didn't know what they'd do if she lost her job, since they already lived on the edge. There was the orthodontist now, and college coming up for Libby with terrifying speed. But Charlie was a gambler and, God help her, there was a certain thrill to it all.

She parked in the outer lot and literally ran to the hotel's distant door, avoiding a tip for valet parking. She had two disgruntled writers to assuage, tease, cajole, and persuade to work together. In a small way, she was getting a name for being able to do just that, and Charlie loved attention as much as anybody.

But through all the thrill of it, the sense of power, two shortened pencils kept floating across her memory vision. They had been sitting on Gloria Tuschman's desk when Charlie talked to

Richard on the phone. Gloria used them always to key in on her computer, press telephone numbers, and work a calculator. She used the eraser ends, holding one in each hand to save her precious fingernails, and she could type faster than anyone in the office who used all their fingers.

That was only one of the reasons Gloria was known as a witch.

2

In the industry, agents can be very famous people. Like producers, they go unnoticed by the public at large, although their clout in real terms can be awesome. Charlie always sensed inklings of that potential at times like this.

She sailed through the Beverly Hills lobby, where the clientele was rich and ancient, to the Polo Lounge, where studio execs and males-with-money sat in curved-back chairs to talk deals in supposed acoustical stealth. Legend had it that the place was so designed that normal conversations in booths or at tables could not be overheard by those nearby. Charlie believed in only the *power* of legends.

One of the execs raised an eyebrow in recognition—a lech to be avoided no matter the mortgage. Another managed a royal wave of the hand—he was just as powerful and had actually thrown a deal Charlie's way, asking only for a minor writing assignment for a niece. He had since tired of the "niece." Charlie passed them both with a smile, winked at the elevator man at the piano, and headed for the patio—that tiny bubble of excitement zipping through her veins like a drug.

She also didn't want to lose this job because she loved it.

The Polo Lounge was a cushioned, padded, draped, and sedate place in a relentless pink and green motif. Outside were pink and green umbrellas with "Polo Patio" and "Polo Lounge" interspersed on the scalloped hang-downs where "Cinzano" would have been emblazoned in eateries catering to Charlie's personal price range. White wrought-iron tables with glass tops, white wrought-iron chairs with pink cushions, little pink vases with little pink roses. It was all too-too for the meeting at hand, and Keegan Monroe's expression admitted as much as Charlie slipped into the chair beside him. There were at least ten places that would have suited better, but Charlie figured the Polo was meant to impress Mary Ann Leffler.

One look at the author of *Shadowscapes* told Charlie that Richard could have saved his pennies. The Montana novelist had been hired by Goliath to write the screenplay on her book. Keegan, who was Charlie's client, was on the payroll to whip the script into usable form both because he was an experienced screenwriter and because he could get along with almost anyone.

He was not getting along with Mary Ann Leffler.

"Adverbs," Mary Ann said the minute Keegan introduced them.

"Excuse me?" Charlie motioned to the waiter. "Would anyone like a drink before ordering?" Maybe she could lubricate away some of the tension here. Then she glanced at the table. "I mean another one?"

Charlie ordered a glass of red zinfandel, Keegan another beer, and Mary Ann Leffler another vodka martini straight up and dry.

"Adverbs suck," the woman said and lit a cigarette off the stub in the ashtray. She wore brown hair cut very short in back, gradually lengthening on the sides until it just curled under the chin in front, all traces of gray dyed to sandy highlights. Her hands were long, strong, and bony—nails trimmed no-nonsense short. The sun had deepened squint lines around eyes that invited no bullshit.

Charlie took a slug of wine and tried anyway. "I'm *so* pleased to meet you, Ms. Leffler, I—"

"Mrs."

"Mrs. Leffler. I'm sorry I missed the meeting this morning. I got caught in traffic, and then there was this mess at the office and—"

"You didn't miss anything—all talk, little food. Now let's go ahead and order lunch before I get drunk and let you have it. This whole town drives me nuts."

"It's a far cry from Montana," Charlie agreed and glanced at Keegan for help.

He just snorted and held up a packet of Sweet'n Low. The patio was canopied by the sprawling branches of a pepper tree, and a jay flew down, grabbed the packet, then headed up to the slanted roof.

"Only in Hollywood," Mary Ann said and leveled a look at Keegan.

"They seem to prefer it to sugar." Keegan leveled a glance back. "Maybe they get a buzz off it."

The author finished off her Polo Club Sandwich, all the while continuing to regale them with her low opinion of Hollywood. Charlie decided to concentrate on her own sweet moist hunks of lobster meat and slices of hard-boiled egg on lettuce and crushed ice, lemon-butter dill sauce, and hot flaky rolls. She figured it was best to let the woman get most of her resentments off her chest before broaching the subject of adverbs. Adverbs. Here was a megadeal, with megabucks involved. So what was the problem with "ly" words?

Meanwhile, all the "frigging" superstars were buying up miles of Montana to get away from Hollywood, having already trashed Aspen and Santa Fe. The film industry was being run by fat old-money boys and kids. "There's nobody in-between," Mary Ann Leffler informed them in all seriousness. "No wonder it's going to hell. Half of them are too old to remember and the other half too young to know. And all those slimy old codgers with squeezes young enough to be their granddaughters is nauseating. Not to mention every third person you meet walking around on their toenails all jerked up on chemicals. I don't know how you two can stand it here."

Well that's show biz, Mary Ann. Charlie choked back a helpless giggle. "About the adverbs—"

"Actually, they prefer steak tartare," Keegan murmured, and Charlie could have kicked him. Pushing away his empty plate, he reached for hers. "Hey, you didn't leave me any egg."

"Who prefers steak tartare," the novelist asked, "the junkies?"

"The birds." Keegan Monroe, like most screenwriters, hated to work with published novelists. He was building a track record, had reasonably steady work, no illusions, and made a lot more money than most of those who had managed to publish books. But he didn't have the prestige. He also had an unpublished novel or two in the back of his closet.

He was fair, soft-spoken, laid-back, and never wore anything but blue jeans and cowboy boots unless he was jogging. Today he had put a corduroy sport coat over his plaid cotton shirt. He wore wire-rimmed glasses and a puny mustache. "I can stand it here, Mary Ann, because of the money. And Charlie here gets off on the excitement. Don't you, Charlie?"

"About the adverbs?" Charlie wasn't just losing control of this meeting, she had never gotten hold of it. "Who's your agent here on the West Coast, Mary Ann?" Let's compare status and settle who gets to do the genuflect thing.

"Irene Webb. She's out of town. I've got a call in for her." Mary Ann stubbed out her cigarette and exhaled smoke. "I got to go to the can. I'll let junior here fill you in on the adverbs."

Irene Webb had the same job Charlie did, that of literary

agent in a talent agency. But Irene Webb did it for ICM, and had more clout in her little finger. And clout was what it was all about in this town.

"Let's face it, Charlie, we're outclassed. She's a novelist and I'm just a hack. And you don't stand a chance against Irene Webb. Here you thought you were going to sail in here and save the day. Talk reason to your old buddy, Keegan, straighten out this cantankerous middle-aged housewife from the sticks who happens to write books." Keegan hooted and held up a piece of French bread.

Charlie tugged his arm down. "You're going to get us kicked out of here. You know they don't want you feeding the birds. Why did Richard send me if—"

"Did he expect you to take on Lady Macbeth there and ICM? Don't overestimate yourself, girl. He expected you to wheedle little old easy-going Keegan into submission."

Charlie ordered a Diet Coke for dessert. Keegan ordered another beer. She'd never known him to sound so bitter. "Tell me about the adverbs."

"It's more than that, they were just the straw." He took off his sport coat and rubbed the cold wet of the beer glass across his forehead. "She comes in from Montana with an adaptation way overdue. And, Charlie, it's damn near a third longer than it's supposed to be. I mean somebody had told her the format but—"

It was rare to ask a screenwriter to collaborate with a stranger like this. He would normally rewrite the author's adaptation to suit the studio, but Irene Webb and Mary Ann Leffler had enough clout between them to tie down a clause in the contract forbidding the use of Mary Ann's name in the credits if she didn't have input on the finished script. And, for the moment, her name was hot. Keegan was both talented and malleable, bless him.

"So I get to help cut it, plus work in all the added suggestions from every bozo connected to the project, plus make the thing workable. And of course by that time it doesn't look a hell of a lot like her script and practically *nothing* like her book. Shit, I just work here."

"So what about the adverbs, damn it?"

"Adverbs, she says, are a product of a weak verb needing shoring up. Okay, I say, so give me strong verbs—see, when I cut her stuff I used adverbs to tighten up, replace whole phrases. But instead of giving me a word to replace them and the weak verb, she gives me whole sentences, and there we go again and the script's still too long. And, Charlie, it's mostly just in the stage directions anyway, like 'Mike walks slowly into the horse barn and stares accusingly at Sally Jean. Sally Jean is frantically putting her clothes back on.'

"And we haven't even got to the polish yet. When we have a shooting script it'll be all jerked around anyway, so what's the fucking difference? We got to take out pages, pal. But no, she says, it will have my name on it and adverbs are sloppy writing and don't you ever read reviews, she says. Christ, Charlie, I was hired to do a job. I did it, and Lady Macbeth can only moan, 'Out, damn adverb.' Well, I feel for you, Charlie, and I know this is going to mess up your day, but good little Keegan is going to have to let you down. I've had it with this project. My dues are paid up at the Guild. I'll collect what I'm owed. Screw the rest." And with that, one of Charlie's most profitable and dependable clients got up and left the patio of the Polo Lounge. And Lady Macbeth never did return from the can.

Having nearly wrecked the Toyota berthing it in its special stall under the FFUCWB of P, Charlie raced to the public elevators only to find them out of order. She noticed the shrink from her floor heading for the private VIP stairs, which were almost hidden beyond a concrete slab that presumably helped hold up the building.

"Dr. Podhurst? Can I go up your way? Elevator's down again." And I can't wait to chew out my boss.

Dr. Podhurst turned to study her with a perplexed expression. His coat sleeves always seemed too short. He reminded Charlie of a balding Abraham Lincoln.

"Charlie Greene," she reminded him. "With Congdon and Morse down the hall? I'm in kind of a hurry and—"

"Charlie, yes." He shook his head but didn't smile. He never smiled. It was creepy. "I was a million miles away. I shouldn't be driving," he joked forlornly, holding open the VIP door for her.

Charlie hoped Gloria was back at her desk. The place was a zoo without Gloria. Was her car still downstairs? Charlie hadn't thought to notice this time. She and Gloria didn't get along that well, but her workdays certainly ran a lot smoother with someone on the front desk to help organize them.

Besides, I need Larry.

She was still so heated up over the fiasco at the Polo and Richard Morse's underhanded conniving she could hear her shoes stomping instead of stepping up the stairs. She was panting by the third floor landing. The good doctor was humming under his breath. His private door was across the hall from the fifth-floor entrance, and when she turned to thank him someone whispered, "Charlie, I'm in the trash can. Help me."

Charlie grabbed the shrink's short coat sleeve, and stopped them both mid-step. "Did you hear something?"

"Hear something, did you say? I don't think so . . . but I'm afraid my hearing is deficient. In fact I've just been to see a specialist—Charlie, your color isn't looking too good. Perhaps you took the stairs a bit too fast. Here, come into my office and sit."

"Do you happen to have a trash can in your office? Is there usually one sitting at this end of the hall?" That's the second time I've heard that call for help. Could I have imagined it twice?

Podhurst and Linda Meyer, his sole office staff, had wastebaskets. He'd never seen a trash receptacle out in the hall, and when Charlie knocked on the locked door of a janitorial closet and called out for Gloria, he began to study her with far too professional an interest. He was one of those guys who could make you feel like a complete idiot merely walking across a room anyway.

"It's just being one of those days." Charlie completed her embarrassment with her inane giggle and scurried off down the hall, knowing he was standing at his door watching her. Charlie had several giggles, but the inane one was the hardest to control. Women on their way up in the world did not giggle.

And I'm going to go in and blow off at the man who controls my livelihood, lose my job and our home because of wounded pride, aren't I? she warned herself.

Having come in the back way, Charlie peeked into the reception area and saw that Gloria was still not at her desk. Tracy, Dorian Black and Luella Ridgeway's assistant, had taken over. Charlie made her way down the office suite's hallway toward the front of the building and her own office. Because of the slant of Wilshire and the slant of the building, Congdon and Morse had four offices with prestige views. Maurice Lavender's, then Richard Morse's—which was on the corner and had the best view, with windows on two walls. Irma Vance had a large office in front of his and a window of her own. She was over fifty, formidable, and in reality second in command. She was presently on vacation, or Gloria would never have dared leave her post without telling anyone. Turning the corner, the next office was Charlie's, and it fronted full on Wilshire.

And last, and Charlie presumed far larger than hers, was Daniel Congdon's. The door was always locked, and she had never seen either it or Mr. Congdon. Richard Morse explained to her shortly after she joined the agency that Congdon was ill. Dorian and Luella had offices with windows that faced the windows of the building across the alley. And that was the lot. It wasn't much for Beverly Hills, but everything was far nicer and more plush than it had been in New York.

And more exciting and more fun and better paying, even though costs are higher, which is why I should not dash into Richard's office in a confrontational manner.

All the assistants had cubicles off the hall guarding the agents' offices. Charlie stormed into Larry's. He looked up, both hands on the computer keyboard and the phone mouthpiece trapped under his chin.

Charlie made hair-tearing motions and continued storming on into her office.

"Sandra at McMullins has been trying to return your call, went home centuries ago, and will try to get back to you tomorrow," he called to her when he was off the phone, then listed four million and two other people who had tried to contact her today. When she didn't answer, he stepped into her office and closed the door.

Charlie was curled up on the couch in a fetal position.

"Three guesses," Larry said. "The meeting at the Polo Lounge bombed, Libby is four months pregnant, or it's PMS."

"The meeting at the Polo Lounge bombed, Libby had better not be four months pregnant, and I don't get PMS. It's degrading."

He sat in one of the overstuffed chairs, crossed his legs, steepled his fingers, and peered over the tops of glasses he didn't wear. "So tell Dr. Larry vot it is dat is the matter, Liebchen."

"Strangely enough, I think it's Gloria the Witch."

3

Charlie's office had too much furniture for the space—a couch and two chairs grouped conversationally around a coffee table, a large desk with floor-to-ceiling cabinets and shelves behind it, and a computer station. The client chair faced her, and her chair faced the window onto Wilshire.

Except for one of her author's bookstore posters Charlie had hung herself, the color scheme was soft blues and pale grays, with accents of lavender and yellow. The whole effect sounded worse than it looked. It had all been done before Charlie's arrival, and the only thing that bothered her was that there wasn't enough room to pace.

Outside the window, palm fronds frisked in a breeze unconnected to the controlled air of the office. A sparrow was busy stripping strings from the emptied sockets of fallen fronds to carry off for nestmaking. Charlie knew all about this because her neighbor, Mrs. Beesom, was seriously into birds. Mrs. Beesom was decidedly unhappy with Libby's cat, because it had decided to get into birds, too.

Charlie leaned against the front of her desk, one pump off and the sole of her bare foot resting up against the other inner foreleg. Charlie did not like funny things of a certain type, and funny things of a certain type had been happening to her today. Gloria would call them unexplainable. But Charlie knew better.

It reminded her uncomfortably of a situation last year in

Oregon. But Oregon was foggy and misty and fey and full of the mysteries of nature, so anything could happen there. Here in the land of make-believe, everything was phony and unnatural for profit, planned that way. It might well be inexcusable, but it made sense.

Larry leaned in the doorway. "Can't seem to scare up Richard. Her car's still down there. And, yes, her purse is in her drawer. And, no, no one notified building security until I did just now, and there is no answer on her home phone, and as far as I can determine no one has seen her, including her husband at the print shop."

The sun hung low over the Pacific when Charlie pulled into the drive of her minicondo complex in Long Beach. It was a good five blocks from the ocean but in a prized old neighborhood. Once a street of modest working-class homes, it had given way to the vagaries of the southern California housing market. Small homes had been built onto, above, and around—filling up small lots with lots of house selling for lots of money. Larger homes had been divided into condos.

Charlie's condo was really a small house attached to three others by a common security wall, driveway, and central courtyard. It was an off-white stucco in a pseudo-Spanish style with arched entryway and windows and a red tiled roof. Stately palms graced the parking area, and a huge bushy one dominated the tiny front yard. This weekend Charlie had to get out and clean up the dead fall around that palm and trim things. Everyone else's yard looked so neat they made hers an eyesore. Hers was one of two fronting on the street. There was a pair in back of the large lot as well.

Maggie Stutzman was an attorney and soulmate whose pink stucco house sat across the drive and was attached to Charlie's by an arched wall with an ornate but heavily reinforced iron security gate. It opened only by private keys inserted in a vandal-proof obelisk or in key boxes in the condos, and closed automatically after a very short interval.

Guests were expected to use street parking, and a little sign next to the drive said so. The little sign had to be replaced about every other week because it was stolen, as was the larger sign that informed criminals that the property was guarded by the dreaded DOG Private Security System. Which told them that anyone messing around on that lot would receive immediate attention from guards armed with Dobermans armed with teeth on instant twenty-four-hour call, and potential perpetrators would not have the luxury of getting in, swiping what they pleased, and leaving before an overworked police department could respond. It also probably told the pro exactly what kind of system it was he had to disconnect before entering.

The obelisk might be vandal-proof (although it was heavily spray painted with obscenities) but the gate lock wasn't, and twice in the time Charlie had lived here all the condo owners had had to divvy up for a new one. And it had been the Long Beach Police Department that had responded to the scene when Mrs. Beesom dialed 911. Apparently the DOG dogs only rushed over when an alarm was set off inside one of the houses. Roving gangs were blamed both times for smashing the lock but were gone when police arrived.

This evening the gate opened obediently. Covered parking for two cars on each side filled the spaces between walled and trellised patios. Charlie pulled into the slot next to Mrs. Beesom's Olds 88, and by the time she got out, the gate to the big bad world had closed her in with Mrs. Beesom, Maggie, and Jeremy Fiedler, who lived in the condo behind Maggie.

Another gate gave access to Charlie's sunken patio, where flowers planted by a previous owner seemed to flourish in spite of Charlie. The back door opened directly into the kitchen, from which vantage point she could hear the sound of television instead of studying. Charlie walked through to the dining room and dropped her shoulder bag and briefcase on the dining room table, which caught all the tiresome details of their lives and so was too crowded to eat on. She stepped out of both pumps and then down into the sunken living room. (Sinking things was supposed to make tiny expensive places worth the expense.) She slumped onto the couch next to her daughter.

"Hi, thought you had tests tomorrow."

"I'm hungry. You didn't say you'd be *this* late."

"There was a whole deli chicken and some coleslaw in the refrigerator. I told you this morning. Didn't you even look?"

"We ate it after school. That was hours ago."

"The whole thing."

"The whole thing."

"We."

"Lori, Doug, and me. We were hungry and started snacking and pretty soon it was all gone. I didn't have lunch, that was my lunch. There is nothing to eat in this house."

"Last week your health and sex education teacher said you should eat a banana a day and you'd be healthier than an old granola girl. Last weekend I bought bananas. As I remember, just now passing through the kitchen, they're all still there."

"Bananas taste like snot."

"Libby—"

"Mo-om, I did not say I wanted bananas. All I said is what Mrs. Hefty said. But no, you make all these . . . these guesses about what you think I mean."

"Assumptions."

"Don't do that."

"Sorry. Let me change, and we'll make a run on the diner."

"You're mad at me." Huge beautiful eyes turned to Charlie.

"Because my friends ate all the food." Huge beautiful eyes filled with tears.

Charlie didn't buy it. This kid was as hard as reinforced concrete. But she said, "You probably eat more at their houses than they eat here."

Hell, one of them has a live-in housekeeper and the other a live-in mother.

Curiously enough, the Long Beach Diner was done in pink and green just like the Polo Lounge. There the similarity ended. The waiters were waitresses, for one thing. They wore shorts and green T-shirts instead of black pants, white shirts, and black bow ties. The soup was canned, the lettuce iceberg, the salad dressing bottled, the bread white, the clientele lower-middle and fixed income, the prices a fraction.

After the day she'd had and the one obviously coming up, Charlie needed comfort food. She ordered the day's special—hot beef sandwich with canned string beans, Jell-O, and a glass of milk.

"Bad day, huh?" Libby ordered her cheeseburger, fries, and Diet Coke. For nine months after they'd moved here from New York, Libby had been a vegetarian. Greenpeace came through the school with some appealing pictures and some appalling horror stories. The intentions were laudable. The problem was Libby Greene would not eat vegetables, nor was she terribly fond of fruit. Pasta, potato chips, and aspartame will take you only so far. Being Libby, she wouldn't cheat on fish, milk, eggs, cheese, or chicken.

A social worker alerted by the school called on Charlie to discuss eating disorders, nutrition, child abuse, and the consequences thereof. Charlie never knew what happened, but one weekend Libby asked to order in pizza. Pizza with everything.

She hadn't been able to get enough hamburger, pepperoni, bacon, or hot dogs since.

"Bad day." Charlie ate half her meal and signaled the waitress to come for her plate. She watched Libby eat all her burger and most of her fries. "Don't you think you've had enough?"

"You're the only mother I know who tells her kid never to clean up her plate. Lori's mom thinks you're weird."

If Charlie were smart, she'd keep quiet and let her child store calories. Her heart sank to wherever it is that hearts sink, watching Libby struggle to think of a way to pose a question or more likely an "I want."

Where Charlie's hair was a bronze color that looked dyed but wasn't and was incorrigibly curly, Libby's was long and straight—a natural platinum half the women in the world would kill for. She'd picked up an even, tawny California tan within weeks of their arrival and never lost it. Her eyes were dark like Charlie's but larger in her smaller face. Right now Libby's smile was full of metal, but when those braces came off . . . if only she'd grow a big ugly nose until she was twenty.

"Mom, are you having a Maalox moment?"

Charlie massaged the skin around her eyes, careful not to dislodge contact lenses. "Gloria Tuschman, our receptionist, has disappeared. And I screwed up a deal with Goliath that could get me fired, and I told you this morning I cannot afford two-hundred-dollar Rollerblades."

Libby said, with no trace of sympathy, "I'm getting a loan."

"For a loan you have to have collateral or at least a job. Who would give you a loan?"

"I'll pay it back when I get a job." The beautiful dark eyes shot sparks. "Grandma told me to call collect if I ever needed anything." Libby slid out of the booth and headed for the door, leaving Charlie with the check.

"Edwina's going to lend you two hundred dollars for Rollerblades?" Charlie asked when she got out to the car.

"Do you still want me to try out for cheerleading?"

"You have to have Rollerblades to be a cheerleader?"

"No, I have to join a sorority, and the two hundred dollars will only cover the Rollerblades."

"You have to belong to a sorority to be a cheerleader?"

"Mom, I do not make the rules, okay? Now can we go home? I have tests tomorrow."

"I don't care if you don't go out for cheerleading. I just thought it might be fun is all," Charlie lied through her teeth. She had wanted to go out for cheerleading once, at Boulder High School. But she didn't, because she discovered she was pregnant with Libby, and her world changed forever in one day.

"Oh I forgot," Libby said as the Toyota slid through the gate into the compound. "Somebody named Keegan called."

"Keegan?" The Toyota jerked to a stop with its headlights drilling through the back gate into the alley as the front gate closed behind them. "What did he say?"

"Just told me to tell you he called. No big deal."

"Libby, that's the Goliath deal. Any other calls you forgot to mention?"

"Some military dude. You're always telling me I have weird friends. Lieutenant Dimple or something."

"Lieutenant Dalrymple?"

"Sounds like it. Just wanted you to call him. I wrote it down on the phone pad. Why, is that some big deal too?"

"That's the Beverly Hills Police Department. I told you Gloria is missing. We called them and they suspect something happened to her because her car and purse are still there."

"Gloria the Witch? What do you care, you don't like her anyway."

"My opinion of her has nothing to do with it." Two small gold orbs blinked on, then off, then on again from the alley where the trash cans were kept. A black, sinewy form with flashes of white slid through the grating. Libby's cat.

"Are you going to park or should I get out here? I don't have the whole night, you know. What's the matter? It's just Tuxedo coming home, finally."

"She said she was in the trash can. She wanted me to help her."

"Tuxedo's a guy."

"Gloria the Witch."

"I thought she was missing. If she's in the trash can, she's not missing. Probably not too comfortable. Mom, don't look like that, okay? You scare me. Did she want you to help her before she was missing?"

"No, after," Charlie said and killed the engine.

Lieutenant Dalrymple wanted Charlie at Congdon and Morse no later than eight o'clock the next morning. She was late because Libby wanted a ride to school, even though it was a straight shot up Ximeno to Wilson High (which was a good part of the reason Charlie bought where she did), and because Libby was very unpleasant to wake that early, and because Charlie's usual trajectory into her parking space was blocked by barricades. So she maneuvered back to Charleville Boulevard and down the alley, only to stop in front of the trash can where she'd seen the woman throw away something red the day before.

It was silly, but earlier that morning at the usual time when Tuxedo tired of floating with Libby on her waterbed and came in to wrap himself around Charlie's head and bite it before trying to smother her, she'd been dreaming about that damned trash can and Gloria the Witch putting something red in it.

Some things you just have to do even if they're irrational. Charlie was late anyway. She got out and lifted the lid. These were extra big green plastic trash cans provided by the city, and this one was empty. She felt sillier but she felt better. Charlie gave a sigh of relief and turned back to the Toyota.

"Looking for this?" Lieutenant Dalrymple stepped out from behind the concrete block wall, one of Gloria's red spike heels in his hand.

4

Lieutenant Dalrymple stood next to Charlie up on the fifth floor landing of the VIP stairs, looking out the darkened glass of the nearly floor-to-ceiling window. She was trying to explain how she had known where to look for Gloria's shoe.

Down below a man took pictures of Gloria the Witch sprawled in the bush tops like she'd been spread out to dry.

From that far away she looked a little puffy, maybe, but really pretty normal. Well okay, she looked dead—but other than that . . .

The tops of the bushes had been trimmed back to expose the body. Some of the fake jewels glued onto the corpse's bright red fingernails sparked in the camera flashes. An ambulance and a gurney waited in the alley.

Gloria seemed to be staring straight up at Charlie. Staring accusingly. (Mary Ann Leffler would have probably said "with a look of accusation" or something else long-winded but pure.)

"You said you were in the trash can, not the bushes," Charlie defended herself, and then realized she'd said it aloud.

"Would you tell me again, please, what you were doing up here when you saw Mrs. Humphrys put Mrs. Tuschman's shoe in the garbage can?" the lieutenant asked apologetically and with just the right trace of vagueness. This guy was good.

On second thought, Gloria didn't really look believably dead. She looked stage dead, the scene playing more like a movie.

They had found the shoe last night, but not Gloria until this morning. Maybe if you were looking for a body you would automatically be looking down. The wall and the bush tops were higher than a man's head. Still, wouldn't someone have smelled Gloria? Or seen drops of blood on the other side of the wall? Or whatever?

The homicide detective was soft-spoken in a sincere, not a silky, way. He was angular, with a pleasant face marred by thick glasses and thin lips. Baldness started exactly halfway back on his head as if drawn up that way by an engineering draftsman, the sideburns long and exact. If Charlie had been asked to type him without knowing, she'd have guessed him to be a college professor in the humanities long before she'd have suspected a Beverly Hills cop. His nonthreatening, slightly bumbling manner invited confidences. He could be a real comfort to a victim's family, a real trap for a suspect.

Right now anyone connected to Gloria was a suspect. Charlie answered him slowly. "I was looking for her, checked the ladies first, then came over here to check the stairwell, and looked out the window to see a woman pick up something off the ground, look around, shrug, walk to the alley, and throw it in the trash. Something red. The way she held it I didn't realize it was a shoe."

"Mrs. Humphrys was on her way to get her car from her garage when she found it. She's lived in that house for over five years."

"This is where I work, Lieutenant. We don't interface with the people who live in the neighborhood. I'd never seen her before."

"You never go out and walk around the block over your lunch hour?"

"In these shoes?" Today Charlie wore high navy blue pumps, sheer navy-tinted pantyhose, navy and white striped seersucker skirt, navy seersucker blazer, and white blouse with navy bow tie. Even her earrings were navy and white. She'd figured a no-nonsense outfit would give her added confidence. It wasn't working. And the lieutenant's eyes hadn't risen any farther than her legs. So much for dressing for success.

"Ah . . . yes." He looked up finally. "So . . . you didn't recognize it as a shoe when Mrs. Humphrys threw it away but as merely something red. But when I showed it to you just now you knew it immediately as belonging to Gloria Tuschman." He paused to feign confusion, obviously not as distracted by her legs as he'd like her to think. "Why would you stop to inspect a garbage container this morning because you'd seen a complete stranger throw something red in it yesterday morning? I'm afraid I don't understand."

"I think my subconscious had picked up on more of this than I had. While I was standing here noticing Mrs. Humphrys put something in the garbage can, I was also noticing something glitter in the sunlight when wind fluttered the leaves of the bushes on top of the wall. I didn't register it as anything to do with Gloria consciously, but Gloria wore a lot of red."

Charlie was trying to be as straightforward as possible without incriminating herself unintentionally, which if you thought about it was probably hopeless. "But when I was talking to her on the car phone I could hear the clicking of her keyboard and had a sort of mental picture of her bright red nails with the fake jewel strips on them."

He flipped a page in his little breast pocket notebook. "That would have been about nine yesterday morning."

Charlie was the last person to admit talking to Gloria the Witch alive and Larry the last to admit seeing her that way.

"Right. And when I went back to her desk after looking out this window I noticed the shortened pencils with the eraser ends she used to type with and press phone keys—to keep those nails so perfect—sitting sort of slantwise as if she'd dropped them in the middle of something and planned to come right back but didn't. Gloria was pretty tidy and usually put things like that in a little trough container gismo. But I'm connecting this now, you understand, now that I know . . . I didn't then. But right after that, on my way to a business lunch, I was thinking about the people I was going to meet there and the business to be conducted, yet still seeing those pencil ends on Gloria's desk."

"Lunch at the Polo Lounge." He checked his notebook again.

"Right. And then I came back and she hadn't shown up yet, so I asked Larry to check if her purse and car were still here and if anyone had notified building security."

"She disappeared from her desk sometime between nine and just after ten in the morning, and no one raised the alarm until approximately three in the afternoon. Is it just me or do you find that strange?"

"If Irma Vance wasn't on vacation, everybody would have figured out something was wrong the minute Gloria stopped fielding phone calls, and a search would have been on. Irma's the office manager as well as executive secretary. But right now we're short-staffed because Maurice's assistant quit and Maurice isn't due back from vacation until today. The rest of us were pretty much in and out, which isn't unusual. Luella just got back from Minnesota. We were all coming and going, and Gloria wasn't here to be a central communication source. It just took a while for anyone to stop long enough for it to sink in that she was really gone and to start checking. I mean just because someone's not at her desk, you don't automatically assume she's been murdered and . . . I forgot the question."

He smiled, keeping his lips together as if he couldn't help himself. "Why you stopped at the garbage can this morning."

"Last night I saw my daughter's cat come through the gate in front of the car lights, and his eyes flashed like we just saw the jewels in Gloria's fingernails do, and we keep the garbage cans in the alley on the other side of that gate. And then he woke me about two and I was dreaming that Gloria was putting something red in the garbage can. How am I doing?"

"And that's when you decided to check the container in the alley behind this building when you came to work this morning?"

"That wasn't until I actually got here and drove up next to it. If the main entrance hadn't been blocked and I hadn't come down the alley and seen the garbage can, I probably wouldn't have thought of it."

He paused to stare at her as if his mind was working to catch up with her logic. And then, still playing for time, he said, "Uh ... I'd like you please to show me just how those pencil ends were lying on her desk."

They were almost past the ladies' room when someone behind them whispered, "Charlie, I'm in the trash can. Help me."

And then, Charlie thought with resignation, there's always that. She leaned against the wall, weak-kneed, aware she looked nothing like a career woman on her way up to the fabled glass ceiling.

"Do you believe in the supernatural?" Dalrymple asked, ignoring her sudden stop yet almost as if he too had heard the whisper. But his expression was too bland.

"No, why?"

"Why not?"

"Not scientific." Charlie, realizing she'd answered her own

question, stared back at the stairwell. Obviously someone alive had figured out how to send a voice recognizable as a dead Gloria's up from below. Someone who knew Charlie's hearing was more acute than most people's. Or perhaps Dalrymple's wasn't any better than Podhurst's.

Maurice Lavender was a compulsive womanizer. Or he wanted every woman in the world to think he was. Charlie liked him but wasn't sure whether or not his charm was the reason, or was it just that he was so different from her distant father. His hair was white but luxuriant, his dress casual. His speech slow, Southern, and suggestive. His face unlined and his smile warm, welcoming, intimate, reassuring—whatever you might order. He would have been insulted to know she thought of him in the same generation as "father."

"I have no idea how old he is," Maggie Stutzman, Charlie's neighbor confidant, said after meeting him at a party Charlie had given in Long Beach. "But those eyes—gawd, you just want to strip and jump in. Not that there'd be anything to land on."

Maurice's specialties at Congdon and Morse were aging female stars and character actresses of daytime soaps and nighttime sitcoms. Generally they were actresses who had gained their initial audience identification in film. He was shrewd, but gently so.

"And how is darling Libby's little mother? I've missed you so, sweetie," he said now, enfolding Charlie in a forceful embrace against a broad, slightly plump chest. Maurice was a boob man, and Charlie barely had any, but he didn't seem to mind. Then he began swirling her around the conference room in a clutching dance step and whispered in her ear, "Dorian tells me the witch is dead. Ding dong the witch is dead. Which old witch? The wicked—"

"Here, you two, none of that in the office," Richard Morse scolded. He'd just breezed in an hour late, his way of one-upping the Beverly Hills P.D.

Meanwhile, Lieutenant Dalrymple watched the gathering together of Congdon and Morse Representation, Inc. with apparent bewilderment.

Charlie gave Maurice a kiss on the cheek and wiggled out of his grasp. "How was Cancun?"

By a bare raising of the brow, a faint constriction of the nostrils and lips, a nearly inaudible moan, and a look of glassy-eyed helplessness Maurice Lavender managed to impart memories of an orgasmic delight beyond comprehension.

"Uh, Lieutenant? You got this all wrong, you know?" Dorian straightened a perfectly straight tie and gestured around the conference table. "You're supposed to question each one of us separately, see? Then at the end get us all together. You oughta watch more television."

"The end of what?" the lieutenant asked quietly.

"Well, of . . . the story."

"This is not a story." He gazed around the table, lingering on each pair of eyes in turn until the owners squirmed. "It is not television. It is not a moving picture, Disneyland, make-believe. It is real, cold-blooded murder. Make no mistake, no matter your opinion of or relationship to Gloria Tuschman, her violent death will alter your lives forever. Nothing will ever again be the same for any of you. And for whoever murdered her, there will never again be true peace of mind."

"Aw come o-on." Richard Morse at the head of the table rolled slightly protruding eyes, flattening beautiful hands on its glossy surface. "Some dopehead bops a total stranger in an alley and he's going to lay awake nights feeling guilty about it? Probably won't even remember."

"The victim was not 'bopped,' as you call it, in the alley, but at the end of the private hallway on this floor." The lieutenant glanced at Charlie when her breath squeaked on the intake.

"Well, you're still gonna be one busy man. That hall is accessible from any floor in the building except the first, and that includes the first level parking. That's all the bank offices on second, third, fourth, plus the floors above." Richard Morse was a well-built man. He looked Greek, Italian, and Jewish and—like Gloria—sounded New Jersey. He had a prominent nose and long eyelashes, hair that was short and curly black with gray patches artfully preserved at the temples.

"Then there's the valet parking staff, and I understand the turnover there is horrific. Cleaning staff have keys. Hoo boy, are you going to be tied up forever if you're looking for your culprit in-house. This is one hell of a big house."

"I've known bigger," Dalrymple said patiently.

But Charlie's boss was on a roll. She could feel the throb in the floor as his knee jumped like he was keeping time to his own private music. "Plus which, Gloria had a life, you know? A husband, neighbors, enemies? She could have buzzed them in the front door. And meantime," Richard continued as if the policeman were not the man in charge here, "you've got my whole agency in this room and this is a business day."

Ironically, most of them would have been sitting in this room at this time on this morning anyway. Beginning with the second, each floor of the First Federal United Central Wilshire Bank of the Pacific had two common conference rooms. One small for staff meetings and another larger one for workshops with related businesses or product displays for sales conferences or whatever. They came with the lease and had only to be reserved. This, the smaller of the two, was reserved by Congdon and Morse on a regular basis two mornings a week. No one was about to tell Dalrymple that.

"Then the sooner we get under way the better," the homicide detective said, unperturbed and, Charlie would guess, unimpressed. "Now, I would like to ask a few questions. The first being, why the late, and seemingly unlamented, Gloria was referred to as a 'witch.'"

5

Charlie looked around at her colleagues, who were doing the same. Had one of them murdered Gloria at the end of the private hall, carried her down four flights of stairs, dragged her past the valet parking attendants—and anyone else using the rear entrance—and out into the alley and around the wall, and thrown her up to the top of the bushes? Wouldn't that take more than one person? Wouldn't there be a trail of blood? Nobody could do all that and clean up the traces completely without arousing notice at that hour of the morning on a business day.

Charlie sat across from Luella Ridgeway—small, quick, wired, ambitious, nice. She had just returned from Minnesota after spending her vacation putting her aging father in a nursing home and closing up the family house. She looked exhausted. She kept herself slim and young-looking to survive, but there were gray roots in the part of her beige hair this morning. Charlie wondered what she'd ever do if she had to put Edwina in a home and close up the house in Boulder. At least Luella had siblings. You didn't return from an ordeal like that and murder a receptionist.

Then there was Dorian Black—cocky on the outside, insecure within. He watched Richard Morse for cues in this most unusual staff meeting. He might be dapper, but he was not muscular.

Next was Tracy Dewitt, a big girl. She was Dorian and Luella's assistant and a funny, pleasant person, but not too efficient. She was apparently a distant relative of the absent partner Daniel Congdon, and if it's who you know instead of what you can do that's likely to get you a job in the world in general, it's the law in Hollywood. Charlie did not know Tracy well, but she couldn't imagine what she'd have against Gloria worth killing for. And although Tracy was a large woman, her size was due more to fat than muscle.

Then there was Larry Mann, Charlie's assistant. His bulges were muscle, yet he was the kindliest, gentlest of people, incapable of harming another.

Maurice the Lover, a handsome gentleman—but really past the age where he could drag bodies around and heave them into bushes. He might love some woman to death, but . . .

And Richard Morse had been covering for Charlie at the Universal breakfast with Keegan Monroe and Mary Ann Leffler and the frantic Goliath producers at the time of the murder. (Charlie's outrage over the misbegotten Polo Lounge lunch had seemed trivial after viewing a dead Gloria.)

She couldn't imagine what Dr. Podhurst could have against Gloria, or his receptionist, Linda Meyer. Linda had often had lunch with Gloria, though.

The Congdon and Morse staff had very little contact with the legal beagles and their support staff across the public hall. They had their own private VIP entrance.

Charlie probably had the weakest alibi, on the face of it. She couldn't prove she'd been in her car on the road on the way at that time. Unless the valet staff had noticed her come in. And that would be iffy. They saw little else but cars coming in and going out all day. Larry at least would have been seen by whoever sold him the Ding Dongs.

It had to have been someone from outside. Charlie relaxed. She liked some of these people better than others, but she still didn't like the thought that the agency could harbor a murderer. Was it the murderer who kept whispering to Charlie? Who else would know where Gloria died?

Her colleagues were looking to Richard Morse to answer the lieutenant's question. Richard was looking at the ceiling, choosing some thoughts. The homicide detective was looking at Charlie.

"It's not that no one laments Gloria's death," Charlie offered. "It's just that murder is hard to take in right away. I don't think we've quite digested it yet. And joking and fooling around is one way to avoid coming to terms with it." She couldn't believe Dalrymple hadn't seen enough of this behavior to know that.

"She's right," Maurice agreed. "And Richard, I think you should consider getting a counselor or two in here. When this really hits all of us it could be pretty bad."

"I expect the health insurance would cover it," Luella said, as if she'd be the first to sign up for counseling. "Wish Irma were back. She'd know."

"Irma is back," Tracy spoke for the first time. She was getting used to contact lenses and looked about to cry—her face screwed up, her eyes blinking like strobe lights. "I came in early yesterday morning," she blinked pointedly at Luella and Dorian, "to get some extra work done. She was at her desk. I don't know when she left. And you were in your office, Richard, talking to somebody. Gloria came in while I was making coffee. And then Larry."

"People pick up pet names in offices, Lieutenant. Bet they do in yours, too." Richard had finally selected a thought and ignored the implications of Irma being back in town after all. "Gloria was called Gloria the Witch because she had those god-awful fingernails and a tongue to match—and because she was actually a witch."

"She practiced witchcraft?" Dalrymple glanced at Charlie yet again.

"She practiced everything. She was certifiable. But a receptionist's job is not going to attract a Ph.D. in physics, you know what I mean?"

"She was insane?"

"She was insane." Richard's head bobbed in time with his knee and with Tracy's blinking. "Let me assure you that insanity is not a unique trait in this town."

"Oh Richard," Luella scolded, "she was not insane. She was odd, that's all. She was into the occult and astrology—things like that, Lieutenant, and tarot and, yes, witchcraft. But I don't think Gloria was focused enough to actually be said to *practice* anything."

Charlie wondered who her boss had been talking to in his office and why he'd come in before Gloria, who usually opened up. And why Irma was back from her yearly pilgrimage to Las Vegas, but not back at her desk. Every year for three weeks Irma Vance, Richard's executive secretary, changed personalities and lived it up in Vegas. And every year some crisis came up while she wasn't running the office. But it had never before been murder.

Charlie also wondered why Lieutenant Dalrymple kept checking her reactions to everything. Did he suspect her above most? Because she looked in that garbage can this morning?

It was obvious why he wanted them all together now, though. Now, before they could get their stories straight with each other by talking on their own. Now, when they could trip each other up. Charlie disagreed with Dorian. This police detective knew what he was doing.

By the time he let them go, the phone lines were flashing. Tracy and Larry worked to steer calls where they were needed. That's why Charlie took the one from McMullins directly.

When she hung up, she let out first a single yip and then a series of them. She could hear Larry's answering howl from the front desk and knew he'd stayed on the line. Charlie met him halfway.

Everyone, including David Dalrymple and two uniforms, converged on them just as she and her assistant high-fived, Charlie leaping up and down on stockinged feet, having slipped out of her heels the minute she'd placed them under her desk. Dalrymple's prosaic expression reminded her how ridiculous she must look and that murder had happened here just over twenty-four hours ago.

It was so easy to get carried away in this business. Most of the time it was pie-in-the-sky hopes and dreams that petered out after great amounts of fantasizing, energy, and planning. But every now and then something jelled, sometimes something grand, producing the same kind of juice that probably kept an Irma Vance going to Las Vegas once a year.

"So? So?" Richard Morse peered into her face, then into Larry's. "You want to share this? Do I have to beg? Do I have to tell you who it is who works for who around here?"

"Whom," Dalrymple corrected and was ignored.

"Hell, you're acting like the *Alpine Tunnel* deal went through," Dorian said. "What's up?"

"It is the *Alpine Tunnel*, isn't it?" That lazy, knowing smile lighted Maurice Lavender's face.

"I thought that was dead long ago," Luella said.

"They turned it down cold last October," Richard told her. "What, Charlie, what? You do not have my permission to do this to me."

"McMullins talked the author's estate into reconsidering Ursa Major's offer."

Now it was Richard Morse dancing Charlie around the crowded confines of the hall until they waltzed up against Dalrymple's expression. "Lieutenant, this is special, you know?" Charlie's boss gave a triumphant hoot. "We're talking history in the making here. We're talking another *Gone with the Wind*, another *Dances with Wolves*."

Dalrymple did not look impressed. But Charlie floated through the rest of her day. She did get partially caught up on her phone log, checking the progress of some of her writers. But she wasn't able to get hold of Keegan Monroe to return his call, although she did make it back to Long Beach in time to pick up buffalo steaks and three bottles of Dom Perignon. If no one could come to her last-minute victory party, she and Libby would eat what they could and freeze the rest. It was that kind of triumph.

As it turned out, everybody came. Mrs. Beesom brought her renowned pasta salad, Jeremy Fiedler his veggie stir-fry and an airhead named Connie. Maggie brought fruit compote. Libby brought droopy Doug Esterhazie. Tuxedo brought one of Mrs. Beesom's wild birds, dead. And very nearly ruined the celebration.

This weekend, she decided, when she wasn't doing the yard work or the housework, Charlie had to find a way to get rid of that goddamned cat—something she'd been threatening to do for almost a year. She turned from the older woman's stricken face to her daughter's unconcerned one. "This is it, Libby. I've had it."

"Mo-om, that's what cats do. They're carnivores like us." She looked pointedly at the bloody juice on the platter, all that was left of a hunk out of a buffalo.

Doug then explained with the restrained patience teenagers reserve for adults that Mrs. Beesom's bird feeders attracted birds. Birds attracted cats. It was all in the nature of things, and Tuxedo shouldn't be blamed for his nature. Any more than Charlie should be blamed for stopping at the gourmet deli on the way home and picking up buffalo steaks. How that kid always managed to put her on the defensive Charlie would never know.

They'd eaten on Charlie's patio, and she stretched out on the chaise longue with her coffee. It felt wonderful to put her feet up. "I'm sorry, Mrs. Beesom. We've been nothing but trouble for you since we moved in."

"Well, life has been more exciting, that's for sure," the old lady said bleakly. Jeremy and Maggie exchanged snide glances. Mrs. Beesom's life revolved around her church, her birds, television, and keeping close track of her neighbors. Maggie swore that the woman went through their garbage to discover their personal habits.

The Beesoms had once lived in an old house in the center of this lot, and when Mr. Beesom died, a developer talked his wife into selling it for one of the new houses he'd build. She was a small woman with a large stomach she kept covered with smocklike tops over polyester pants. Her thinning hair had turned from gray to white, but she seemed to have a fair amount of energy.

"I saw on the news tonight about the woman in your office that was murdered. It must be awful for you, Charlie," she led the way to the topic everyone had been too polite to bring up over buffalo.

"Yeah I know, and here I am celebrating," Charlie admitted. "But the whole agency would be tonight if it wasn't for Gloria and the police running around and everybody having to avoid reporters."

As she'd told them at dinner, this *Alpine Tunnel* project was one she'd brought with her from New York when she'd come to Congdon and Morse. The only best-selling author Charlie had ever represented died after one book, and Charlie lost the account to another agent when the estate took over the rights. But the literary agency where she worked in New York, Wesson Bradly, often used Congdon and Morse as its Hollywood connection, and Charlie served as liaison. So when Richard Morse went after *Alpine Tunnel* for a now-defunct independent production company, he used Charlie to begin negotiations with the author's estate through the new agent. The publisher got into it and decided on a new huge printing to tie in with the film, but the indie went under, the author's family hadn't liked the screenplay, and Goliath had brought out a similar historical that flopped like a beached salmon.

When Richard talked Charlie into coming out to work for him, the deal had a little life left because McMullins was still interested in the tie-in and had interested another indie, Ursa Major, in the deal. McMullins and Ursa Major brought Congdon and Morse and Charlie back into the picture, another screenplay was written, excitement mounted once more. And last October the family had said no. Flat out.

Last week the book's editor hinted that something was yet again in the wind, but Charlie had kept it quiet. And yesterday the deal was on again, but Congdon and Morse found out a day late because somebody murdered Gloria.

The night was warm and soft and filled with the sweet, tangy scent of lemon blossoms. Charlie could just hear the ocean over the traffic and emergency sirens. Jeremy sprawled on the other chaise fondling Connie with one hand and Tuxedo with the other. One of them was purring.

"What's all this witch business?" Jeremy asked. His eyes were open wide and seemed to glow in the city-dark like the cat's. "Was it some kind of a ritual murder?"

"In an alley behind a bank?" Charlie began to see why everyone had accepted her last-minute invitation. Once again she was the center of attention. But not for the reason she wanted to be. "She was always claiming strange powers and going to strange meetings with stranger people. Nobody at the agency paid much attention to it all."

Until she starts talking to you from the end of an empty hallway after she's dead. Is that a strange power or what?

That was a very alive person playing a very cheap trick, Charlie reminded herself.

At least she was able to sleep that night. After the heavy dinner and the champagne, and after closing her door tight to be sure it latched and kept Tuxedo out, she had barely closed her eyes before the alarm went off. A short time later, Libby perched on the nearby clothes hamper while Charlie stood in front of the bathroom mirror preparing hair and face to meet the world.

"Mom, what are you now, thirty-two?"

"Thirty-one. Don't make it any worse than it is."

"Here you are, thirty-one years old," Libby drew it out mournfully, "with a fifteen-year-old daughter. Don't you think it's time you thought about getting married?"

6

I know you're under a lot of stress, and I'm sorry if I upset you just now, okay Mom?" Libby blocked Charlie's exit from the john.

"I'm in a hurry. We're late. And what makes you think you upset me?"

"You just sprayed your hair with bathroom deodorant."

All the way to Wilshire on the interminable freeway, did Charlie scheme and fantasize and rejoice in the possibilities about to come out of the *Alpine Tunnel* deal? No.

Did she consider the ramifications of a murder at the agency and mull over the possible candidates for murderer? No.

Did she get on the car phone and call New York? She did not.

Charlie spent the entire time trying to figure out the connection between two-hundred-dollar Rollerblades, cheerleading, high school sororities, and her own unmarried state. She knew Libby. There was a connection somewhere. And whatever it was, it would cost Charlie bucks.

This weekend when she wasn't trimming the yard, cleaning the house, getting rid of the cat, doing the laundry and grocery shopping—she and Libby were going to have to take the time for a long talk. Charlie had never known the bliss of matrimony, nor had she known the desire. Motherhood was already more than she could handle. Libby had made it this long without a father figure, couldn't she hang on just a few more years?

Jesus, some kids have to go without food.

Riding up the public elevator to the fifth floor of the FFUCWB of P with Maurice Lavender, Charlie received the requisite hug-grope and continued congratulations on the *Alpine Tunnel* deal. And then Maurice raised a handsome brow. "What is that wonderful perfume you're wearing, sweetie? It's vaguely familiar, but I can't place it."

"*Eau de Potty,*" Charlie, who wasn't wearing any, told him and sidled away to the door just as it opened.

She stepped right into Lieutenant Dalrymple's chest. "Miss Greene, here you are. I was hoping for a few words with you before all the excitement starts. Have you had breakfast?"

Before she'd even set foot in her office, Charlie found herself, instead, facing the Beverly Hills Police Department over omelets and coffee at Sidney's.

"Have you had any thoughts about who might have killed Gloria Tuschman and why?" he asked pleasantly and as if they both had all week to laze around the breakfast table.

"Not really. That's your job. I have one, too, you know. Lieutenant, do you have a family?"

"A wife and two grown children, why?"

"Did your wife work outside the home while raising the children?"

"Once they were in school, certainly. You know a policeman's pay."

"Did she have time to solve murders, too?"

"She barely had time to clean the house, and I was no help, with my hours—ah, I see what you're getting at. I do realize you're busy. And I understand you have a young daughter."

"More like frantic, and she's fifteen, and I'm raising her

myself. Between home and office and freeway, I barely have time to read submissions. Which is a big part of my job, but there's no time for that during working hours. And I know this is going to sound incredibly cruel, but I've barely given poor Gloria a thought since I last saw you yesterday." Charlie pushed her plate away and reached for her coffee. Neither she nor Libby ate breakfast at home, and this was the first cup of the day. She sniffed the warm pleasure of it and took a gulp, continuing before he could interrupt her. "Right now you are concentrating on Gloria and those murders assigned to you. Do you have time to worry about or concentrate much on those assigned to other detectives?"

He'd hardly begun on his omelet, and now he paused to break and butter a muffin. "You are a very persuasive young lady."

"That's my job, too." She looked pointedly at her watch.

"You're overlooking something important." He took a bite of the muffin and spent forever chewing it. "Murder takes precedence."

"Lieutenant, I really have to get on the phone to New York soon. I've already lost a day. This *Alpine Tunnel* thing could well be a megadeal here."

"Yes," he said dubiously and cut another piece out of his omelet, "is this something to do with Switzerland or skiing?"

"*Phantom of the Alpine Tunnel*, the novel."

"Never heard of it."

"You must have. It was on the *New York Times* best-seller list for twenty-eight straight weeks. Of course that was a few years ago, but—"

"Unlike murder, fame is fleeting," he mused and continued enjoying his food, his movements precise, unhurried. "You're not the only one who seems untouched by the receptionist's sudden absence."

"But we all are, don't you see? That place is a madhouse

without someone on the phones and filtering traffic through the front door and the fax ... a hundred things. Clients will have seen about it on the news and be calling in worried that their business is not being seen to, that we're so preoccupied by the murder that opportunities are being overlooked and it will affect their careers. Actors are paranoid, and so are writers. I just hope Irma came in today to take charge."

"Gloria Tuschman's death, then, is an inconvenience rather than a grief?"

"I feel sorry for her. Nobody wants to be dead."

"But you didn't like her. I have the feeling no one did. Why?"

This man was not going to be manipulated, hurried, or put off. Charlie might just as well bite the bullet and consider Gloria. "She grated on people. I never felt comfortable around her, and I doubt the others at the agency did, either. But she was very good at what she did, and I don't think Richard realizes how hard she's going to be to replace."

"How did she grate on you? What was it she did that made you uncomfortable?" When Charlie just shrugged, he added, "Miss Greene, consider this a business breakfast. Time worth spending. Because it is, you know. Murder's a nasty business but every bit as exciting as show business if—"

"Can't you talk about anything but murder?"

"It's not going to go away, and neither am I. So, why did Gloria Tuschman make you uncomfortable?"

"I honestly can't put my finger on it. You can probably tell I love my job. It's exciting and wonderful and I wouldn't be anywhere else for the world. And she made it easier by being a good receptionist and keeping things running smoothly. We're all in and out of the office so much, and you could always count on Gloria to know where everybody was. I just never spent a lot of time around the front desk. I'd breeze by on my way in and out. Larry picks up my mail and keeps track of my calls. I didn't stop and talk to her much."

"You never had lunch or coffee breaks with her?"

"Lord no. I'd grab a cup of coffee on my way in and drink it at my desk. If I didn't have a lunch meeting, I'd probably had a breakfast meeting late and wouldn't want lunch. One of the assistants would take a break with Gloria while another covered for her at the desk. At lunchtime she put the phones on the answering service and went out with other secretaries in the building. If I'm in, I find that a very good time to get caught up."

"If you had no contact with her, how could she make you uncomfortable?"

"There was some contact of course. But I always had the feeling that if I stayed around her very long, she'd want something I didn't want to give her, or try to tell me something I didn't want to hear. I know it sounds dumb, but I avoided her whenever possible. Which doesn't mean I killed her."

"Something you didn't want to hear. Something like the fact that she thought you might be sensitive to certain stimuli or even be psychic?"

"You've been talking to Larry Mann." Charlie was forever passing on her irritations to her assistant.

"I overheard you talking to a dead woman, Miss Greene." His omelet was finally gone, and he wiped his lips carefully, folded the napkin, and placed it beside his plate so it looked like it hadn't been used. He took out his little spiral notebook again. "'You said you were in the garbage can, not in the bushes.'"

"I was just talking to myself."

"I don't think so. And another thing. You have never once asked me about any of the details of Gloria's murder. I would think natural curiosity would lead to questions here. Whether you liked her or not, this is a woman you actually knew." The mild-mannered homicide detective was going on the offensive. And he had all the clout in this deal. "One explanation for that could be that you already know the answers."

"It's only been two days, and there's been a lot else going on. And sure, I have questions, but I figure that when the proper authorities find the answers, we'll all know. You're not going to answer them until you're ready anyway. Why waste the effort? All I can tell you is I did not kill Gloria and I am not psychic. I was involved in a murder investigation last year, Lieutenant. In Oregon. And all I did was mess things up by asking questions. I learned my lesson. I will leave it all to you." Like the good little citizen that I am. If you think I'm going to go through all that again with the *Alpine Tunnel* deal pending, you're out of your mind.

"Yes, I phoned Sheriff Bennett of Moot County this morning. He spoke highly of you and sends his warm regards."

David Dalrymple waited for Charlie to respond to this easy opening. Actually, she had some warm memories of Sheriff Bennett that she figured were warming up her complexion about now, which probably said it all anyway. She must be on some interpolice computer thing just for having been involved in that murder at Moot Point last summer.

"So what are the questions you would ask me if you thought I'd answer them?" he said. "About the murder."

"I don't believe this. You're the expert on murder."

"But I didn't know Gloria alive. Help me, Miss Greene."

"My questions have nothing to do with knowing Gloria. They're the same you'd ask yourself if you had as little information as I do. What was Gloria hit with and where is that weapon? I mean in front of all of us Richard mentioned she'd been bopped, and you didn't contradict him, so I assume someone hit her with something. How did she get from the private hall on the fifth floor, dead, past all the people who are around that time of the day, to that back alley entrance and then up into the bushes? Where were her friends and relatives at this time, like her husband, Roger, for instance? What do the guys down on valet parking have to say about all this? There's nearly always an armed security guard hanging around somewhere, too. What about the people in the coven she claimed to be part of? I mean she was into séances, Ouija boards, you name it. The questions are endless, Lieutenant, and unless you've got all the answers, you have your work cut out for you. And so do I. Please? Unless you've decided to arrest me this minute, I need to get back."

"On one condition." He picked up the check. "I want you to walk with me to the end of that fifth floor hall again."

Much to Charlie's relief, Gloria, or someone pretending to be Gloria, did not speak to her when she and the lieutenant walked to, stood around and waited in, walked from, turned back and repeated the process, and then left that particular VIP hall on the fifth floor of the FFUCWB of P building. David Dalrymple was noticeably disappointed. But as far as Charlie was concerned, David Dalrymple was seriously weird.

Thank God Irma Vance was at the front desk when Charlie snuck behind her by way of the back hall with an unseen salute. Charlie, having come in via the VIP stairs, was now officially back on the premises unnoted, which might mean she might get something done—like work.

"Has Keegan called? Get me a line to Keegan. Hold everything else except McMullins, Ursa Major, *Alpine Tunnel* things. Line up how many calls I need to get through to New York otherwise. And, Larry, hurry, that damned Dalrymple has put me so far behind already—"

Charlie was actually through his cubicle and behind her desk, her pumps kicked off, her computer booting up, before she registered what her eyes had seen while her mind had been so organized. She rushed back to the cubicle that protected her office. "Larry? What's wrong? Larry?"

Charlie hadn't realized how high the stacks of screenplays, treatments, teleplays, manuscripts, and proposals had grown since last she'd noticed. Larry was a large person. There was his chair behind his computer keyboard, a small visitor's chair just inside the door, a towering drop-leaf file cabinet alongside it stuffed with proposals filed alphabetically by author, and a narrow path to Charlie's office door. Every other inch of space was stacked with material as yet unread and unalphabetized.

Larry was slumped over a pile of submissions next to his keyboard, his head buried in folded arms.

"We'll call in Harry and Lucinda to screen some of this, and I'll help you organize the rest right away. Hey, this is doable, trust me. Larry?" Harry and Lucinda were outside readers the agency hired on contract to help Charlie and Larry paddle through the flood. Most of the paying business came from contracted work like Keegan's, but every now and then there was a possible *Alpine Tunnel* in the pile worth wading through the muck to get to.

She closed the door to the hall. "I just hate to see a beautiful man cry."

He finally raised his head to stare at her dry eyed. "And I just hate people who say things like 'doable.'"

"It's not the backed-up work load, is it?"

"No, it's Gloria."

7

he backed-up work load would have been easier." Charlie slumped into the visitor's chair.

"I don't see how you and Richard can just blow this off and continue working like nothing happened. A woman we know was murdered right here in the building."

"That's work for the police, Larry. When I think of something I can do about it, I'll stop and do it. What do you want me to do, just be upset or what?"

"When you didn't know she was dead, but were worried about her being missing, you were upset enough to be hearing voices in the back hallway. Then when you find out she's murdered, you seem to feel better about it."

"Well, I could have maybe done something about her being missing. I can't do anything about her being dead."

"You're fucking pragmatic for a woman."

Charlie was never sure how to take him and didn't want to hurt or insult him. A good assistant was worth his weight in yen, and Larry was good. So now she said carefully, "Larry, you and I are just different. We're neither one right or wrong, just different. You see, to me pragmatic is a compliment."

He worked up a grimace. "You know, don't you," he said, "that you're everything I detest in a man?"

"Hey, if you want to take the rest of the day off, I'll fight it out with the Vance."

"There you go again trying to avoid things. What I want to

do is talk about Gloria, not go home and stew about her murder alone. I don't understand you, Charlie."

Charlie didn't understand him, either—why would you want to talk about something you were helpless to influence instead of something exciting like a megadeal you could participate in? But she had Irma hold her calls and took her assistant to the couch in her office so they could discuss Gloria in comfort. Maurice was right, Richard should get some counselors in here. But Charlie couldn't picture him spending the money. "Excuse me for sounding pragmatic again, and I'm not questioning your feelings, but Larry, you were not that immensely fond of Gloria."

"And you know it could have been one of us who killed her. Her husband was probably at work and has witnesses to prove it. I don't think the police are going to buy the theory that a coven of witches waltzed in here unnoticed to do her in. You'll notice this Dalrymple is spending a lot of time hanging around the office."

"Around the building. There're all kinds of offices in it. Larry, what's really bothering you?"

He had a male model's square jaw. When coming into the office he usually wore stylish cotton pants and a white shirt, with the sleeves carefully rolled up above the elbow and the neck open. A lightweight sport coat with patches on the elbows and a necktie in the pocket hung behind the open door to the hall for the occasional dressy lunch. He looked indefinably mussed and rumpled today, and his tan had taken on an unhealthy hue.

"I don't believe anybody at the agency has the airtight alibi they think they do. And I'm the only one strong enough to heave a body up into the bushes like that. I'm scared, Charlie."

"You had no motive. And it was not necessarily just one

person involved. Do you know who Richard was talking to in his office earlier that morning when Tracy heard voices?"

"Mary Ann Leffler and Keegan Monroe."

"Before the breakfast at Universal?"

"Yeah, and that meeting didn't last a half hour. Charlie, when I left to go over to the Chevron practically everybody was here."

"But Gloria told me over the car phone that most everybody had come in and then left on business."

"Probably just to needle you. She was always trying to make people feel guilty."

"Richard, Keegan, Mary Ann, Irma?" she asked and he nodded with each name.

"And Maurice, I think. Dorian, I know," he said. "And Tracy. I'm not sure about Luella. And when I came back the office was completely empty."

"Have you told Dalrymple all this?"

"I don't want to implicate myself, or irritate a killer, or lose my job."

"You think Richard did it?"

"All I know is that now that Gloria's gone, I'm low man on both the seniority and the clout totem poles around here. I'm not making any waves until I know what this is all about. And I was gone a little longer than just over to the Chevron for Ding Dongs for Gloria. I slipped in another errand first."

And if he raised the first alarm about alibis someone else would probably figure that out and call him on it in front of Dalrymple. "How much longer?"

"Half hour, forty-five minutes." He leaned forward in probably his most endearing pose, the butterscotch hair tumbling across his forehead. "You know, Charlie, I think you and I need to look into this whole business on our own before we go to the lieutenant? We know each other didn't do it. And we'll know better what we're getting into that way."

Charlie stared at her quiet phone and blank computer screen. All she wanted was to be happy and do the work she loved. Was that so much to ask of the world? "*We* did not go on this errand together," she said, "so maybe *you* better fill *me* in?"

"I had to meet a friend. It has nothing to do with Gloria or the agency or any of this, I swear."

"A friend? Larry, I thought you and Stew were solid." Stewart Claypool was Larry's significant other.

Color flowed back into her assistant's complexion. Anger pushed him to his feet. God he was something—sort of a combination Superman and Mitch Hilsten, Charlie's favorite superstar. "Stew and I *are* solid, Charlie. Just because you don't need anyone doesn't mean you know shit about relationships or that just because I meet someone it has to be about sex."

He slammed the door on his way out and, having propped her feet on the coffee table in front of the couch, she stared at the run in her hose as it zipped up from a big toenail to a knee. She stared at the lavender and beige dried arrangement in the dark blue pot in the center of the coffee table. When did that arrive? She honestly couldn't remember seeing it before. Hadn't there been something similar but with yellow in it? Irma must see to these things, too. Charlie watched the palm fronds droop outside the wall of window. They reminded her of droopy Doug Esterhazie.

What did he mean she didn't need anyone or know anything about relationships or sex? Why did life have to get so damn complicated just when it was getting so good? Charlie slipped out of her ruined hose and into one of the spare pairs she kept in a lower drawer.

Besides being an irreplaceable assistant, Larry Mann was an irreplaceable friend. "Know why you like him so much, don't you?" Richard Morse had said to Charlie no more than a month ago. "Because he's safe. You, lady, have a problem."

I do *not* have a problem.

Charlie slipped back into her killer heels and marched out to the cubicle. "You think you're so picked on," she told her assistant. "You don't have to go home to Stew and hear about cats who kill birds and two-hundred-dollar Rollerblades and sororities, huh?"

"Charlie?"

"You get me Keegan Monroe on the line and no more bullshit, understand? And after that be ready to plug back into *Alpine Tunnel.*"

"And where are you off to?"

"If the good Lieutenant Dalrymple is not lurking nearby, I'm off to beard the Vance about *our* little problem. But the deal is, my friend, that we mix business with snooping or *you* are back on *your* own. Right?"

"Right." He flashed her that smile. His parents must still be paying off the orthodontist.

Which reminded Charlie that this weekend when she wasn't doing all the other chores she'd promised fate—she'd better pay the bills. Was it any wonder she didn't look forward to weekends?

The Vance—Irma Vance, harridan of the paychecks and the paper clips, and scourge of Las Vegas—was appropriately paper thin with skin dried to parchment, her hair so long dyed that the expected glassy auburn had leaked to pink-tinted puffs resembling rice noodles. But her eyes soon laid to rest any illusion that she might be old-lady fodder for con artists.

"Charlie," she grimaced, her capped teeth too large for a shrinking face, "how're the adorable Libby and her harried mother surviving since last we spoke?"

People of Charlie's generation might have said something like, "Yo, Charlie, how're you and the kid doing these days?"

Charlie countered with, "Irma, I'm dying to hear all about Vegas. Did you win? Why are you back so early?"

"Yes, I won. That's why I'm back so early. Good morning, Congdon and Morse Representation. May I ask who's calling, please? Oh yes, Mr. Monroe, she's right here." Irma Vance flashed her caps again, this time with a wink. "It's for you, dear."

Larry, it turned out, had not located Keegan. He was calling from across the street on his own initiative. He said he needed to meet for a talk and would reveal little more over the agency line than that he meant right away.

They met in the lobby of the Beverly Pavilion, and Mary Ann Leffler was with him.

"Were you followed?" Mary Ann whispered.

"Hell, anything's possible now that there's been a murder at the agency. You two decide to work together? Why all the secrecy?"

"Let's take a walk," Keegan said and took her arm.

"In these shoes?" But Charlie found herself tugged along between the two writers to the end of a hall and out a service door, past a dumpster in which a man rummaged for food or aluminum.

Charlie would never get over how quickly Wilshire could end once you turned onto a side street. Richard Morse maintained that a Wilshire address was money in the bank. It was a wide, sun-drenched street with palms and flowers and imposing structures of glass and concrete and marble—elegantly proportioned, clean and bright compared to New York City standards—as if to announce that here there was so much money they didn't *need* to build too high.

But turn off Wilshire and you could be in a residential neighborhood in less than a block, sometimes with a buffer of small apartment buildings and sometimes with no buffer at all. Charlie couldn't help but notice how much better kept the tiny front lawns looked here than did hers in Long Beach.

"You realize you guys are being pretty silly. The Beverly Hills P.D. is not the gestapo. So out with it."

Mary Ann coughed something up from her knees and lit a cigarette while she walked. "We'll cooperate on the screenplay and have it in, in less than a week if you'll help us."

Charlie pulled them all to a stop. "You two have tied up development, damn near killing off the project because of scheduling problems, which you knew about.... Last time I saw you guys you were barely speaking, and now you're going to cooperate?"

"Before we met you at the Polo Lounge," Keegan stared at the pointy toe of his cowboy boot, "Well, we'd been to the agency first."

"Same morning that secretary was killed," Mary Ann added needlessly. She was wearing blue jeans, a T-shirt, and running shoes. The letters on the front of her shirt read, "Grandmother" surrounded by four arrows, pointing up, down, right, left. Charlie's own grandmother had worn polyester pantsuits, and her great grandmother wore dresses gathered big at the middle that needed ironing.

"What are you two worried about? Mary Ann, you didn't even know Gloria. And, Keegan, about all you ever knew of her was to have her buzz you into the office. I realize writers are paranoid, but I really don't have time for this. I hate to disillusion either of you, but yours is not my only project."

Keegan fronted the pointy toes of his boots up against the toes of her pumps. Since Charlie's heels were higher than his, he was no more than a few inches taller, and she could feel the warm breath of his sigh tickle her forehead. "Charlie, did you ever really read *Shadowscapes*?"

"I read so much, I can't remember all the details of everything forever—uh, it's about witchcraft and a ranch and Indians, but very intense and literary and full of meaning." And the film adaptation will probably be about men in mid-life crises with government agents breathing down their necks while they try to save beautiful heroines from something they're too stupid to realize has put them in mortal danger. Keegan, I do not want to discuss this in front of the author, okay?

"Witchcraft," Keegan said. "Witchcraft."

"I knew Gloria Tuschman," Mary Ann said.

Charlie was beginning to look forward to the freeway and Libby.

8

Mary Ann Leffler had been a noted novelist as a young woman, hit a long dry spell, and reemerged, years later, with *Shadowscapes*.

"The *New York Times* and the *Rocky Mountain News* said 'Grandmother writes another book!' You ever see, 'Grandfather, Clive Cussler, writes another book'? 'Tony Hillerman, grandfather, writes another book'?"

Mary Ann had taken up a few other hobbies when her books stopped selling to publishers. One of them was alternative philosophies and a newsletter on that subject.

"Well, I had to do something. Being a housewife can drive a sane woman crazy, and if you've been writing fiction very long, your brain's too dead to be good for much else."

"So how did you know our particular witch?" Charlie asked for the third time. She'd yet to meet an author who could come out with a straight answer. They always had to fill in the backstory.

"She'd been a fan of mine for years, and we'd corresponded." Mary Ann stared down at Charlie with a sideways slant as if one eye saw a lot better than the other. "It may take a year, but I always answer my readers' letters personally, and just because I wasn't selling to publishers didn't mean my readers had given up hope."

"About Gloria?"

"She offered to put the newsletter on a computer, print out a

master with columns and everything. Hell, before *Shadowscapes*
I couldn't even afford a computer. Her husband owned a print
shop and had a fancy system that did mailing labels. They sort
of took over publishing the thing. Made it a lot easier for me.
All I had to do was write my part of it and edit the stuff that
came in, send it on to Gloria and Roger Tuschman, and forget
about it."

"So you'd talked to her on the phone and written her. Had
you ever met her before the morning of the Universal breakfast that I just learned, by the way, didn't take more than a
half hour?"

"I'd been out here doing research for *Shadowscapes*, stayed
with Gloria and Roger."

"Why? It takes place in Montana."

"Well, there's lots more good stuff on witchcraft here."

"Mary Ann, get to the point," Keegan said, "Charlie's attention span is atrocious*ly* short."

"The point is I didn't know any witches in Montana, and
the Tuschmans offered to help me. Simple as that."

"That's why you're worried about becoming involved in
Gloria's murder?"

"No, Charlie," Keegan spoke through a grimace of impatience, "*Shadowscapes* was starting to make some money."

"And damned little of it trickling down to the author," Mary
Ann stomped on a cigarette butt. "Try to tell that to Gloria
and Roger."

"But the Tuschmans wanted a piece of it," Keegan added.

"Oh-oh," Charlie said.

"Right," Keegan said.

"Shit." Mary Ann Leffler lit another cigarette.

That evening, sweeping in on the 405 and getting off on
Seventh, Charlie stopped at Ralph's for makings for BLTs.

There was a white Porsche sitting in front of her house that she figured was visiting at a neighbor's until she'd parked in her courtyard slot and reached the top step to her sunken patio.

It wasn't dark yet, but a candle flame fluttered in an elegant cut-glass thing Charlie had never seen before, sitting on a tablecloth she'd never seen before, either. It covered the perpetually dirtied glass top of her picnic table. There were matching cloth napkins folded into fluted shapes on china she'd kept locked in a glass cupboard. The table was set for two.

Never mind that, who's the guy?

A man in a white dinner jacket stubbed a cigarette butt in one of Charlie's flowering plants and stared at her, as if this were his house and she'd just walked in uninvited.

"Hello?" Charlie asked. He did look familiar, yet she could swear she'd never seen him before.

He had one foot up on the edge of a planter set into a low concrete wall, an elbow resting on the raised knee, looking over his shoulder at her. He stepped back and straightened, his eyes moving from her shoes to her face. "You can't be Libby's mother."

Libby strikes again. Jesus, now what?

A slow smile replaced the shock on his face. "You weren't expecting me, were you?"

Before Charlie could answer, Libby rushed through the kitchen door to grab the grocery bag, briefcase, and purse from her arms. "Dinner's almost ready, Mom. Don't you want to change into something more comfortable?"

Like what, shorts and a T-shirt? "Libby, what's going on?"

The man who'd apparently come to dinner laughed behind dark-rimmed glasses. He had dark hair and graying sideburns like Richard Morse. Add the dinner jacket, and he looked like an ad for Dewars. "Those kids are up to something. I thought I was the only one not in on it. I'm Ed Esterhazie."

"You're droop . . . I mean you're Doug's dad?" She finally walked down the three steps to her own patio to shake his hand. "You don't look like an Ed."

But he did look a little like droopy Doug, who appeared from nowhere with a pewter tray Charlie had last seen hanging on her dining room wall. It held two drink glasses, each with an ice cube and a lemon slice floating on amber liquid. The kid wore a sport jacket over dirty shorts and one of her dirty dish towels over his arm. "Charlie, I'd like you to meet my father."

"Doug, who's doing the cooking?"

"Libby."

"Oh God." Charlie grabbed a glass.

When Doug was gone, his father sat in a chair, still grinning. Charlie collapsed on a chaise, took a slug of scotch and soda, and had a good laugh herself. "How did you get roped into this, Ed?"

"I'm still not sure. I was made to feel I would be a cad, a subhuman, if I did not accept your dinner invitation. You were presumably prepared to jump off the Queen's Way Bridge if I did not grant your wish to meet me. Libby is very persuasive. The kids painted you as a poor lonely heart adrift in the world who wanted nothing more than to spend the day preparing me a gourmet meal. Instead, I arrive and find you not even home from work yet."

Yeah, well maybe so, but don't you think the dinner jacket's a little much, Ed? "Every night I come home to a new surprise. All I can tell you is that whatever's going on has something to do with Rollerblades or cheerleading or high school sororities or all of the above and that your dinner will be unique."

"Now that you mention it," he said when the feast was set before them. "I don't believe I have ever had Dom Perignon with macaroni and cheese before."

"There was a bottle left over from a party we had last night." She added quickly, in case he thought Libby was right and she really did like to cook, "Sort of a potluck with the neighbors . . . to celebrate." Then, of course, she had to go into her work and the agency and the *Alpine Tunnel* project and the murder—wishing all the while she hadn't started this in the first place.

But Ed Esterhazie was flatteringly attentive. All Charlie knew about him was that he and his ex had split the children, Ed taking Doug and she taking a daughter. The ex had remarried and lived in Florida and Ed and Doug lived with a housekeeper in a house, worthy of Bel Air, a few blocks away. He traveled extensively, mostly for pleasure as far as she could tell. Anyway, he was not the macaroni and cheese type.

She broke off finally with, "You know, actually you're lucky? I make Libby cook dinner one night a week, and it's almost always beanie wienies."

"With ketchup?"

"Of course with ketchup. You can't eat beanie wienies without ketchup. But I do think we might be wise to make our own coffee."

When they carried their dirty dishes inside, the kids were in with the TV and didn't even notice.

"What's that smell?" Ed asked.

"Just rotten bananas," Charlie assured him.

"Don't you ever pull a trick like that again," Charlie rounded on her daughter when they were alone. "I'll make my own social arrangements, thank you." God, my life's a sitcom.

"No you won't. You don't ever go out with guys. All you do is work and complain that I cost too much money. Do you know that Doug's father belongs to the yacht club?"

"I am not the yacht club type, and I like my work, Libby."

"Here I go to all that trouble and planning. I was just thinking of you. But do you appreciate it? Noooo."

"Yeah, well you'll notice who's doing the dishes." Charlie straightened from bending down in front of the dishwasher, wanting to take back that last remark but knowing it was too late. You didn't get a second chance with Libby Greene. Charlie realized again and with that same little shock that Libby was taller than she was.

By the time she reached the office the next morning, Charlie was still drained from the verbal knock-down-drag-out she and Libby had had the night before and the icy stone-cold silence of mutually hurt feelings instead of breakfast.

Libby had finally come up with the ultimate weapon ... well no, that would have been, "Guess what, Mom, I'm pregnant." What she had come up with was a new euphemism for Charlie, "UM." It stood for unwed mother.

Charlie's mood was foul. Maurice Lavender was fortunate not to share the elevator and his friendliness with her on this morning, and Lieutenant Dalrymple was lucky he wasn't lurking outside the public door with a breakfast invitation. There were already five or six manila envelopes leaning against the door, and an intense young man with a juvenile mustache and sparsely bristled chin lurking near the public restrooms at the end of the hall. He did not look like a reporter.

He started toward her as she pressed the buzzer. She was frantically searching her purse for the card that would gain her entrance when the Vance asked who was there.

"It's Charlie, and I'm being followed." The latch clicked

open and she slipped inside but then couldn't close the door behind her because there was a boot in it. Charlie shrugged an apology to Irma and raced to the back corridor to her office while the formidable executive secretary, sounding as cold as Libby, asked the hopeful if he had an appointment.

Charlie slammed the door to the hall and leaned against Larry's emergency sport coat.

He gave her his long-suffering glance and reached into a lower cupboard beside his chair. "If it's a Maalox moment, I just happen to have a spare fifth."

"Now she's trying to marry me off."

"Libby."

"Libby. To the yacht club, no less."

He knew her moods well enough to let her get halfway through her calls and some of her mail before he slipped into her office. "So, did you learn anything yesterday? Why did Irma come back early?"

"Just because she won, she says. Knowing Irma, she wouldn't want to risk her earnings by staying. Then again Irma knows she has more than enough will to quit when she wants to. I'm not sure it holds water, but it sure doesn't lead to murdering Gloria." She told him about Mary Ann Leffler. "Far as I can see, her worries are groundless. I'm amazed that Gloria and Roger would do such a thing, but it's no motive for murder, either. I can tell by your expression that you have news that can hardly wait. Run get us some coffee first, okay?"

"On my way, boss."

Charlie hated it when he called her boss. But at the same time she kind of liked the idea of it.

But before they could get to his news or the coffee, the phone rang again. This time it was Richard Morse. He wanted Charlie up to his house on the double. He gave a ghoulish laugh, "The phantom is arising. Grab your file, have Irma collect mine, and bring her along. Put The Kid or Tweetie on the phones." Tweetie was Tracy Dewitt's office name. If you walked her too fast her breathing made chirping sounds.

Larry ended up on the front desk. Like he said, he was low man on the totem pole now that Gloria was gone. "When you have her alone in the car, ask the Vance about the famous party at Gloria's house," he whispered with knowing nods and winks to Charlie while Irma was still off collecting Richard Morse's paper file on previous *Alpine Tunnel* negotiations.

"I can remember getting a call like this seven years ago," Irma said, clutching the Toyota's armrest and pumping the rider's phantom brake as Charlie careened through traffic heading for Bel Air. "And guess who was sitting in Mr. Morse's living room when I arrived? Mitch Hilsten."

"Is he that gorgeous in real life?" Charlie had never met him, but she'd had the fantasy hots for him most of her adult life.

"Oh ho, the silver screen does not begin to do that man justice, Charlie dear."

Charlie, not being the detective her assistant wanted her to be, and thinking about Mitch Hilsten the superstar, forgot all about trapping Irma into divulging guilty secrets about some party at the Tuschmans'. She couldn't imagine Irma mingling socially with the office receptionist anyway.

The Beverly Hills police drove black and whites, but Bel Air had its own private security force driving white cars. The fences and privacy hedges bordering plebeian thoroughfares here were as forbidding as the chain link fences around maximum security prisons. The lawns fronting the winding inner streets were as precisely kept as the homes behind them. The only people on the sidewalks were Hispanic gardeners and Oriental cleaning ladies.

"I wonder how much of this we pay for by not demanding a raise," Charlie quipped to the executive secretary as the Toyota swept between stone pillars to join the lineup of far more impressive cars on the paved semicircle of drive. She received an icy stare for an answer.

There was no Mitch Hilsten at this meeting. But there was fresh-ground coffee, fresh chilled fruit, hot breakfast rolls with real butter, and mimosas to celebrate. And no, it wasn't what a lawyer or a real estate agent would call a closing, but in fantasyland it was a lot closer to a done deal than could be said to happen ninety percent of the time.

9

Unlike Ed Esterhazie last night, Richard Morse was not dressed for the occasion. He lounged at poolside in shorts and sports shirt, tanned and gregarious, passing fresh strawberries and hunks of pineapple and melon to the producer and the money men and Edna Thurlow's daughter and grandson and their lawyer, all of whom were dressed for success. So were Charlie and the Vance, the only females present except for the daughter and the Vietnamese maid with the coffee and the mimosas.

Talk about a coup—to have the head of an agency hosting this at all and at his home to boot. Charlie scanned the holes in the prickly hedge guarding the huge pool and tiny lawn for the legs of a reporter from *Variety* or the *Reporter.* She gazed at her boss with new respect.

And he noticed. An eyelid notched three-fourths of the way down one protuberant eyeball and stayed there as if stuck. He was the only nonanimated creature she had ever seen who could do that. It said, "Stick with me, kid."

"Are you his wife or ... something?" Edna Thurlow's daughter, Tessie, asked Charlie behind her hand. Tessie's body had grown middle-aged lumpy, but her complexion made you want to reach out and stroke her cheek.

"I work at his agency. I was your mother's agent in New York when we sold *Alpine Tunnel.*" And Charlie could hear

Edna's soft Louisiana blurring in her daughter's speech. Why an elderly lady from Louisiana would choose to write a first novel about narrow-gauge railroads in the Colorado Rockies had always been a mystery to Charlie. "Why did the family change its mind about this?"

"My brother passed on. He was the one who never liked the way the story was going to be changed. My sister and I have too many children needing college. Mama would understand. She'd always wished Flora and I had gone to college. It was one of her greatest disappointments when we married right out of high school. Now we're both divorced with nine children between us. Earl was an attorney and only had one son, so he could afford to be fussy."

Charlie would never understand how a mother survived more than one teenager. Tessie's son, Sonny, looked a little older than Libby—and essentially wholesome, responsible, healthy, mature, boring, safe. Charlie wondered what it would take to get him to Long Beach for beanie wienies on the patio.

"What do you think, Charlie?" Richard Morse asked, and literally everyone turned to her expectantly.

"What?"

"*Do* you think Keegan Monroe will be finished with his current project in time to be considered a possibility to script this project?"

"Oh absolutely," Charlie lied happily, "no doubt about it."

While Richard went on to sing Keegan's praises and list his credits, she paused to run close-ups of Keegan's recent moods through her mental camera lens. Something was bugging him. Something besides Mary Ann Leffler and her adverbs. Something neither he nor Charlie needed right now.

And then without warning the conversation turned to the recent murder at the agency. Apparently, Congdon and Morse had made both *Variety* and the *Hollywood Reporter*, and for all the wrong reasons, and the witchcraft angle was being played to the hilt.

"Don't worry," Richard assured Murray Goldstein, from Ursa Major. "It had nothing to do with business or the agency. It was a fluke. And Beverly Hills' finest are hot on the scent, and besides, we have our own in-house detective. Matter of days, maybe hours, and poor Gloria's murderer will be named and we can all forget about it."

Charlie thought those last a poor choice of words and tried to smile reassurance at Tessie and Sonny.

"Yeah, Charlie here solved a murder case up in Oregon just last June. She's got a sixth sense about these things. She'll probably finger the murderer before the cops, huh, Charlie?"

"Finger the murderer?" Charlie yelled at her boss when all but she and the Vance and the maid had left. "What was that all about? I was the prime suspect in that case, not a detective."

"Charlie, baby, relax. You realize how close this is to coming together? A little exaggeration at a time like this is not going to queer the deal. And you *are* the only one in the agency who's ever been near a murder investigation, let alone a part of one." His head nodded in accelerated motion, and his knee kept time. "Wouldn't hurt if you'd help out a little, you know. Not like the rest of us never did anything for you."

"Richard, Lieutenant Dalrymple and the men with him are professionals. And if you want a private investigator, you can hire one. I'm a literary agent."

"You already work for me, why hire somebody? Just promise you'll keep your eyes and ears open and think about our problem a little. Never know what it'll turn up. You got a good head. You just need to focus it better. You let it scatter like buckshot."

"Only if you'll tell me how you got this morning put together so fast. Got Edna's daughter out from Louisiana and everybody else who was here? It's only been two days."

"Only been two days. Your time, it's only been two days. By the time McMullins found out about it the whole thing was already in the works out here. Murray and Ursa Major were lighting fires in three different places before your little editor friend in New York knew there was smoke in the air. And the daughter was already out here." He was forever pointing out to her how uninfluential were her contacts in New York. "Listen, I'll take Irma back to the office with me. You go scare up Keegan, see what you can get burning under him. Get him excited, Charlie, take him out to lunch, whatever—but if you get him worked up over this project—not that it's an offer yet—maybe he'll get off his can and wrap the script with the Leffler woman. He got anything else besides his novel lined up? This thing's made for him. And you got anything better to do?"

"No, but I promised Tina I'd go with her when she pitches CBS Monday. For moral support. I can't let her down." And before that a weekend with not enough hours. When am I going to read, damn it? And who in the hell has time for murder?

But Charlie jumped back in the Toyota and headed for Coldwater Canyon sucking antacid tablets. And practicing her own pitch to Keegan. "You're getting a belly full of working with book authors, right? *Alpine Tunnel* will be all yours. The author's dead. And there'll be lots of nice money. This is going to be big, I just know it."

But when she pulled off onto the secluded drive, she found Lieutenant David Dalrymple had beaten her there.

Coldwater Canyon had growths of huge pine—so different from those she'd grown up with in Colorado—the better to secrete pricey little houses. Charlie wondered if she'd ever be able to afford such a neighborhood. She had two writers who could. It kept them busy working for her instead of on their novels, though. Keegan's house was larger than Charlie's, but it was small for Coldwater Canyon. Built into the hillside, it was made of natural rock and glass. Instead of redwood decks it had rock terraces connected by stairs along one end.

Lieutenant David Dalrymple leaned over the metal-pole railing that reminded her suddenly of the ones in the back hall at the agency. He stood on the middle terrace and watched Charlie approach. The lower level was given up solely to writing. Keegan had walls removed to make it one large den with a storage room at the back. The middle level held kitchen and living room. The upper level was for sleeping. Keegan moved a girlfriend in every now and then, but she'd inevitably begin to make demands on his writing time and he'd move her out again. He was such a lamb, women tended to mistake his innate politeness and good nature for wimpdom. Even though he considered himself a hack, and even though he grew impatient with the treachery in show business, he was devoted to his craft.

"Well, well Miss Greene, how interesting to find you here. Doing a little sleuthing after all?" The sun lit up the exposed front part of his scalp through holes in the tree branches. He still looked nothing like a cop, and the ones on television certainly didn't talk like this guy.

"Just visiting a client on business matters, Lieutenant. What brings you here?"

"Murder, Miss Greene, as always."

There *was* something familiar about his speech pattern, what was it? "I don't see the point. Keegan hardly knew Gloria."

"But, if I'm not mistaken, he worked closely with Mary Ann Leffler."

"Mary Ann's been murdered?"

"Mary Ann is missing. And it doesn't look promising."

"Oh shit." Charlie grabbed a rail and swung around to sit on a stone stair.

"Your client's words exactly." Dalrymple sat down beside her and took out his little notebook. "Now I would like you to describe to me completely your last meeting with Mary Ann Leffler. Leave out nothing, even if it seems unimportant."

When she'd described the conversation she'd had the day before with the novelist and Keegan on their stroll off Wilshire, he stopped writing long before she'd finished. He'd already gotten this from Keegan.

"Witchcraft again." He raised his head to peer sternly at her down through the magnifying arches at the bottom of his glasses. "Why didn't you come to me right away with this information?"

"There is so much going on at the agency right now, other than murder, and I just didn't think it was all that important."

"That's for me to decide."

"Oh come on, Lieutenant, you know people aren't going to come to you with every little thought, suspicion or half-formed uneasiness that crosses their minds. You're getting ready to charge one of us with murder. You made it pretty clear you don't think it's an outside job."

"Sheriff Bennett said you'd put it something like that."

"I suppose he also told you I'd just run out and do my own detecting. That's why you keep setting me up for it."

"No, as a matter of fact, Mr. Morse at your agency informed me that if I didn't hurry and 'wrap' the investigation so that business can get on as usual, he'd sic his own in-house detective onto the case and clear it up in hours. I realize this is show biz, Miss Greene, but does everybody in that place live in a fantasy world?"

His bewilderment was obviously genuine this time, and Charlie bumped his shoulder gently with her head and laughed. "We probably all seem nuts, huh? The frenetic energy, bursts of excitement, incredible optimism, improbable dreams?"

He peered down at her from the tops of his lenses now. His eyes were still huge. "That was very well put. Right on the money, as they say. Perhaps you should consider writing instead of agenting other writers' work."

"Nah, that came straight from a manuscript somewhere. As I remember it had to do with football." But she suddenly had a take on what was so familiar and yet incongruous about his speech. She'd bet the mortgage he watched mysteries from England on PBS.

"If you come across anything else, I would appreciate your passing it on promptly."

Charlie smiled and promised him nothing.

He rose to leave and turned back several steps down. "And, Miss Greene, the insider's view, the mind unclogged by routine and past failures, the fresh approach, is often quite helpful. Obviously there's much I can't divulge, but if I can help you in any way I'll try."

Jesus, he must read the stuff too. Charlie waved as he turned his unmarked car in the driveway, stood, brushed off her skirt, and went to find her writer—realizing she hadn't even asked the details of Mary Ann's disappearance. Keegan would know.

Charlie and Keegan sat on the balcony of the Pane Caldo Bistro on Beverly Boulevard. She picked at the calamari (chewy squid) bits littering her pasta al dente (tough spaghetti). She'd already eaten at Richard's but wanted Keegan Monroe well fed and happy to hear her pitch. Instead, he wanted to talk about nothing but fucking murder.

"Thought you gave up swearing because you were a mommy," he said, and she realized she'd let her thoughts trespass on her tongue again. She had to quit this. Show business was largely subterfuge, and one should never lose control of one's pitch.

"Thought you gave up smoking," Charlie countered and nodded at the ashtray, where he'd left a smoldering butt when his cioppino was set before him.

"What do you expect? The guy practically accused me outright of killing Gloria and Lady Macbeth and then stuffing Lady Macbeth someplace he couldn't find her." He broke open a dripping clam shell and left bloody tomato-goo drops on the tablecloth as if in emphasis. "You got to do something here. Ask around, you know, like you did in Oregon? My dad said you worked it all out before he did, and he knew everyone involved in that murder."

First Larry, then Richard, then Lieutenant Dalrymple for God's sake, and now Keegan. Keegan was a very intelligent person. "It's got to be television," Charlie pointed her fork rudely. "Everybody watches too much television, and they're starting to believe that stuff. Keegan, you're a writer. You make it up. You know better. You know it's make-believe. Don't you?"

He didn't answer her, just dunked a piece of garlic bread in the cioppino broth, glanced around to see who might notice he was lunching with his agent.

"I mean, having nonprofessional people solve crimes is good for entertainment purposes, but we're all supposed to know better. It just makes you feel good to think you maybe could. But, Keegan, I didn't solve anything or figure anything out in Oregon among your dad's friends. I stumbled, no, bumbled into a nest of amateur killers who any cop will tell you are very dangerous, and damned near got myself killed."

And I'm not real anxious to jump into that little sauté pan again, let me tell you.

But Monday you're going into CBS with Tina Horton to support her pitch of a television series based on just such a premise—that a little old lady veterinarian in Sun City, Arizona can solve crimes the Phoenix police can't figure out because she has raised eight children and treated thousands of animals and therefore knows all there is to know about the human condition. You are a fake, Charlie Greene.

10

It was a hot day for April, and heat waves shimmered off the Writers Guild building down the street. Traffic noise and exhaust stink swam up from Beverly Boulevard to the Pane Caldo's balcony. Charlie would have preferred to eat inside where they didn't have to yell over the Boulevard.

"Hey Charlie," a man leaned from a table across the aisle, "what's Congdon and Morse up to now, knocking off secretaries just to get mentioned in *Variety*?" He wrinkled his nose like a rabbit. "Just kidding."

Charlie couldn't place him, but his red plaid sport coat and brown pants screamed agent. She gave him a smile filled with a lack of humor and ignored him. "Look," she said to Keegan, "Mary Ann Leffler probably got her snoot full of the show biz set, and to make a point, lit out for someplace to cool off without telling anybody. She'll turn up."

Mary Ann had been staying at a beach house in Malibu owned by one of the muckety-mucks at Goliath Productions. After she and Keegan talked to Charlie yesterday afternoon, the two writers parted, making a date to meet at the beach house that evening. Keegan was to bring Chinese carry-out, and they planned to stay up all night wrestling the *Shadowscapes* script into line. (It was a fact that many of Charlie's writers worked best at night.) But when Keegan and the carry-out arrived, he couldn't get Mary Ann to answer his knock. She'd always kept the doors and windows locked tight.

He waited around until one of the producer's yes-men showed up to see how they were doing. He and Keegan broke in. No sign of Mary Ann. They warmed up the carry-out and ate it, got on the phone, and started calling. Mary Ann and her rental car were missing, but her things were still at the beach-front house.

"She didn't even call her kids to let them know." Keegan didn't find Charlie's solution reassuring. "She's a devoted mommy, too, remember, and grandmommy. The husband's up in Canada fishing."

"That's probably where she went. I don't know why everyone is jumping to the conclusion something happened to her."

"Because, Charlie, she had a connection to Gloria Tuschman. And Gloria was murdered." He studied the glass of milk she was nursing. "Ulcer acting up again?"

"I do *not* have an ulcer. Merely an easily upset stomach. Indigestion. Okay?"

Today he wore a bolo tie with a big piece of turquoise and silver holding it together. His mustache looked weedier than usual with cioppino spots dotting the light hairs.

She figured one of the reasons he was so successful was that he was nonthreatening. Which was not an asset that normally played well in the industry, but somehow worked for him. Maybe it was the clear, dead-center sort of thinking his eyes persuaded you he was always doing. The wire-rimmed eyeglasses with deceptively expensive tinting suggested honesty, dependability, keenness.

Most of Charlie's writers lived from hand to mouth, had mates with honest work, or shagged part-time jobs wherever they could. She figured that's how valet parking came to be invented. She even represented one who worked nights as an armed security guard. But a handful like Keegan had hit it hot early and remained consistent. And he had a good head for a writer. Lived well but not lavishly, didn't spend a lot on his women, had few illusions about the industry. However, lighting a fire under him, as her boss asked her to do, was not an easy job.

"You're a workaholic," he said. "You know that."

"And you're not, I suppose?"

"I'm dedicated. That's different."

"You don't want the *Alpine Tunnel* script?"

"No, but I need it. And you know that, too. Someday, oh Siren of the Checkbook, I will write the screenplay of my own published novel, and I might even let you run the deal. But don't count on it."

"I promised I'd send your novel out for you when you finished it, didn't I? How far along is it now?"

"I've started over. It got too long."

"I told you to just finish it and then go back and cut and shape. You have room to explore and invent, surprise yourself and me. You're not under contract, you can do what you want."

"I will. This is the last start-over. I promise."

"Too many adverbs, right?"

He always had great concepts for novels, but somehow they got lost in the mechanics. He rewrote all the freshness out of them, worried them to death, often never completed them. Charlie loved writers, made her living off them, but would never understand them.

While they waited for the parking valet to walk five feet to collect Charlie's Toyota (there was no avoiding the ransom here) they watched Guy Matell, the executive director of the Writers Guild, pull in in his new Jaguar.

"Must be slumming," Charlie muttered.

"He has to deal with money and power for the rights of some seventeen hundred writers," Keegan whispered through his teeth—not an easy thing to do. The Guild provided the

Jag. A new one every year. One of the perks of the privileged. "He's not going to cut much green in a Chevy."

While they waited to pull out into traffic, Keegan said in that reasonable, innocent manner of his, "I assume we're heading for the print shop."

"Print shop?" Charlie had planned to hurry him back to Coldwater Canyon and then herself to Wilshire and the agency to find out any new developments in the *Alpine Tunnel*–Ursa Major deal and to try to make another dent in her phone log. "What print shop?"

The Kwick Kinky Kopy Shoppe was in Pasadena. It sat in a dying shopping center—two newer, more upscale malls were nearby—weeds sprouting in the outlying concrete cracks of the parking lot, the shop windows on either side of it empty but for "For Lease" signs. There was a "Closed" sign next to the one announcing that Kwick Kinky Kopy was open eight days a week, twenty-five hours a day.

Keegan got out to read the small hand-lettered card taped to the glass door and returned to the Toyota. "Closed for Gloria Tuschman's Memorial Séance and Dance."

"Maybe we can talk to Roger next week. Right now—"

"We go to Gloria Tuschman's Memorial Séance and Dance."

"Keegan—"

"Sign says it's in Happy Valley Canyon, 1132 Honeah Place. Number 568. I never heard of Happy Valley Canyon." He started pawing through the glove compartment. "You got a *Thomas Brothers Guide*?"

Happy Valley Canyon was all the way back the way they'd come and then a good forty minutes north and west. 1132 Honeah Place backed onto a commercial grove of orange trees now in bloom. Electric voltage hummed through multilayered wires overhead, and down below bees by the zillions hummed around the trees. The air was almost too sweet to breathe. The clingy dripping fragrance of orange blossoms always reminded Charlie of gardenia. Gardenias always reminded Charlie of a drink at Trader Vic's. She took off her suit jacket and threw it in the back of the Toyota.

She stood on the paved parking lot behind an old stucco apartment-turned-condo complex that appeared to be its own community. It spread to either side as far as the curvature of the earth allowed, and you could tell it was old because the stucco had metallic glitter flakes in it. The orange grove was planted in straight lines like a field, with irrigation pipes set to dump water in tidy trenches carefully maintained between them.

Heat roiled off car roofs. Most of the condo dwellers were down in the city at work this time of the day, and the lot was more than half empty. But a familiar forest-green sedan was parked next to the fence. It looked a lot like the unmarked one Lieutenant Dalrymple had been driving that morning in Coldwater Canyon.

"Here to study the suspects?" Keegan asked, following the direction of her gaze and her thoughts. There was another note taped to the window on the back door of Number 568. "Through the gate and into the woods." Charlie and Keegan followed the fence line to the nearest street, where half of a vehicle gate stood open, posted with "No Trespassing" signs and warnings that the fence was wired with electricity.

The road beyond the fence was dirt, with an assortment of shoe prints snaking along in the dust. The skin under Charlie's pantyhose and bra itched as if demented fire ants were dancing on her body before she and Keegan came to the end of the shoe tracks. A lone drop of sweat tickled between her breasts down to her navel.

No one danced. The road was one lane wide and blocked completely by a circle of people sitting close together on webbed lawn chairs and folding stools. Lieutenant David Dalrymple knelt on one knee between two elderly ladies. He alone was watching their arrival. The rest had their eyes clenched tightly as they gripped the hands to either side of them.

A man sitting next to Gloria's husband, Roger, looked as if he were undergoing a helium enema—face puffed scarlet with purple highlights and body arched.

Everyone dripped sweat and chanted, "Glor-e-ah, Glor-e-ah."

Bees droned and high-voltage wires hummed backup. It could have been church.

Another man stood away from the group over in the shade of an orange tree, a suit coat hooked over his shoulder by an index finger, his other hand shooshing bees with his handkerchief. His hair was cut in the old astronaut crew. His expression was plenty fed up. He looked a lot more like a cop than David Dalrymple.

The man who appeared about to explode relaxed a little, and, opening his eyes, said, "Wait, I think I'm getting something finally." He looked up into Charlie's cynical gaze. "Gloria?"

"My name's Charlie."

He was a large man with lots of hair and eyebrows and muscle and belly, maybe in his mid-fifties. Hair bristled in his ears and over the top of a V-neck T-shirt and on the back of his arms and hands. He wore tan work pants and hiking boots. Charlie had expected the person in charge of the séance would be a woman in, say, a long skirt, sandals, beads, graying hair dyed to pink—an old granola girl. This guy looked more like an ill-used stunt man.

"Won't you join our circle, Charlie?" His color was calming down, but his breath still came in gasps. "Gloria needs help."

"Talk about your understatement." Charlie grunted when Keegan Monroe stabbed an elbow in her ribs.

They all stared at her now, and the circle of aluminum chair bottoms were scooted apart to include her.

The man under the bees and blossoms curled a stick of chewing gum into his mouth and, cranking up one cheek and both eyebrows, grinned at her discomfort. Keegan gave her back a gentle prod. David Dalrymple, from across the circle pleaded, "Please, Miss Greene?"

Charlie plugged into the hands on either side, but she'd be damned if she'd kneel in the dirt or close her eyes.

Roger Tuschman didn't close his eyes, either. They were puffy with exhaustion. It was obvious he had not expected her to be here, and interesting that no one at the agency had been notified of this ceremony. Charlie had met him maybe four or five times, once at a Christmas office party Richard Morse swore he would never throw again. It had been at his house, and Gloria had soaked up some mood-altering substance and pushed Roger in the pool. Which was a boring and passé thing to do, but Roger had felt the loss of dignity out of all proportion and left without Gloria.

The sun hammered on Charlie's head, setting up her own buzz to match the bees and the wires. It made her slightly dizzy. The man on her one hand was young, his grip hurt as he got back into the spirit of things. The lady on her other was past middle age and into early seniordom. Her clasp trembled. She looked more like a medium than the big guy in charge. Both hands were sweaty. Charlie's stomach was not a bit happy with this whole scene and her feet hurt. Damn it, Gloria, speak up and let's get this over with. I haven't got all day.

"I think that's a great idea," the big hairy leader said and stood. Everyone dropped hands and began to gather themselves and assorted seating.

"Charlie, are you okay?" Keegan put an arm around her waist and started walking her back down the dirt road.

"What's a great idea?" she asked him and Dalrymple, who came to flank her other side.

"Don't you remember?" the lieutenant stopped, and the other cop left the shade to join them, really leering now.

"You don't remember, do you?" Dalrymple turned her to face him. "Or are you just toying with us?"

Keegan said quietly behind her, "You told the medium what to do, Charlie."

"I just told Gloria to hurry up so I could get out of here." But Charlie could swear she hadn't said that aloud. "What did I tell the medium?"

"You said, 'touch my things,'" Keegan answered. "I can't believe you don't know."

"Oh my God. Did he?"

"Did he what?"

"Touch my—"

"No, no," Dalrymple hurried her along now, and the other cop guffawed, "not you. Gloria. She spoke through you."

A set of Gloria's acrylic fingernails, complete with jewel strips, and a red dress, much like the one she'd worn to die in, lay spread across the dining room table in Number 568. Lieutenant Dalrymple added a ladies' wristwatch, a pair of white earrings with red polka dots, and the red stiletto-heeled shoes.

Marvin Grunion, the spiritualist, sat, and everyone else stood. He placed all the bright red acrylics on the dress, and they blended so well that if you didn't look closely all you saw were the tiny fake jewels. He hummed a soft monotone like he missed having the bees as backup and added the earrings and watch, then the shoes. He bunched the dress around the assortment. A stiff white shoulder pad popped out of the neckline so suddenly someone squeaked a choked-off scream. More people were arriving, but fell silent once they entered the room.

Charlie had a low tolerance for weird people. Too many at one time was threatening. After all, she had never been that comfortable around even just Gloria, and this was a real assortment of all ages and dress and styles. But no one in particular you'd look twice at walking down the street. Then again, it was southern California.

Marvin Grunion rearranged the dress and stuffed the shoulder pad out of sight. He circled the earrings and the watch with the acrylics and looked puzzled about what to do with the shoes. The wall behind him was covered from floor to ceiling with shelves of different heights and widths, some small enough to feature pewter miniatures, two large enough to hold ornate candle holders, and all sizes in-between. One of the candle holders was empty, the other held four white candles with a red one in the middle.

One shelf sported what appeared to be a lemon with nails driven through it at odd angles. Another held the sort of thick chalice actors in medieval movies spilled wine from while gnawing turkey drumsticks and leering at actresses' cleavage. A metal cross sat upright with a chain dangling from a ring at its top like a necklace for a giant. An assortment of bells, the statue of a unicorn, strung beads falling out of a little treasure chest. None of the odds and ends looked valuable. Some looked like what you'd use to decorate the bottom of a fish tank.

The reason Charlie paid so much attention to these knick-knacks was her embarrassment at the antics of old bristle-haired Marvin. He was passing his hands over Gloria's things in slow-motion swishing gestures as if he were treading water, all the while murmuring in tongues. She stood right across the table from him like the guest of honor (or the main sacrifice), unable to back away or move to either side because of the press of bodies.

The sweet smell of orange blossoms couldn't get through the crowd, either. Charlie could smell herself and other over-heated, excited bodies. And maybe she could smell a hint of something else. Something that suggested these weren't just clothes yanked from Gloria's closet for the memorial séance and dance in her dead honor, but the exact same clothes Gloria had lain in in the bush tops for a sunny day and then a whole night. . . .

If I don't beat rush hour getting Keegan back to Coldwater

Canyon and me back to the office, this is another day blown to hell, and me with deals happening.

Charlie, a woman has been murdered.

And I can't help her now. That's work for the police and Marvin the Shaman here. If I'd been murdered I wouldn't expect Gloria to turn off the phones and door buzzer and quit work.

Marvin picked up Gloria's skirt and wept into it.

Oh Jesus.

"What's happening, Mr. Grunion?" Lieutenant David Dalrymple whispered as if they were in church.

"I'm Gloria Tuschman and I'm dead," Grunion answered.

"What's happening, Gloria?" Dalrymple asked with a straight face. He might have been ordering pizza with mushrooms. He was definitely some kind of nut who had infiltrated the Beverly Hills Police Department. "Gloria, it's important. Tell me what you're doing right now."

"I'm talkingeh to Charlie Greene. She's caught in traffic on the 405, she says. But she's got this kid she can't really handle, and she's not always reliable."

"Where are you?"

"In the office. I usually am first thing in the morningeh. But she's always late. I don't know why Mr. Morse puts up with it. I mean, she knows she's got a kid when she takes the job. The agency shouldn't be responsible." This all coming from a weepy middle-aged man with sweat stains spreading all over his shirt. But the inflection, the nasal whine, the wheedling, the irritation sure did bring to mind Gloria Tuschman. "I am much more important around here than most people think, know what I mean?" There was a sly threat to this last pronouncement. That was like Gloria, too.

"Gloria, is that really you?" Poor Roger Tuschman looked

near collapse. He was short and slightly beefy, wore a striped shirt open at the neck and lots of jewelry. A gold chain, a small loop earring in one ear, a lavish watch band, and three rings. And one sideburn was much longer than the other. Perhaps he'd accidentally shaved one off this morning. "What can I do?"

"You, I'll talk to later," the shaman snapped back at the poor man, but in Gloria's accent.

"Why are you dead, Gloria?" Dalrymple persisted.

"Because that Charlie won't help me. I'm in the trash can."

That did it. Charlie, who had promised herself not to validate this charade by speaking up, lost it right there. "You are not. You're in the morgue. How can you be a ghost if you don't even know where you are?"

"You never did like me, did you Charlie?"

"Did Charlie Greene murder you, Gloria?" Roger Tuschman started pushing at people to get around the table to Charlie. The other cop, Detective Gordon, stepped in to stop him before he got there.

David Dalrymple said calmly, "Tell us who came in the office after everyone left, Gloria, came in while you were alone. Tell us who did this to you."

But Marvin Grunion rolled his eyes up under his eyelids and passed out.

When Charlie finally made it back to the agency, it was closed for the weekend and dark except for her office, where the cleaning lady was getting an early start. No one had left any exciting word on the *Alpine Tunnel* deal. If there had been any, Charlie had missed out on it. Thanks to Gloria. How could anybody be even more irritating dead than alive?

You always think of yourself as a decent person. How can you be so callous?

Charlie *was* beginning to feel guilty, and when she reached home to find a note that Libby was spending the night at Lori's, she decided to emulate the office janitorial service and get a head start on a grueling weekend. Maybe she could clear time to do some reading on Sunday.

By eleven that night Charlie collapsed in the breakfast nook with a peanut butter sandwich, a glass of milk, and the *L.A. Times*. But the house was pretty clean, and the week's wash had a good start. She'd always insisted Libby help with the household chores, but her daughter increasingly arranged to be gone when they needed doing. And if Charlie wasn't there to crack the whip and work alongside, Libby was useless. Which is exactly what Charlie had done to her own mother at this age. But that did not make it right.

Libby's cat landed square in the middle of the world news, narrowly missing the half-empty glass of milk. When Charlie looked up startled, Tuxedo met her nose to nose. Then he meowed. Then he stared.

"Do you want to go out?" I've been talking to ghosts, might as well talk to animals. Charlie got up and walked to the door. Tuxedo got up and walked to his food dish. "Did she not feed you? I thought you'd eaten before I got home." Tuxedo wound himself in and out and between and around Charlie's ankles, rubbing his neck and his jaws on her legs.

"I told the two of you the deal was that she feed you and change the litter box and all that, or you couldn't stay. I'm planning on getting rid of you anyway."

The cat had been a starving stray kitten Libby brought home once when Charlie was out of town and which she'd been unable to dislodge on her return. Now he was a large, sleek houseplant eater who delighted in keeping Charlie up nights. Charlie looked in the cupboards but could find no cat food. She finally dumped some Cheerios and pieces of bread crust in his dish and poured the rest of her milk over them, he set to, able to carry on a rattling purr and slurping noises at the same time.

The house full of fleas all summer, kitty immunizations that cost more than Libby's, stinky litter box—Charlie let him out when he went to the door. Maybe he'd get run over tonight, and she wouldn't have to deal with getting rid of him tomorrow.

Charlie could remember Edwina complaining about having to care for Bowzer the Schnauzer, a stray dog that followed Charlie home from school one day and stayed to die of old age after she'd left home. Charlie had promised to care for Bowzer if her parents would let him stay, just as Libby had.

"Don't let Libby be like me," she told the goddamned cat when she found him out in the alley and brought him in where it was safe before she went to bed. "We both know she might not be at Lori's tonight. She might be out doing something we don't even want to think about." The animal had moaned warning and hissed when she picked him up in the alley, but let himself be carried inside without biting her. He was all black except for his chest and stomach and four white paws.

"If we call and she's there, she'll never forgive us for not trusting her. She could be out riding in a car with some drunk teenager and we could get a telephone call that she was horribly killed in a wreck. No, they'd come and knock at the door."

If Tuxedo wrapped himself around her head that night, she didn't know it. She woke up feeling guilty that she hadn't lain awake to worry.

But at least no one had come to the door to inform her of a death in the family. Charlie put another load in the washer and drove to Von's for groceries. When she got back, Libby was still not home, so she grabbed some garden gloves, a rake, and clippers and headed for the front yard.

It was immaculate.

Charlie stood stupidly holding open the security grate that guarded the front door with her heel so it wouldn't close on her. She'd meant to prop it with something, but she stood there surveying her domain, tools in hand. Her domain was probably twelve feet square if you didn't count the parking. And now it looked just like her neighbors'.

Charlie heard the music before she heard the gunning motor, but not by much. She knew Libby was home even before she saw the shiny new Jetta pull up to the curb, where it disgorged the girls and then squealed off again. Charlie counted three boys and a surfboard still inside.

"Who was that?" Charlie sounded exactly like Edwina.

"Just some guys. They gave us a ride." Libby tried to push past Charlie, who stood her ground. "We're starved. You been to the store yet?"

How old are they? Have you really been at Lori's? Were her folks home? But Charlie said, "Libby . . . did you clean up the yard?"

"No way. Jesus did it. Looks great, doesn't it?"

Lori waved and giggled a greeting, and somehow the girls were inside and Charlie was still standing there holding the rake, her foot against the security grate.

She took one last look at her perfectly spruced-up property and followed them into the kitchen, where they'd already turned the radio to blast, found the donuts, and were pouring milk. Lori was everything Libby wasn't. She was short, plump in a pretty way, bouncy with a regular waterfall of dark, wavy hair. Her expression was persistently jovial.

They took their food to the breakfast nook, and when Charlie switched off the radio, both looked up as if astonished to find her home.

"Jesus cleaned up our front yard?"

"Yeah. When I got here after school yesterday, he had it all done, so I let him in and he did the patio plants." Libby dunked her donut in the milk and opened the morning paper to the comics.

"Libby—"

"Mom, don't make a big deal out of this, too, okay? Everybody in Long Beach but us has a gardener."

"Jesus wants to be our gardener?"

"We've got a gardener," Lori helped out. "And so does everybody on our street."

"Yeah, he goes by and sees our yard's a mess and figures we don't have a gardener. He's coming this afternoon to get paid. Mom, even Maggie's got a gardener. It's embarrassing."

"Maggie doesn't have a daughter to provide for. She can afford—"

"Oh sure, blame that on me, too. Everything is my fault. Even the fucking yard. Just because of my existence, right? Well, wrong, lady, my existence is the one thing that's not my fault." Libby stormed out the back door.

"I think it's pronounced 'Hey-zeus,'" Lori said meekly.

When the gardener arrived, Charlie took one look at him and said, "Jesus."

"Hey-zeus." He was probably somewhere in his late teens. He sizzled. He smoked. He smoldered in that dark, stunning, macho Mexican manner that says, "I'm a tolerant man. If she behaves herself and makes me happy and begs hard enough, even a pale little gringa can have my baby." And that sultry, languid, devastating gaze was locked on Charlie Greene's nubile daughter.

12

If you turned a hose on that guy, all of Belmont Shore would go up in steam." Charlie sat in Maggie's kitchen over a glass of wine as her neighbor tossed a chicken salad. "Jesus."

"Hey-zeus." Maggie refilled Charlie's glass and opened the oven door. The room swelled with the comforting aroma of toasting garlic bread. "You got Libby on the pill?"

"Says they make her swollen and fat. Won't take them."

"She has a point," Maggie conceded, and divided the feast between them. It was Saturday night, and Libby was baby-sitting.

"Says she doesn't need them anyway. Says they don't protect you from AIDS or herpes and other social diseases—thank you very much, Mrs. Hefty—Wilson High's sex and nutrition guru." Charlie paused to taste what was between her teeth. "What is the dressing on this? It's marvelous."

"Honey and mustard and cashews and Maggie Stutzman's oh-so-special herbs." Maggie was a displaced homemaker, displaced in that she was an attorney instead of a happy house-wife. "But, Charlie, you can eat it all, because I gave you half of mine." She passed the basket of garlic bread. "So it's only half to begin with."

Maggie Stutzman was about ten years older than Charlie, with jet-black hair and pale, fragile-looking skin. She was growing too beefy through the butt and hated it. Without planning to, she was also growing into a specialist, handling

Workers' Compensation cases, and she hated that, too. She resented the limitations that came with stereotyping, and the lack of variety. But it was the irrepressible gleam of fun and mischief in her green eyes that had attracted Charlie to begin with, and thank God it still flashed when all the other emotions didn't crowd it out.

"What do people like me do without people like you?" Charlie asked with a sigh over coffee.

"They get married. Now fill me in on the murder or pay good money for your dinner."

They jabbered on half the night until Maggie brought out the popcorn and the brandy.

On marriage—given the right opportunity, Maggie said she would marry in a minute. "I envy you Libby, Charlie."

"I'll give her to you, and all the bills and all the guilt that goes with her. You're such a fake, Stutzman. You wouldn't put up with some demanding guy just to have a kid. Wait, I've got it, have Libby set you up with Ed Esterhazie."

On Libby's cat—Charlie was taking him to the animal shelter first thing tomorrow, no matter what.

"Saw you unloading bags from Von's this morning," Maggie said. "Buy any cat food?"

"Well yeah, I guess I did. Just habit . . . I'll take it to the shelter, too."

"You're such a fake, Greene. Tomorrow's Sunday, and the shelter will be closed, and you know Tuxedo will live to be twenty sleeping on your bed, curled around your head. Under that tough exterior, you know what you are? Mush."

On Maggie's latest case—"Same-o, same-o. John got screwed, Allied Sheet Metal got screwed. Only winner was the insurance company."

"I don't understand—if John lost, why didn't his employer win?"

"John did not get compensation for most of his hospitalization, but Allied Sheet Metal still paid the same premiums. And the insurance company didn't have to pay up because they got off on a technicality. Allied pays through the nose to insure its workers. It's the system, Charlie, it's all dicked-up. It was meant to protect the employee, but it's bleeding the employer dry and enriching the insurance company. It's wrong, but the way the system works the judge had no choice. Her hands were tied."

"She?"

"Yeah, Workmans' Comp is just another of the frustrating boring household drudgeries of the legal profession. Pays like shit, too."

On Libby and money—"Well, what do you expect when her mom brings home champagne and buffalo steak to celebrate? This is supposed to teach a kid to be economical?"

"That's the first time in my life I've ever even bought a bottle of champagne."

"And you buy Dom Perignon."

"It was a special celebration, Maggie. We're talking *Phantom of the Alpine Tunnel* for God's sake."

"I know you say it was a best-seller, but Charlie I never heard of that book."

"You too, huh?" Charlie reached for the brandy bottle but Maggie grabbed it away.

"Not until you bring me up to date on the murder, Greene."

"Aw come on, who cares about a friggin' murder?"

"Everybody. Now give."

Charlie started in on the story of her frustrating Friday and didn't get halfway through before Maggie grabbed a sofa pillow and doubled over it like she had menstrual cramps.

"Memorial séance and dance? Stop, I hurt. Oh Hey-zeus."

Charlie was launched well into marvelous Marvin's treading

air over Gloria's effects and had Maggie really pleading for mercy when Libby strutted in with a squirming Tuxedo. "Caught this creep sneaking up on a mockingbird. Figured Mrs. Beesom'd have a nerd attack." Libby pretended to take in the room and the situation and scowled. "You girls boozing it up again? You know you can be heard all the way to the beach, don't you?"

Maggie pulled Charlie's daughter down on the sofa and put the popcorn bowl on her lap. "You gotta hear this. Your mom should be a stand-up comic."

Charlie's personal camera shot her a close-up of Charlie the stand-up comic continuing her sit-down monologue while the voice-over explained how aware she was of Maggie's warm soft undemanding living room and friendship. Cut to Libby breaking up when Charlie explained how everybody thought Charlie Greene, the experienced amateur detective and natural psychic, ought to take time out of a busy work schedule to solve a puzzling murder case for the Beverly Hills Police Department.

"You know, I just noticed how nobody really close to me thinks I can do this, and everybody who isn't thinks I can. Always interesting to find out who has confidence in you."

"Oh sure, Mom, right. Like in Oregon when you practically got yourself arrested for murder? Charlie Greene, the Great Detective."

"I am stung," Charlie said, only half kidding by now. The goddamned cat chose that moment to barf all over Maggie's coffee table. "That does it. Next weekend that animal goes to the shelter in search of a new home. And we'll just see about that great detective business, too."

Tuxedo stopped washing his puss long enough to give her a look of utter contempt. Her daughter and best friend broke up into new paroxysms of hilarity. Something wrong with the script here.

Charlie had a similar thought Monday morning during Tina Horton's pitch at CBS. Tina had done a format for the Sun City veterinarian-detective series on speculation, and Charlie had shown it to one of the story editors at ZIA Productions. He'd liked it well enough to take Tina in to pitch it to the vice president in charge of project development, who loved it and took it to a producer at ZIA, and they made an appointment at CBS for Tina to pitch it there. ZIA had made up a fancy, bound presentation booklet and treated Tina to a special atta-girl breakfast before the appointment where they'd pumped up her confidence and self-esteem.

Tina was one of Charlie's up-and-comers with a few minor credits to her name but a major off-the-wall imagination. Unfortunately, her professional calluses were still paper-thin, and the least hint of disapproval nearly destroyed her. She'd practically had a nervous breakdown before going in to this pitch.

"Just remember," Charlie whispered to her client as they walked into the building, "if he starts squirming after five minutes, wrap fast and get out of there. The day will come when you'll want to be invited back. But if he starts asking questions and interrupting, it is not meant as an insult or a put-down but a sign of interest—so slow down, pump the hype, relax. You've got fifteen minutes, but if he's interested he'll give you a half hour or more. And, Tina, your career does not begin or end with this series or this pitch. This is just the beginning, no matter what happens in that conference room."

Charlie sure hoped that her words and her smile and her

support were convincing to her client, because her own stomach was doing handstands, kneebends, convulsions, and flips.

Tina Horton was small, bottle blond, thin—all to her advantage in this town, but Carl Shapiro was five minutes late and came in with five CBS yes-men (vice presidents of everything) and a glass of Alka-Seltzer. Tina visibly aged ten years in that five minutes of waiting—not a good thing in this town.

"Wait, now let me get this straight," Carl Shapiro said finally. "This woman produced eight children and had a full-time career as a veterinarian. She is now retired and living in Sun City, but all her neighbors have pets who get sick and she's nice enough to doctor them and in the process is privy to mysterious happenings in Sun City."

"And because she is so successful there she gets called into investigations in Phoenix," Tina added, "out in the desert, across the border, you name it. This woman is not confined to kittens and grandchildren and knitting."

"Make her a little bit out of the ordinary if she didn't like knitting and baking cookies and typewriting, wouldn't it?" the CBS executive said thoughtfully.

"Oh she doesn't. She's not at all stereotypical. She's a retired career Grandma."

"We could be talking Tony Hillerman—there's got to be Indians out there someplace—Jessica Fletcher, Golden Girls here," the studio exec said. "Who'd you have in mind for your lady detective?"

"Someone like Angela Lansbury or Betty White?"

"Or Ellen Maxwell," Charlie spoke up for the first time. Ellen was a client of Congdon and Morse.

"Ellen Maxwell . . . now there's a thought," Carl Shapiro said. "Whatever happened to that old girl?"

Charlie reflected that Ellen was younger than Carl Shapiro. "Summer stock, commercials . . . "

"Not those old lady diaper things, I hope," the exec's prominent lip swelled with disgust.

"No, cornmeal, baking soda, American Express—"

"Who's her agent?"

"Maurice Lavender."

"Never heard of him."

"He's with Congdon and Morse, Carl," Barry Zahn of ZIA came to Charlie's aid. "And the desert scenes we can film cheap. The budget on this could come in sweet."

"Okay, so who's the guy?" asked a yes-man when he saw it was safe to express some interest. He had to be all of twenty-three.

"The guy," Tina took a beat, "oh the guy. Right. Well, Thora Kay has all these sons, and the youngest is always around to help her out. You know, the strong-guy stuff."

CBS had given Tina and ZIA forty-five minutes out of the fifteen allotted, and Charlie hugged her screenwriter in the parking lot. "The strong-guy son stuff was inspired, Tina. You did great."

"Awful how natural that question seemed. I've been in this town too long, Charlie."

13

Lieutenant Dalrymple had a uniformed officer waiting for Charlie when she returned to the agency. So instead of joining Richard and Dorian for lunch with a New York producer she'd hoped to interest in a manuscript with a similar story line to a picture he'd made some years ago, she rode to the beachfront house in Malibu in a squad car, her stomach rumbling.

Detective Gordon, the one with the Marine haircut and the smirk, opened her door when they reached the Goliath beach house and nodded the driver away.

Charlie had actually been to a party at this house one night with a crush of people dressed in dress and undress you'd have to have seen to believe.

It looked very different now, empty and in the light of day. There were signs of wear on the redwood decks that sported two hot tubs and a flowering vine–coated arbor that sheltered a padded picnic booth. All this bordering the walkway to the entrance, which was down a stairway. The door was in the roof, and you could see the ocean over it from the decks.

The house below spread along a low cliff, opening every room but the kitchen to the sea view, a back hall running the length to give access to each room. It was an odd arrangement. First you entered the kitchen, which looked over cooking islands and countertops onto a vast living and entertaining area surrounding it on three sides. You saw there free-standing fireplaces, wet bars, and several conversation nooks on both sides of the sunken dining room. Everywhere were bleached wood floors with oriental area rugs and sand scratches, and side tables graced with dust catchers and lamps. All this punctuated by floor-to-ceiling pale rose sheers blowing in the salt breezes, a narrow balcony, a stretch of beach, the Pacific Ocean, the horizon, the sky.

It almost seemed as though you could invite the whole world into the room, and the heavens, too. The side walls were mirrors that made the room and the view even more limitless. How could Mary Ann and Keegan ever have concentrated in such unstructured space?

David Dalrymple startled Charlie when he rose from a couch in front of a far mirrored wall, looking like two men, one front and one back. The room was so disorienting—or else it was her empty stomach—that she would have tripped into the sunken dining room had Detective Gordon not caught an elbow to steady her until she regained her balance.

"Have you had lunch, Miss Greene?" Lieutenant Dalrymple asked.

She shook her head, and even in a room this large the rumble of her stomach was an audible answer. She had not accompanied Tina to her atta-girl breakfast and was operating on one Diet Coke.

"We have some quarter-pounders and fries on their way by patrol express. We'll be happy to share them with you."

"I take it you've found Mary Ann."

"Before we discuss that, I'd like you to relax and be comfortable," he motioned to the pillowed couch he'd just risen from, "and be quiet for a moment. Tell me if you sense anything unusual here. Try to forget about your busy day for a while."

"I take it that means she's dead, too." But Charlie sat and leaned back into the pillows. If the burgers and fries didn't arrive soon, she could always take a nap.

"Don't worry about that just now. Sit quietly and rest, see if you can tune into the atmosphere here. It's important. I'll be back in a few minutes."

Charlie closed her eyes and propped her feet on the coffee table. For some reason her thoughts meandered to Jesus Garcia. Libby had said he didn't go to Wilson High. Charlie wished she'd told him to never return, but the whole situation had conspired to make her feel mean and greedy, especially with the girls standing there watching. She told him he could come only on Saturday mornings. She'd see to it Libby had chores to do on Saturday mornings. Which would guarantee Libby wouldn't be home on Saturday mornings.

Charlie didn't sense anything in the atmosphere of the house until she smelled lunch. She considered making up something just to get even, but shared the greasy repast with Gordon and Dalrymple, grateful to assuage the painful demon in her belly.

Charlie nursed her shake. A recent column on the health-fad pages of the *L.A. Times* assured a worried public that milk products and slimy fat coatings did not really soothe angered stomach linings. They were wrong. The burning went away. But it was followed by a bloating nausea. Did doctors work on weekends? Did Charlie really need one more thing to worry about?

At Dalrymple's request, Detective Gordon left them alone in the massive room, and for a time they sat quietly, he chewing on cold limp fries and Charlie sucking in air up her straw.

"You're not cooperating," he said finally.

"What is it with you? I know most of my impressions of the police are stereotypes from TV and novels, but I really can't believe you're serious about this psychic stuff. I mean, I know you could not do the work you do and be gullible enough to believe in Marvelous Marvin Grunion and the like. What I don't know is why you're pretending otherwise. It's frightening."

"As a matter of fact, I increasingly find my colleagues imitating TV cops, Miss Greene, and *that's* what you should find frightening. Life imitating art, if one could be so gullible as to call that art. Maybe the phrase should be 'fact aping fiction.'" Definitely a PBS kind of guy. He removed his thick glasses and polished them absently with a handkerchief. With their removal, his eyes became tiny and sunken—his entire face appeared smaller. "I hate to disillusion you further, but scratch an ordinary policeman and you'll find all the foibles and weaknesses inherent in mankind, with some submerged and others hardened to allow him to function in law enforcement. Or her," he added quickly.

"You don't really think I can help you in any psychic way. You suspect me of murdering Gloria or knowing who did. I can't even defend myself, because you don't say what you're thinking. And now I suppose you think I did something to Mary Ann, too."

"Granted that, until we find the motive and the murderer everyone involved is suspect, you among many, I am still sincere in asking for your help. Please hear me out," he said when she groaned and started squirming. "Let me tell you a story."

Like most people, most cops didn't believe in what he called the paranormal. And until about six years ago, David Dalrymple didn't, either. He had been working in Las Vegas at the time. There was a particularly grisly murder of a child. Kidnap, rape, torture, murder, dismemberment. It had been so monstrous even the hardened investigators handling the case had severe difficulties with it both in their work and in their personal lives.

"In order to live anything remotely resembling a normal life, to get on with family and the civilian population—people in law enforcement, rescue work, emergency and long-term medical care and similar professions have to separate their personal and professional lives and feelings. If they don't they become dysfunctional in both." He leaned forward with forearms on knees, staring past her out to sea between blowing curtains. He sounded like a textbook, but he looked like a deeply troubled man who was, in reality, staring within.

"The case was getting a great deal of press, my kids were talking about it, my wife was teaching school, and everyone she met at work wanted to know the latest on our attempts to track the killer. It was the same for my colleagues. There was no relief from the nightmare, day or night. And when there is notoriety with a case, the nuts come out of the woodwork. They all claim mysterious powers and knowledge that will help solve the crime."

"And help them cash in on the publicity."

"Some shun publicity, send their information in anonymously. But they are all so vague and mysterious that they end up half-right and half-wrong, so they never come out looking like they missed totally. In many ways, like politicians and preachers. It's an art."

"But this time somebody came up with the right answers," Charlie prompted, trying to hurry him along.

"This little girl, her name was Deborah Ann—she was wearing a hooded sweatshirt jacket when she was abducted."

"In Vegas?"

"It can get quite chilly at certain times of the year. Anyway, it was pretty much intact. It was a cheap little affair, red, with the regular drawstring through the hood and zipper up the front. It was all there but for one arm, which we later found on one of her arms lying across the top of a slot machine in one of the better casinos. But the first trace of her we found was the rest of the sweatshirt jacket hanging from its hood by a clothespin on a wire draped with Christmas decorations in another casino. A description of what the child was last seen wearing had been heavily publicized, and an alert security guard called the department immediately. The jacket plus a recent photo of the child was shown on the local television news in hopes the two together would trigger a memory in someone who might have seen Deborah Ann without realizing it."

"And the nuts came out of the woodwork."

"One woman became so hysterical in my office that I finally let her see and hold the jacket. She was on vacation from Chicago, the exact stereotype of what you'd expect, an aging sixties flower child. Made her living as a psychic. Told fortunes, performed séances, complete fruitcake. Pretty, in a maternal, well-worn way. Comfortable woman when she was in control of herself." He stood and walked over to the sheers, their billowing motion arranging and rearranging the lighting in the room, the shadows on his face, and the bald swath of scalp above it. "Did I tell you my daughter's name is Deborah Ann Dalrymple?"

"Bummer," Charlie said and meant it. Then when he turned back to the sea and didn't speak, she added, "Look, for all I know this is a hoax and you're really pitching a true crime or a novel or even a treatment. But I'm hooked, okay? Don't blow it now. She takes a hold of the jacket, and—?"

"She took the jacket and told me where the child's head was. And then through her sobbing she told me things I could no more write about than I can tell you now. But things I will take to my own grave."

"Things like—?"

"How confused a four-year-old child can be when a beloved

uncle hurts her, how she feels sure she's done something wrong to deserve this—even that young they feel it's somehow their fault." The homicide lieutenant's voice broke, and he stood silent for a few moments, staring at the toes of his shoes and shaking his head at his own memories. "We started calling him Uncle Christmas around the department."

"Her uncle?"

"We were out rounding up known child abusers and creeps. We'd looked at family and neighbors first thing, of course, and found nothing. The uncle was a forty-five-year-old airline pilot with a solid twenty-year marriage, three kids with no records, and his only recorded offenses were two traffic tickets and a personal bankruptcy. A churchgoer, no heavy drinking or drug habits. A man in good health. We found out later his one verifiable vice was visiting porno movies when out of town—which was often, considering his occupation—but who knows?"

"And you just took this flower-child fruitcake's word for it? I can't believe I never heard of this case."

"You might have. Something makes the national newscasts one night, maybe two. So much goes on in our world that if the threat doesn't appear in our own community it sort of blends in with all the horrors on 'News from Around the World with' . . . the latest blow-dried network celebrity. But if you live in the same area, the fear factor aids memory immeasurably. And nobody believed the middle-aged fruitcake. Including me. But if you'd been there and heard her, you'd be haunted for life anyway. I told my superior about it. I was the psychic's only witness, which had been a stupid mistake, but I hadn't wanted anyone who worked with me to know I'd been a wuss and let her in to begin with. Great way to lose your job, for one thing. Anyway, we had a good laugh and no good leads, so he said to take a day or two and follow it up and we'd run a check on the fruitcake from Chicago."

"And you found she wasn't who she said she was."

"She was exactly who she claimed to be, a respected psychic by people who respected psychics, and who was at home in Chicago when the kidnapping occurred. Deborah Ann's head was exactly where she said it was, in the uncle's storage locker at a small municipal airport—in north Vegas, where he kept his private plane, not McCarran."

"It would begin to smell, wouldn't it?"

"We don't know to this day how long she was kept in a casino hotel room and molested and tortured before the butchery began. The storage locker was in an air conditioned building, but there had been some unheeded complaints, as it turned out. It was in late December—Merry Christmas, Deborah Ann, from Uncle Mike."

Charlie rose, and he followed her out to the cool Pacific breeze and warm sun and fishy ocean smell that cleaned the sinuses and bathed the contact lenses. "It's a gripping story, but I am not a psychic who can help you."

"You know the funniest thing about it all? My fruitcake had it all right, everything. We never gave her credit. She didn't want any, as a matter of fact. And the body parts showed up as she predicted. We followed the uncle delivering the last two of his morbid messes before taking off on a flight. But the strangest part of it all is, my fruitcake from Chicago was lousy at gambling. You'd think she could psych that out, too, wouldn't you? Anyway, the whole situation was treated like an oddity and an embarrassment best forgotten, and I soon was too, even though we got a signed confession. But I was so bowled over by it—I was the only one, remember, to actually hear the child speak through this woman from Chicago—I couldn't leave well enough alone."

"That stuff can be faked, Lieutenant. I don't see how holding something that a dead person has worn can connect you to them—or sitting around in an orange grove holding hands, either."

"I have come to believe that *some*times *some* aspect, that I don't pretend to be able to identify, of a dead person lingers behind and *some*times on or near personal effects and that *some* people can form a link with it *some*how."

The atmosphere in the Vegas P.D. had soon convinced him to begin hunting a job elsewhere. The Beverly Hills Police Department was a great deal more tolerant of the inexplicable. "Not that I'm encouraged to pursue investigations in this manner, but as long as I get results, my methods are tolerated. I just don't believe in closing off any possible avenue when tracking down a murderer."

"And you're right, he's a kook," Detective Gordon said behind them, "but he gets those results in spite of himself."

14

Mary Ann Leffler's clothes still hung in a corner of the walk-in closet over her shoes, her empty suitcases on the floor in another corner. Two drawers in one dresser were half-full of things that didn't hang. A laptop computer sat open on a bedside table. Makeup and toiletries were scattered sparsely across a bathroom the size of Charlie's bedroom.

Mary Ann's presence hadn't made much of a dent in all this space. Neither did her absence. Charlie obediently ran her fingers over the terry-cloth robe hanging behind the bathroom door, parted the clothes on the hangers—mostly blue jeans, sweats, sundresses, and informal cotton knits. She picked up a shoe. "So is she dead or what?"

"You're supposed to tell me," Detective Gordon said as she passed him on her way to the balcony.

"I'm not getting a feeling either way. I don't think I'd know it if I did." And I don't like pawing through other peoples' things. It's sad.

"I heard you up in the orange grove." Besides a bull neck and a smirk, Detective Gordon had freckles, lots of freckles. "'Touch my things,' you said."

There had to be an explanation for that, too. She just couldn't think of one. Charlie didn't believe in psychics, but if there were such a thing a person wouldn't reach the ripe old age of thirty-one before knowing she was one.

If I was psychic—whatever that is—I'd know where Libby was last Friday night and how she feels about Jesus.

The wind was growing stronger and seemed to blow sound as well as sand in circles. For instance, she could hear the wind chimes on the deck above and behind her, but not the voices of the two men on the beach in front of and slightly below her.

Keegan Monroe and David Dalrymple stood in that peculiarly male pose of discreet discomfort—hands deep in pants pockets, eyes glued to their shoes, rocking back and forth, shrugging with their elbows. Less cerebral types would probably be spitting, as well.

If something had happened to Mary Ann by the same hand that did in Gloria, the only people that Charlie knew who were even acquainted with both of them were herself, Keegan, Richard Morse, and Roger Tuschman. But their common connections to weird types could be infinite. Or Mary Ann could have seen who killed Gloria and been a threat. Anybody who thought Charlie had some kind of pipeline to dead or missing people or any innate expertise in matters of murder simply did not know Charlie Greene. She grinned, remembering her daughter and best friend going into hysterics at the very idea last Saturday night, and heard herself tell Detective Gordon, "She's in her car."

"Who, the Leffler woman?"

"What?"

But he yelled to Dalrymple, "She says she's in the rental car."

The homicide detective and the screenwriter hurried across the scuttling sand. The wind chimes went bonkers.

Oh that's just great, Greene, now what are you going to do, put on a turban and buy a crystal ball? How about some tarot cards?

"Where?"

Dalrymple's sharpness surprised her into saying, "Underwater somewhere. Maybe somewhere not too far."

He drove her up and down the coastal highway, into and out of every beachfront and access road and even some driveways before he gave up and let Keegan drive her back to the agency.

"How do you know she's in her car underwater?" Keegan asked.

"I don't. I don't even know why I said that. It's like I'm trying to get out of work, for God's sake." Charlie checked her watch and groaned. "You know what I think? I think I'm the only sane person left in this world. I think I'm letting you all talk me into something here. I think you're right about the ulcer."

"You know what I think? I think there's a great story in Lieutenant David Dalrymple."

"He told you about Deborah Ann and the Chicago fruitcake, right?"

"Charlie, think of it—a homicide detective sympathetic to the paranormal arts. Sounds like a great concept for a TV series to me."

"I don't know, Keegan, it's pretty original."

"Yeah, you're probably right."

"Of course, you might make the cop a woman. It would have to be on spec. Write up a treatment and I'll show it around." She told him about Tina Horton at CBS that morning.

"She pitched to Shapiro himself? Think he'll pick it up?"

"He was very interested. My gut feeling is it has a chance." My gut feeling is also that he'll want to buy Tina out and get a name to write the pilot, offer her her own show later. The name will be a guy, they'll move the location to Seattle, and Tina will get screwed out of the credits and her own show later will never materialize. I'd sure like to be wrong on this one. "So if something has happened to Mary Ann, where does that leave *Shadowscapes*?"

"All but finished. Second act needs shoring. But if I can unplug her suggestions, I could have it in in two days." There was an odd catch in his voice as if the emotion behind his words threatened to choke him.

Charlie glanced at his profile and then back at the traffic. Could this frustrating business have broken one of her best clients? Could Keegan have done something awful to Mary Ann Leffler? Could the woman simply have offered one too many frustrations for this normally even-tempered man? Or did Charlie actually know him as well as she thought she did? Writers had many hidden places in their psyches.

"So tell me again about Lady Macbeth in her submerged car," he said carefully, as if aware of her sudden attack of paranoia. "I can't buy the business about our talking you into saying what you did back there."

"Have you ever been hypnotized? No? Well, I have. By a guy years ago at a party in college. I can remember him to this day telling me while I was supposedly under that I wouldn't remember anything that went on. I also remember him telling me that later on in the evening long after I'd awakened, I would go up to this other guy and kiss him, but that I would not remember that my hypnotist had suggested it. And I did."

"Did what?"

"Did go up and kiss this guy and *did* remember that my hypnotist had suggested it. And I really couldn't tell you if the kiss was a lark or if the suggestion was so powerful I couldn't help myself even though I knew full well where it came from."

"The power of suggestion."

"The power of suggestion. And when they find Mary Ann alive and well or find her dead but not in her car underwater we'll know I said that because everybody has been on my back because of this psychic thing. I am *not* the L.A. fruitcake."

All hell had broken loose at the office. The Vance was on the front desk because The Kid and Tweety had had it out. Richard Morse was bouncing off the walls because so much was happening at once and Charlie wasn't there.

"Christ, you been in Malibu all day? I'm going to start hittin' up the police department for your commissions. Listen, Steve took the manuscript home, says he'll get back to you on it in two, three weeks."

"Dorian got Steven Hunter to look at *The Corpse That Got Iced*? I'll believe that when I get that phone call."

"Ay, don't underestimate Dorian. That's your problem. You underestimate people just because they're men. Listen, babe, you're on a roll here. First the *Alpine Tunnel*, and now ZIA wants a call back, get in there. Oh, and CBS is even asking about Ellen Maxwell. Thanks for the mention. Maurice is on the line to her now."

"But Tina just pitched this morning."

"She pitched to Shapiro himself, right? Things can happen fast when you start at the top. That's your problem, no confidence. All you women are like that. Good luck comes in threes you know."

"How about bad luck?"

"Well, yeah, that too, but that's everybody's problem."

When Charlie Greene the agent staggered into the condo in Long Beach that evening, she was greeted by a frantic Libby before she could kick off her pumps.

"Hurry, Mom, we're invited to Doug's for dinner tonight and Mrs. McDougal gets rabid about tardiness. I tried to call you at the office but the lines were busy, and then when I did get through, Larry was so pissed about something he kept on sputtering and I couldn't make him listen. What are you doing, Mom? Hurry."

Charlie Greene the mother was leaning her spine against the kitchen door trying to focus. "Libby, I'm exhausted. I wish you wouldn't spring this stuff on me. And Mr. Esterhazie and I really aren't—"

"Mom, on top of everything else . . . are you a les?"

"Whaaat?"

Dinner at the Esterhazie mansion was certainly a step up from macaroni and cheese with Dom Perignon. The Greenes and the Esterhazies dined in a small informal room just off the kitchen that overlooked the bay window that overlooked the lighted swimming pool in the backyard. They sat at a cozy round table that seated four comfortably—could have handled six—and were served formally by Mrs. McDougal. The catch was that to get to this cozy back room you had to walk through the intimidating formal dining room, where the table could have handled twenty-four without blushing.

"She won't sit with us when we have guests," Ed explained in a whisper. "It's embarrassing, but what can I do? I think there are laws against harassing housekeepers."

"Too bad there aren't a few against harassing parents." Charlie smiled sweetly at Libby, who grinned a nasty, braces-filled reply.

Dinner was a simple little shellfish casserole. Individual casseroles, actually. Simple chunks of shrimp, crab, oyster, lobster, and asparagus tips floating in a rich cream sauce and baked in paper-thin pastry. Served with a white wine Charlie could actually stomach, stuffed artichokes, and crusty rolls. Brie and fresh strawberries for dessert.

Ed was in sport shirt and slacks tonight, but even they looked pricey and tailored. Charlie was still dressed for the CBS meeting in black skirt, hose, and pumps with a black shell and red blazer. She would gladly have killed to get out of the pantyhose.

The kids conveniently disappeared afterward, and Mrs. McDougal served coffee in Ed's study. Ed's study was three times the size of Charlie's office on Wilshire Boulevard.

"The dinner was marvelous," Charlie told the housekeeper, whose face completely rearranged itself when she smiled. Thin, pale, tired, and sinewy was Charlie's first impression of the woman. And disapproving. Definitely disapproving. But the thick gray hair was cut short and stylishly brushed upward, and when she smiled, all the droop lines tilted up to join the haircut and she was lovely.

"Don't forget the amaretto and the fire, Mr. Esterhazie." And Mrs. McDougal left them alone in the dim lighting.

"I wasn't kidding about the dinner, but how do we scotch this arranged romance, Ed? Libby practically accused me of being a lesbian if I didn't come tonight, and frankly I've had an incredible day and am this far from passing out."

"We do have a problem here, Charlie." His lips had been fighting a curl all evening, and he finally let them catch up to the grin in his eyes. "For one thing I think they have an accomplice in Mrs. McDougal, who really runs this place. And you played into their hands just now with your compliments on the dinner."

"You're not going to build a fire? That would really put me out."

"Tell you what, I'll pour the amaretto and forget the fire. You take off your shoes, loosen your tie," he pushed an enormous brown leather ottoman up to her chair, "rest yourself, and we'll make our plans."

"They're probably watching from somewhere." She tried to see through the French windows next to the fireplace, but they only reflected the room.

"I'm sure of it." He sat on the ottoman near her bare feet and poured tiny cut-glass glasses full of liqueur. "Charlie, are you currently involved with someone special?"

"No, but that doesn't mean I'm a lesbian."

"Well, I am."

"A lesbian?"

"Involved."

"That's our answer." She took a grateful sip of coffee. "I can just tell Libby that and—"

"It's not so simple. We have two major problems here. One is that your Libby can talk my son into anything."

"That I can believe."

"And the other is that neither he nor Mrs. McDougal approve of my current."

"What's the matter with her?"

"She enjoys cooking and other domestic arts, which my housekeeper finds threatening, and she's a frustrated mother, which my son finds threatening. I think they have decided that you, as a dedicated career woman, are the answer. What I am not sure of is what Libby hopes to get out of it all."

"Well, this is pretty fancy living compared to our little nest. Maybe she wants to live in style. Which is moot because next week she'll want something else. I have a lot of trouble believing she wants a father. Another parent would just double the rules and expectations she's determined to avoid now. She does keep mentioning your belonging to the yacht club though, seems incredibly impressed by that."

"You know, that might be it? What exactly do you know of the local social strata?"

"Absolutely nothing. I get my self-esteem from the size of my commissions. Why?"

"The social life of a certain set of young people revolves, particularly in summer, around the pool at the yacht club and selected social events. Although families belong in a manner of speaking, they do so through the auspices of a male head of household."

The good old boys strike again. "Now that sounds like something Libby would connive for."

"What's the best way to get her to stop wanting something?"

"Give it to her. Once she's got it, she doesn't want it anymore. Goes on to new wants."

"What if we pretend to go along with their little plans?"

"Ed, what about your current?"

"Dorothy? It would just be for a week or two. She'll understand when I explain why we're doing it."

Boy, what Ed Esterhazie didn't know about women. Charlie could only stare at the man.

Charlie, who are you talking to?" Luella Ridgeway said, and Charlie very nearly choked on her Maalox tablet.

"I was just talking to myself."

Luella peered down the stairwell at the end of the back hall on the fifth floor of the FFUCWB of P.

"Luella, can I borrow your nail file?"

"Sure. Listen ... we've talked Richard into calling in Dr. Podhurst. This whole thing has been wild. Why don't you talk to him? I'm going to. . . . Charlie, what are you doing? That's the janitor's closet."

"Gloria has decided she's in a trash can in the closet. I figure it's this closet."

"Gloria is at home in an urn."

"I know that. You know that. Gloria does not know that."

"Much as I ache for some free counseling, I think you, Charlie, should be the first to talk to Dr. Podhurst."

And much to Charlie's amazement, the janitor's closet could be unlocked with a simple nail file, but since there was no knob or handle, she broke Luella's file in the lock pulling it open.

"Sorry."

"No problem."

And no Gloria and no trash can in the closet. There was a portable broom-closet trolley on a metal frame with a heavy canvas bag hanging from it. A mop, a bucket, a push broom were attached at one end—spray bottles of cleaners, paper towels, and heavy-duty rags at the other. Charlie wheeled it out in the light and peeked over into the canvas bag. It was empty now, but easily big enough to hold a doubled-over body with maybe a few baskets of paper waste spread on top. Industrial-strength bearings made it roll with silent ease.

Luella was nearsighted like Charlie and wore contact lenses for distance but then couldn't see close up to read. She'd had a new haircut and color job since the murder, and her eyebrows arched up under puffy bangs as she peered over the tops of the little half-glasses she wore around the office. Curls curled onto her face to cover the sun wrinkles—bright blue eyes, bright red lipstick, pale sage-colored suit with flashy blue costume jewelry and pumps.

You could easily move a dead Gloria in this thing, but it wouldn't wheel down the stairs. The canvas part was meant to unhook and throw over your shoulder like a duffel bag and carry out to the dumpster in the alley. But even the security guards probably wouldn't notice if you slid around the concrete block wall with it. And from there you might take Gloria out and toss her up into the bush tops to hide her.

Luella looked twenty years younger than she had when she'd come home from her unpleasant tasks in Minnesota.

But you'd have to be big and strong and dressed like somebody who would look normal carrying out bags of trash to the dumpster. There was a dumpster just behind the end wall sheltering the parking barn. Why hadn't the murderer thrown Gloria in it? It would have been closer and easier. No extra uniforms in the closet. Charlie pushed the janitorial rig back and slammed the door on it.

Nice try, Gloria, but you obviously still don't know what you're talking about.

Then again, if Luella had committed a murder, that would

have taken its toll on her looks—that is, if it bothered her. And it would have bothered her. She was small and could be fierce when bargaining for what she believed in, but Charlie couldn't imagine her being mean, knowingly. She was kind of a neat lady, really.

"Hello?" Luella folded her arms and tapped the toe of her tiny blue pump. "Larry told me you were going to play detective again. Charlie, are you sure it's what you want to do?"

"No. It's what everyone else wants me to do. I don't have time for this, Luella. I pay through the nose in taxes for a police department to solve crimes. But if I don't at least make an effort, nobody lets me work at the job I get paid to do. Can you please explain this to me?"

Charlie asked Dr. Podhurst the same question. He had a new hearing device in one ear. It was so small Charlie couldn't really tell which ear, but he kept turning his head to catch her words just right. It seemed to her he was concentrating more on the novelty of how he was hearing them than on the sense of the words themselves.

"How would *you* explain it, Charlie?" Even sitting down he looked gangly and all wrong for his clothes and the chair, too. But he didn't look strong enough to carry a body in a duffel over his shoulder down four flights of stairs and past the security guard and parking valet attendants. Then out into the alley, around the concrete wall. Then throw her up into the bushes. And he was so strikingly odd that even disguised in a janitorial coverall he'd be recognized in a minute. Disguised in anything but a total gorilla costume or as Abraham Lincoln, he would look exactly like Dr. Evan Podhurst, no question.

"Charlie?"

"Humm? Oh, well I'd explain it the same way I'd explain hearing Gloria Tuschman speaking to me in the hall. It's nuts. Either that or it's a conspiracy."

"Are you telling me that a murder in your office and the fact that the homicide division of the Beverly Hills Police Department is pressuring you into solving the crime for them strikes you as either nuts on their part or a conspiracy?"

"Sounds paranoid, doesn't it?"

"Or as though you had not thought this through too clearly. Or perhaps have misinterpreted the intentions of the police in this matter. But let's come back to that, Charlie, let's talk about your home life. Is there anything there that could account for your self-admitted paranoia or such fantasies?"

They discussed Libby Greene and her grandmother, Edwina Greene, for three times as long as they'd devoted to the effects of murder and the Beverly Hills P.D. on Charlie's personal and working life.

Charlie did not feel better when she left Evan Podhurst's office. She felt like a crazy paranoid whiner who couldn't look at anybody involved without suspecting them of murder.

"So what happened yesterday between Tracy and Larry?" she asked Dorian Black when she found him alone in his office on her way back to her own. "I can't get him to talk about it."

"He called her a pig and she called him a fag." Dorian faced her over a desk as neat as his clothes. "Don't know what the problem is. They were both right."

"Anybody ever tell you you're a real sweetheart, Dorian?"

"Ay, can I help it?" But Dorian was pretty sure it started over who had to man the front desk. "I mean hell, Tweety's got two agents to carry and fetch for. We can't spare her out there on the phones."

Dorian possessed a captive housewife, and they had two children. He doted on the children, but Elaine could do no right. Elaine was a lot younger than he, and Charlie figured the abuse was only verbal. But once Elaine grew up, Charlie hoped she'd shuck this guy. He womanized openly, yet all his clients were male. Still, she couldn't see him doing anything so messy as murder.

"So what, Charlie, what? You going to just stand there and stare at me? Since Tweety is on the desk right now I don't have time to sit and watch you stare at me. You want to do a strip or something, doll, I'll reconsider."

"Dorian, how well do you know Mary Ann Leffler?"

"Seen her around here a couple of times, read about her—but don't know anything you wouldn't know a lot better. Famous novelists are your meal ticket, remember?"

Tracy Dewitt was no happier about the fact she was manning the phones and the door buzzer than was her co-boss. "Charlie, Irma Vance has the whole office to oversee plus the business of the head of the agency. I am the lone support group for two very busy and important talent agents. Larry is responsible only for your office work, and all you handle are writers. I mean, it's obvious to anyone with eyes that in an emergency he should take over the receptionist job so the real work of the agency can continue with the least disruption. But here I sit doing Gloria's job while mine piles up. Even Irma serves a shift out here. It's lunacy."

"Well, Larry takes a turn out here."

"Right. He takes a turn. He should replace Gloria full-time until her permanent replacement is hired, since his work is the least vital to the entire agency on a minute-by-minute basis. I've written to my uncle about this." Tweety watched Charlie for a reaction, squinting, and one eyelid twitching. Why would anybody listen to an eye doctor and opt for hard lenses? "You can bet if he weren't a guy this whole problem would never have arisen." She took a bite off the top of a Snickers, crunched the peanuts, pulled in a stray string of caramel with her tongue.

"Maurice Lavender handles as much business for this agency as both Dorian and Luella put together, and he is currently without a secretary. And as far as I can see the agency is still afloat. You want to explain that to me, Tracy?"

"Secretary? You think I'm just a secretary around here? Well I have news, Charlie Greene, I—"

"Did I say secretary? I meant assistant. But that doesn't change the—"

"Do you know lovely Larry, your sec-re-tar-eee, practically accused me of murdering Gloria Tuschman? Huh? Asked all sorts of personal questions? Told me you had asked him to? *You* want to explain that to *me*, Charlie?"

"Wait a minute. Your uncle. Is that Mr. Congdon?" Charlie had always wondered what the relationship was there. "Is he well enough to be bothered by all this? I mean I understood he was . . . do you see him often?"

"No, he travels." The telephone tyrant tinkled—soft but relentless. "Congdon and Morse Representation," Tracy Dewitt answered sweetly. She had a piece of chocolate wedged between her teeth.

By her own admission Tracy Dewitt was in the office the morning Gloria was murdered. She could disguise herself a lot easier than Dr. Podhurst ever could. But Tracy couldn't carry a body over her shoulder down four flights of stairs and out to the alley. Then again there was always the elevator. She'd have had to push the trash cart through the office and out the public door to the elevator and then out to the alley from the first floor hall and then over halfway across the covered area where the parking valets lurked to get to the alley. Certainly wouldn't be easy.

"Tracy, how well did . . . do you know Mary Ann Leffler?"

"I know she was a famous author, which didn't impress me at all. I think books are for the squirrels myself. If it's any good they'll make a movie out of it, and I'll go see that."

"*Was* a famous author?"

"Well, what has she written since the Goliath pic? You know, the shadow thing about witches." But Tweety had hesitated and reddened before she'd answered. A suspicious reaction to a normal question. Unless something had happened to Mary Ann and she knew about it. "Don't you start in on me now. And stop looking at me that way, first the police, then your tame fag, and now you. I don't have to take this, you know."

"Larry and Lieutenant Dalrymple asked you about Mary Ann?"

"No, about Gloria and witchcraft, and everybody knows Mary Ann was into that, too, and I am not getting snared by that old guilt-by-association thing." Tweety refused to say another word, but she was clearly shaken by something. Or was that more of Charlie's fantasizing?

Charlie walked thoughtfully down the hall toward her office, stopped when she saw Irma Vance at her desk in front of Richard's closed door.

"Irma, what's the deal with Daniel Congdon? Is he terminally ill or is he a world traveler? And why does he never even pay this office a visit?"

"He is not well, but I certainly hope he's not facing death anytime soon. Still, that is not something any of us can foresee, is it?" Irma pointedly returned her attention to the papers on her desk. Audience over. But Charlie lingered.

"You still haven't told me why he never comes in."

The Vance's exasperation was evident. And that was unusual—not the exasperation, the showing of it. "Mr. Congdon is what is known in the business world as a silent partner, Charlie. He helped to capitalize the founding of the agency, participates in the profits, is consulted occasionally about business crucial to its survival, but leaves the management up to Mr. Morse."

"Then why does he maintain an office here?"

"He's entitled to do so if he wishes. The agency does bear his name."

"So what's so silent about his partnership? He's got top billing. Have you ever seen this guy?"

Irma squinted like Tracy, tapped her pen on the desk, pursed her lips around her reconstituted teeth. But she didn't answer Charlie's question.

Back in her own office Charlie returned some calls and then called Larry in, asking him to close the door.

"Right, chief, I've got the goods on everybody here." He pulled out a small spiral notebook like Lieutenant Dalrymple's and glanced at the comfort of the couch.

But Charlie pointed at the client chair on the other side of her desk, trying not to linger on the memory of Ed Esterhazie suggesting she loosen her tie. "First order of business, Larry, lay off Tweety . . . I mean Tracy."

"That cow? Christ, Charlie, she—"

"I mean it, Larry. No excuses. No explanations. No bullshit. No whining. Just lay off Tracy Dewitt."

"I hate it when you get macho."

"I know. But that's the bottom line, so let's cut the crap and get on with your report."

He licked a finger and turned a page, peering over the little wire spirals of the notebook to see if she might have softened. She hadn't. "First person I questioned was Linda Meyer, Dr. Podhurst's receptionist. She became involved in witchcraft through Gloria Tuschman."

16

Charlie watched the palm fronds outside her window stand perfectly still. Even the traffic on Wilshire couldn't stir the heat today. Larry had been summoned to his cubicle by the phones, having barely begun his report on the suspects. They didn't dare ask Tweety to take messages for Charlie right now.

Mary Ann Leffler, Keegan Monroe, and Larry Mann had all asked Charlie to look into Gloria's murder unofficially, because they were worried their alibis were shaky. Did the fact that they asked her to snoop around mean they were innocent? Mary Ann had withheld the fact she knew the Tuschmans personally. But Charlie could swear that when she saw them at the Polo Lounge the day of the murder, Keegan and Mary Ann's only concern was their inability to get along while writing the screenplay. What did the three of them have in common? This agency and *Shadowscapes*.

But Larry's role in the deal between Goliath and Keegan Monroe on the scriptwriting was only some of the paperwork and a few phone calls. His actual involvement with Mary Ann had been, to Charlie's knowledge, nil. Larry was definitely strong enough to haul a body around and toss it up into the bushes. Keegan kept himself in good physical shape and might well be able to. Charlie had no idea how strong Mary Ann was. Any of them could probably disguise themselves.

"Edward Esterhazie?" Larry called in from his workstation.

"Oh boy. Is he at home? Get a number."

Charlie heard her assistant explaining that Ms. Greene wasn't in her office right now but would call Ed back, while she was remembering Mary Ann Leffler's apparent vision problem, her odd manner of looking at people. That didn't seem to lead anywhere. Richard Morse had also asked Charlie to investigate, but that was because he was cheap and she was already on the payroll and he liked to get all he could out of an employee. Which simply sounded like good business unless you were the employee. Which brought up another thought. Most of Charlie's income came from commissions, and if she spent time snooping instead of hustling, she'd come up short when it came time to pay the mortgage.

"This one's New York. It's Phyllis."

"I'll take it. Hi, Phyllis, I've been meaning to call you back. I've got none other than Steve Hunter looking at *The Corpse That Got Iced.* That just happened yesterday, so don't mention it to the author until we hear something." But Phyllis really only wanted to talk about the murder at Congdon and Morse. She had also heard that Mary Ann Leffler was missing. Charlie got off the line as soon as she could politely do so and went back to her dark thoughts.

What was the use of tallying up the people who asked her to investigate, anyway? She realized she was trying to eliminate people instead of track one of them down.

Who else had Gloria turned on to witchcraft besides Linda Meyer? Larry had met someone when he left the office to get Ding Dongs for coffee break and had come back late. Sooner or later Charlie was going to have to make him tell her who. Did Dalrymple know about this? Did he think she could get Larry and perhaps others to confide things he couldn't? Was he maybe really more interested in her ability to do this than any supposed psychic talents Charlie might or might not have?

Dalrymple didn't make any more sense than Gloria Tuschman's murder.

"It's Sheldon," Larry called.

"What's he doing up at this hour? Tell him I'll call—no wait. I'll take it." Sheldon Maypo was Charlie's security-guard screenwriter. He usually worked all night, slept all morning, and wrote all afternoon. "Shelly, I've got a tickle is all on your latest" (Jesus, she couldn't even remember its name), "but very high hopes. There hasn't been much time."

Sheldon Maypo was downstairs at a pay phone in the hallway next to the public elevators. He had come to the FFUCWB of P for two reasons. One was to fill out an application for building security guard and the other was to see his agent.

"You lost your job at the Spaghetti Factory?" Why was it *that* she could remember and not the title of his screenplay? "Just a minute. Larry, what's on the docket for lunch?"

"Nothing but murder."

"Where can you get me a reservation for two for lunch this late?"

"El Torito would be about it." Larry sounded petulant again. By rights the two of them should have lunched together to get away from the office long enough to discuss the information in his notebook. But Charlie had just discovered a need to talk to an unemployed security guard who also happened to be a damn good writer.

"Shelly, have you got plans for lunch? You like Mexican?"

"Charlie, just because I'm suddenly unemployed, you don't have to—"

"It's on my expense account, and I need some advice from a security guard."

"In that case I'm your señor, señorita."

"It's really more pseudotrendy Sante Fe, which is trendy-pseudo Navajo or something, but—"

"El Torito Grill, right? They got great booze and great beans. Besides, us working stiffs get hungry enough to eat anything."

But on her way out of her office and well into Larry's cubbyhole, Charlie came up against the boss. Hard.

"You women, always complaining about glass ceilings. No wonder. You can't even navigate in front of you." Richard Morse regained his balance. "Listen up you two, party at my house tomorrow night to celebrate the *Alpine Tunnel* deal. I want you both there, and bring somebody so it looks more like a crowd. Kid, Stewart's fine, I love Stewart. Charlie, you can even bring Libby. I know how hard up you are. But we're going to do a bang-up celebration before—"

"Richard, I just got a call from Phyllis? New York? They've already heard of Gloria's—"

"Everybody's heard of Gloria, it's the *Alpine Tunnel* I want to—"

"And the fact that Mary Ann Leffler is missing. Phyllis wanted to know what Congdon and Morse knew about it."

"You know how hard it was to set up caterers and all this fast, Charlie? You want to know the names of the reporters who'll be there? Do you want to know how bad this agency needs to do this, or how many people might be there that you should speak to while investigating the mess your agency is in, through no fault of its own? We put off the celebration because Gloria got herself killed. We better hurry up before we find out Mary Ann did, too, huh?"

"If I take time to do what you ask, I do not earn commissions or enough to pay the mortgage. I want a raise. I want it before I commit to one more of your demands for extra work."

"That's the problem with your generation, Charlie, you

always expect instant gratification. When I was your age, my parents—"

"I *am* a parent." Charlie sat down in the cubbyhole's visitor chair. It was considered impolitic to ask—but Charlie figured the bigger agencies paid big salaries. At Congdon and Morse, and some of the others of its size that Charlie happened to know about, the base wage encouraged young agents to hustle for commissions. Truth be known, Charlie sort of enjoyed the challenge of this system. Her stomach sort of didn't. It was considered even more inappropriate to discuss wages in front of another employee. Larry seemed to enjoy it, though.

"Don't push your luck, honey," her boss warned.

"Might look funny if I didn't show up at the party tomorrow night," Charlie said.

"Wasn't my idea to buy an expensive condo way off in Long Beach," Richard said.

Charlie didn't answer.

Richard checked his watch. "I have a lunch meeting. Talk to me later this afternoon. But be there tomorrow night."

"I have a lunch meeting, too. I'll decide about tomorrow night after we have our discussion this afternoon." Charlie's heart was beating so fast she worried she sounded breathless.

Richard swore and left the cubbyhole and then added over his shoulder on his way down the hall, "Three o' clock sharp. You be here. And bring a man tomorrow night, damn it."

Every one of Larry Mann's beautiful teeth warred for space in a gigantic grin.

"Get me Edward Esterhazie, quick." Charlie tried to swallow adrenaline. Her stomach didn't like that, either.

The El Torito Grill could do fabulous margaritas, and Charlie made the mistake of having one with her favorite unemployed security guard. She spilled the beans before hers arrived under some soothing huevos and mildly serious salsa.

Sheldon Maypo looked a lot more like his name than he did a security guard. He was short and grizzled with a good-humored but highly intelligent look in his eyes. He had a white manicured beard and a black belt in karate. He took out little drugstore half glasses, similar to Luella Ridgeway's, to read the menu and forgot to remove them. Regardless of the black belt, he had a large bulge in his torso to fit it around. Any time Charlie had seen him, Sheldon wore suspenders instead.

"Shelly, I'm sorry. Here you are unemployed, and I haven't sold any of your stuff yet, and I can't believe I'm dumping my problems on you. It's not fair. Must be the margarita."

"You need another, and so do I, and do not apologize. This is wonderful. Who knows? There might be material here. God, there's got to be. I feel privileged to even get in on it."

"Don't you writers ever quit working?"

"We can't. You think *you* have trouble making a living." Shelly's hair was sparse, and white like his beard, but his movements swift and strong, almost jerky. It was like they'd put a teenager in an old body. Charlie had felt his physical strength only in benign ways, but she had no doubt Sheldon Maypo could physically do away with anybody and hide the body as well. Which again threw out all her suppositions about those at the agency who might have killed Gloria Tuschman. The only people at Congdon and Morse smaller than Shelly were Charlie, Irma, and Luella.

"You know," Shelly said, "if you could find out who in your building could put in a word for me and get me on the security squad there at the First Federal United Central Wilshire Bank of the Pacific building, I could question the security staff and parking valets in less threatening ways than you or your dippy homicide cop could. And now that I know something of the problem, I might even be able to nose around that party at your boss's tomorrow night—among the staff, you know, if you could figure out a way to get me in. Hell, this all sounds like fun."

They walked back to the agency in the curiously still air. If it was this hot in April, what would summer be like? El Torito was not far from the FFUCWB of P, and Shelly had left his car there. "There's one thing that puzzles me more than all the rest."

"Which is?" Charlie's stomach felt a lot better now than after her talk with Dr. Podhurst. Maybe two margaritas and half a plate of huevos rancheros had stunned it into submission.

"Why throw the body into the bushes?"

Charlie steered her security guard up the alley, past the dumpster and the first off-alley private parking spaces, to the concrete wall. "To hide it?"

Once around the wall, victim and murderer could be seen only from the alley or by someone standing directly behind the gate to the house yard. A dense hedge about ten feet or more high protected the backyard of Mrs. Humphrys' house, and the approach to the gate was angled so that you couldn't see in from this side. Out of curiosity, Charlie tried the gate and found it locked. She had to step back halfway to the garage to see the window of the back hall on the fifth floor where the agency was located.

"I saw Mrs. Humphrys put what turned out to be Gloria's shoe in here when I was standing at the window at the end of our hall." The green plastic garbage can sat to the side of the garage in the alley. Did some essence of Gloria Tuschman cling to that shoe and make her think all of her was in the garbage can? Then why did Charlie imagine she heard Gloria talk about a closet this morning? "It's got to be somebody pretending to be Gloria talking to me. And who better than her murderer? But why?" Charlie asked Sheldon Maypo. "And why me?"

"Granted, it's the most likely, but it wouldn't have to be someone at Congdon and Morse who did in Gloria or even someone who worked in the building. Do you have any clues as to motivation and strength of alibis here, Charlie?"

"Not really, other than that Gloria was more needed than beloved at the agency and that I'm finding out that some of the alibis I thought were solid are turning out to have holes. I suppose I can ask the lieutenant. He hinted the other day that he would share what information he could with me so I could put it in my crystal ball and come up with some kind of magic. Shelly, do you believe in psychics and crystal balls and communication with the dead?"

"Only if I'm pitching to Disney. No Charlie, there's a human explanation to all this if only we can unclutter our minds of that paranormal junk and see it. You know, sometimes when I'm writing, I'm sitting there and nothing's coming, or more likely all the wrong things are coming—like problems in my real life or fantasies about how rich and famous I'm going to be when you sell whatever it is—and I suddenly become aware of a quiet but shyly persistent voice, so far in the back of my skull it could be in my hair, trying to feed me the next line."

He was inspecting the bushes next to the wall with his back to her, and she surreptitiously checked to see if there was anything interesting in the green garbage can. It was empty.

"Really?" She loved to hear her writers talk about their mysterious thought processes, keeping in mind always that they were congenital exaggerators. "You mean like the muse or something?"

"Or something. It's like some part of me has already written the whole thing. All the questions and all the answers. See, it's done, maybe while I was asleep, I don't know. I just have to clear my mind of extraneous stuff and let it flow."

Broken branches and bruised red blossoms showed where the body had been heaved into the bushes and, later, moved during the job of getting it down. "Charlie, how did the police know she was killed up in that hallway? You said there wasn't any sign of blood that you saw that morning. How do we know Gloria didn't walk out here, with the killer maybe, and then get bashed?"

I sure hope I'm not going to turn out like you," Libby said over dinner at the diner that night.

"Me too." Charlie looked down at her side order of mashed potatoes, cream of cauliflower soup, and glass of milk. "You'd have to give up eating again."

"I don't want to go to college and have a career and end up working myself sick." Libby pointed a ketchup-tipped french fry at her mother. "Women should get married and stay home and have babies."

"Libby, have you been talking to Jesus?"

"You mean church or 'Hey-zeus'?"

"The friendly gardener. You know, the Mexican stud."

"You are so prejudiced. It's embarrassing." Libby picked the lettuce and tomato off her cheeseburger and took a big bite off the front end of it. Condiment and meat juices mingled to drip out the back end.

Charlie fought a bout of nausea. "You didn't answer my question."

"I don't even know where he lives. I haven't seen him since Saturday. But you're right, he does know how to fill a pair of Levi's."

Charlie ordered her voice to stay down at a normal, controlled octave. "So . . . your ambition is to become a happy housewife. Name me two couples since your grandmother's generation who've made a success out of that."

"Lori's folks, and ... Mrs. Hefty. And she has kids to support too, just like you. But she doesn't make a huge deal of it because she has a husband to help."

"Are their last names Hefty? The kids? Was this her only marriage?"

"I don't know. They're little. She just talks about them by their first names. You're weird."

"Yeah, well you better warn your good friend Doug of that, because I'm taking his father to an agency party at Richard's house tomorrow night."

"You are? Really?" Her daughter came alive so suddenly Charlie worried the kid would swallow her Coke straw. "When did this happen?"

"When the *Alpine Tunnel* deal jelled again, but because of the murder at the agency we couldn't celebrate it then and so—"

"No, I mean when did you invite Ed?"

On the way home Charlie had to pull the Toyota over. She got her door open just in time to spew cream of cauliflower soup and something dark that wasn't mashed potatoes or milk all over someone's carefully tended rocks and cactus. Probably some Jesus would have to come along and clean it up while he wasn't impregnating the daughter of the house.

"Mom? What are you doing?" her own daughter whispered when Charlie sat back and closed the door. Libby's tan had turned a sick orange under the yellow glow of the sodium vapor streetlight. "You can't be sick."

"How do you figure that?" A welcome breeze moved air into Charlie's window, and palm-leaf fans shifted the shadows on the windshield and hood.

"You're all I've got."

Charlie's mouth had acquired a coating that tasted like Tuxedo's kitty litter smelled. Prickly sweat coated the rest of her.

"I mean, I can't drive us home. Well, I could but . . . I don't have a license."

The sign on the lamppost in front of them said, NO CRUIS-ING. THREE TIMES PAST THE SAME POINT WITHIN FOUR HOURS IS CRUISING.

"Besides, you have to go to that party tomorrow night."

"You'd sell your own mother just to get into the yacht club?"

"Mom, Ed's rich. You wouldn't have to work so hard for us and worry so much you make yourself sick. Do you think it's more than just indigestion?"

"I'm seriously beginning to wonder, honey. I can get us home. Just let me sit a minute."

"I mean like . . . stomach cancer?"

"Let's try to be positive and go for maybe an ulcer, huh?"

Maggie Stutzman forced Charlie to down two pieces of dry toast and some warm milk that night. And forced a promise out of Charlie to eat breakfast and call for a doctor's appoint-ment from the office the next morning instead of waiting for the weekend.

Libby even offered to walk to school.

"I should get sick more often."

"Mom, why do you always have to wreck the good moments?"

"I don't know. I do appreciate the offer. But there's time. Get your stuff. I'm so used to going right by there."

"Not until you finish your Cheerios."

Since no one in their family ate breakfast, those Cheerios dated from the Mesozoic era. Charlie continued to regret them all the way up on the 405. By the time she hit the Santa Monica Freeway, Charlie remembered that Maurice Lavender had thought he had an ulcer some months ago. He'd found a doctor somewhere close enough to the office but still out of the Beverly Hills fee area.

As it turned out, Maurice didn't have an ulcer—or even, God forbid, stomach cancer. He had indigestion. That sounded like a good kind of doctor to go to.

Charlie was so caught up in her survival fantasy that by the time she reached Congdon and Morse she wasn't thinking logically and rushed into Maurice's office unannounced. An easy thing to do since his new assistant had not yet been hired.

She came to a skidding stop in front of Ellen Maxwell. Maurice smiled wryly but rose to hug Charlie. "Ellen, you remember Charlie Greene, our talented literary agent? And, my dearest lady, the very one to suggest you as the perfect actress to play the part of Thora Kay, the retired veterinarian detective."

Ellen was every bit as gracious, grandmotherly, and sweet as she appeared on recent commercials and occasional guest shots. On those she'd worn a gray wig to cover her hair. In real life she wore it beige. She'd had just enough neck tucks and face and eye lifts to look lively for her age, yet still softly feminine—without resorting to that scraped look.

Legend had it that Ellen Maxwell had danced on Broadway, but she was best known for a string of sweet wifely roles in comedy films and a long series of supporting roles after that. She'd won an Oscar for one of the latter, had done some theater work in the boonies, and begun to fade away like all the rest when American Express picked her for the traveling grandmother who knew how to make the most of her golden years by seeing exotic places while kept in comfortable safety by that magic little card. And she had been chosen because of the recognition factor of her face rather than her name. She'd appeared often enough on the screen that she was familiar, trustworthy.

"Of course. Charlie, how can I ever thank you?"

"Things are all still at the talking stage, aren't they?"

"Yes, but oh, I have just such a good feeling about this. I just know it will come to pass and I will be Thora Kay. I've just been to my astrologist, and the signs are all there, Charlie. Darling Maurice here and I were just discussing whether or not to commit to any more commercials at this point. They would pay so much more if I were the star of my own series, you know. It's just all so exciting."

Ellen gushed on and Charlie waited it out, making all the right nods and faces until she could interject the request for the doctor's number and *just* get out of there. Astrologist? Oh boy.

Between a deluge of phone calls and regular office business, Larry was able to get her an appointment with Dr. Williams for the next day and then continue his little spiral notebook report.

Irma Vance had gone to a party at Gloria's, and there was some flap over it Larry couldn't tease out of anyone. "Everybody stonewalled me on that one. But I overheard Tweety mention it to Gloria weeks ago, maybe months."

Irma refused to divulge even to Richard how much she had come away from Las Vegas with. It was enough, she said. Charlie had never heard of anyone winning anything in Las Vegas they hadn't lost again before they left. Except for the Vance.

"I can tell Richard the Clever is worried about losing her," Larry said. "He keeps pestering Irma to find out how much she won. She loves this job so much he needn't worry. She'd stay here if she won the lottery, but I'd be willing to bet she's gonna get your raise, because she's his right arm. The law being—the more you have the more you get."

"Larry, that's all supposition. You can't know any of it." But Charlie hadn't been offered a raise. She'd settled for an unspecified bonus if she was instrumental in clearing up the irritation of Gloria's murder. Which was really just another commission. Charlie had to admit the boss *was* clever. Heartless but clever.

"Oh but I can sense, intuit, and reason this by pausing long enough to be sensitive to the vibes around this place, Charlie, which you are too work-oriented and self-centered to bother with. Let's face it, you need me as much as Richard the Lionhearted needs the Vance."

Nobody could quite pin down the office name for Richard that would stick.

Keegan might have a motive to knock off Mary Ann, but not to kill Gloria. Mary Ann might have a motive if the Tuschmans had threatened some form of blackmail to force her to share the proceeds from *Shadowscapes*. Anybody could have a motive that Charlie didn't know about, a relationship with Gloria that Charlie didn't know about. Larry was right, Charlie had not paid close attention to the office gossip.

"What if Gloria stepped out to the private hall to use the john and saw something happen there and got bonked on the head to keep her from telling anybody what she saw?"

"Gloria wouldn't have left the phones at that time of the morning," Larry reminded her. "She'd be fielding half the calls from New York about then, and everybody was in and out of the office. She'd have waited for somebody to come back in and take over for her."

"Unless she was suddenly sick. Or unless someone lured her out there. Tracy said she was in early that morning. Where was *she* at the time of the murder, I wonder?"

"Says she slipped over to the Chevron to buy some candy bars for coffee break." He pushed the dark blond hair out of his face, not bothering to hide the bitterness never far from the surface. "I'm sure she's told Dalrymple she didn't see me buying Ding Dongs there. What I can't understand is why he isn't hanging around asking me why."

"I'm asking you why, Larry. Where did you buy the Ding Dongs? You said you went to meet someone. Who did you see that morning to make you late getting back?"

He stared at Charlie without quite meeting her eyes, his watery blue ones literally swimming now. These weren't actor tears. His jaw muscles twitched dramatically before he managed to whisper, "It's all so unfair, Charlie."

They sat facing each other across her desk, now both of them avoiding eye contact. It was a long time before Charlie could find a breath and her voice under the weight of a premonition that dropped on her like a piano in an old Laurel and Hardy flick.

She watched his Adam's apple ripple as he swallowed more tears. "Larry, have you . . . been tested?"

"Have you?" he snapped back and stood to face the tinted window instead of Charlie.

"Oh, please don't do this to me."

"It was negative." But he was still choking on something, still didn't turn. "Satisfied?"

"You don't seem to be. Is that where you were that morning, being tested? Or finding out the results? If so you have an alibi, Larry. You don't need to worry."

"That's not where I was." The big shoulders shrugged. "I have to be checked again in six months. And so does Stew."

Charlie left her chair to walk around in front of him, standing close, careful not to touch him. Stew was a contact man, had a hug or a handshake for everyone. But Larry didn't like to be touched by anyone but Stewart Claypool. At least that's what she'd always thought. "Is Stew . . . ?"

"Not that we know yet. But he's been helping take care of a friend of ours who's dying of this . . . this monster. You know Stew—always thinks of other people first. He may not have been careful with needles and rubber gloves, and who knows? A public nurse finally stopped in on her rounds while Stew was there and went bonkers when she saw his medical procedure. Blew the whistle on all of Terry's keepers and their lovers."

"When did all this happen? I haven't noticed a major change in you. This has got to be a horrendous thing in your life."

He drew himself up and stared down his nose at her in that infuriating way. "I'm an actor. Remember?"

And that, amazingly, was what was bothering Larry the most. Word of this could squelch any dreams he might have for future acting jobs, and it might even cost him this one. Richard Morse might cheerfully overlook Larry's sexual preferences—he was only an assistant after all—but the taint of AIDS was a very real stigma in this town, for all its fund-raising campaigns and verbal support for those afflicted.

Stewart Claypool was in the social services, alcohol and drug rehab, as Charlie remembered. He, too, worried this would cost him his livelihood and health insurance.

Charlie carefully slipped Larry's spiral notebook out of his hand and flipped it shut. "Come on, I'm taking you out to lunch."

She drove him to a mom-and-pop diner off the fast track in West Hollywood that Larry had introduced her to shortly after she'd come to Congdon and Morse. She brought him here because it was homey, and if she tossed her cookies or cried, the proprietors and patrons might be a little less offended.

Larry had pizza. Charlie had homemade chicken soup. The place was called Mom and Pop's.

"Next thing I know," the gorgeous man across the table from her said, "you'll be sending flowers for my desk." He batted thick lashes.

"Actually, I was thinking of nominating you for Secretary of the Year. Who did you meet that morning?"

Larry cut a steamy slice of the homemade bread that came with Charlie's luncheon special, spread it thick with real butter, and handed it to her.

Charlie's assistant told her of meeting a man with whom he'd had a "dalliance" to warn him of what had happened to Stew and thus to Larry Mann. "It was not a pleasant encounter. I really did stop at the Chevron across the way for Ding Dongs on my way back, though."

"I don't understand. You said you and Stew were solid. Like an old married couple." I never worried about you because I thought you were monogamous.

"We are, mostly."

Homemade chicken soup with thick homemade noodles and little spicy green things floating in it really was comforting, restorative. It gave Charlie the strength to ask, "Why do I have the feeling I haven't heard it all yet? I admit I'm no detective and no psychic. But even though I'm an insensitive workaholic bitch, I'd like to think I'm your friend. I'm missing something here and I just can't track it. I don't see why any of this, as awful as it is, makes you worry about your alibi for the time Gloria was murdered."

"Oh, didn't I mention it?" Larry pulled a thread of melted cheese into his mouth with his tongue, reminding Charlie of Tweety doing the same with a string of caramel the day before. "Our Gloria took the call from the stupid nurse at the clinic, reporting I'd tested negative but that it was so soon after the possible exposure it would take another test in six months to validate my health and humanity."

If it got around the office that Larry and Stew had been ordered to be tested, the insurance company that covered Congdon and Morse, albeit marginally, might threaten to drop the agency. Larry Mann would find himself without a job. And that could just be the beginning. Even if he was still negative in six months. All in all a pretty good motive for murder.

18

The way her day was going, Charlie wasn't surprised to find Lieutenant Dalrymple waiting for her when she returned to her office. She settled him on the couch with a cup of coffee, told Larry to hold all but life-threatening calls, closed the door, and waited for another Laurel and Hardy piano.

He studied her, the coffee, the dried flower arrangement on the coffee table, and seemed to be waiting, too.

"So," she said finally, hugging her middle and the comfort of the chicken soup for courage, "have you found Mary Ann yet?"

"No," he said thoughtfully and watched her.

"Well, that's a relief."

"You're relieved she's still missing?"

"I'm relieved you didn't find her in her car underwater. I honest to God don't know what made me say that."

"Oh, I think you do."

"What's that supposed to mean?"

"What I came to discuss ... " he said slowly and reached into the vase. "Are you aware that your flowers are wired, Miss Greene?"

She looked at the tiny buttonlike thing in his palm, the comfort of the chicken soup slowly draining away. "That's not a wire."

"We'll call it a bug, if you like, but it is a listening device. Have you any idea who might want to keep track of your conversations?"

Yeah, you. "No."

"May I use your phone?" But he already was.

David Dalrymple took Charlie into the back VIP hall while two cohorts scoured the agency for the device that listened to, and perhaps recorded, what the bug picked up in Charlie's office. All Charlie could think of was the conversation she'd had in that office just before lunch with Larry Mann. She hugged her middle even tighter, but the comfort was gone.

"What I really came here to discuss with you is what you might have learned in your informal, insider investigation into Gloria Tuschman's murder and Mrs. Leffler's disappearance—which we might assume are related until we learn otherwise. Apparently, I'm not the only one interested."

"I haven't learned much. How could I? I don't know alibis, times, motives—I don't even know what Gloria was hit with. And are you sure she actually died here?" They stood at the end of the hall by the tinted window. From up here the bushes and their red flowers flouncing on top of the white brick wall looked undisturbed by murder. "I mean it would be awfully hard to get her down there unnoticed."

"Gloria didn't tell you?"

"Now she thinks she's in the closet," Charlie heard herself say, but this time knowing why she said it. Anything to keep from talking about Larry's secret. Anything to keep from thinking about who might have overheard it.

"Closet?"

Charlie pointed to the door of the janitor's closet. "She's a dip, always was. Lieutenant, we all know she's been cremated but Gloria. It's typical."

He turned his back on her and did something fancy, because, without Luella Ridgeway's nail file, he had that door open in no time. The inside of the closet and the inside of the canvas trash bag looked about the same as when Charlie had broken in.

"So, she gets knocked out by something, dumped in that bag, carried out to the wall and the bushes—by who?"

"Whom."

"Past the security guard and the parking valet guys, and we're talking in the morning—busy time. It just doesn't play, Lieutenant. But say I killed her up here. How would I get her down there? I couldn't."

"Not in those shoes," Dalrymple agreed with only a hint of the sardonic behind the owlish glasses.

"The only way would be to push her through the office in that trolley and out into the public hall and down in the elevator, halfway across the parking garage, past security and valet people, to the alley—at that time of day there could be people in the halls, the elevator, everywhere. And if you're dressed for the office you're going to look pretty silly pushing one of those things around. And somebody's going to remember it."

And somebody bugged my office. How long has that device been there? Did someone want to overhear what I said about business instead of about Gloria's murder? Could it be another agency? Or another agent in this one?

It all seemed farfetched, but Charlie suddenly felt threatened around here by more than just Gloria. And it dawned on her how odd it was that she hadn't felt afraid before. Here in the place murder had happened. It had simply not occurred to her that it could happen again. And since she didn't know why it had in the first place, she couldn't know the casting requirements for a future victim.

She did know it must seem odd to the man standing next to her that no one at Congdon and Morse had shown much fear at the terrible, sick thing that had happened in their daily lives. Was everyone really that remote, estranged from Gloria? That

busy and self-centered? That jaded by the violence everywhere around them? Or were they all so sure it wasn't one of
them who had done it, that it was someone in Gloria's life outside the office, the motive unconnected to them?

"Murdering your receptionist is one thing," Dalrymple said
softly, "but someone bugging your flowers does rather get
your attention, doesn't it? Let's try your idea." He pulled the
cart out into the hall. "How often do you see someone pushing
these around during the day?"

"Now and then, I guess. Most of the cleaning is done at
night when the offices are empty, but I suppose there'd have to
be someone around during the day. I assume the janitorial
work is privately contracted, but I don't know that, either.
Haven't you questioned whoever manages these things? Let's
try what idea?"

David Dalrymple heaved a leg over the side and crawled
into the canvas bag. "Let's continue to pretend you murdered
Gloria. I am Gloria and you want to take me out to the alley."

"Why would I do that? Why wouldn't I just leave you in
there and in the closet and pretend someone else did it? I
mean, when we were looking all over for Gloria, we didn't look
in that closet."

"Good point. But let's try this, and maybe something will
occur to us." He had scrunched down so far in the bag that he
was only that soft voice.

Charlie felt silly, but she pushed the cleaning trolley along
the hallway to the agency door, surprised at how easily,
smoothly, and quietly it rolled with a whole man in there. The
cart had handles on each end, and the agency door opened
inward. All she had to do was open the door and pull it
through.

"How we doing?" came the disembodied voice from the
canvas trash bag.

"Piece of cake." She went back to pushing. Past Tweety's cubicle. Her workstation was slanted to see people coming the other way. Charlie looked over her shoulder but Tracy Dewitt was calling in a caller into one of her agents' offices and was looking over her shoulder, too. Next, the little utility niche with sink, coffee pot, copier, fax, and small refrigerator, but no one to see Charlie pushing a cleaning cart. Down at the end of this hall, Irma Vance's door was open, but only a corner of her desk showed. There was no assistant in the cubbyhole shielding Maurice's office to see her. She turned into the reception area, where Larry sat with his back to her in the semicircle of Gloria's desk.

"Don't ask," was all she said when he looked up as she passed. It didn't take any release switch from Gloria's desk to get out of the agency, and they were soon in the public hall.

"What's this?" Dalrymple asked when she threw a manila envelope in on top of him. It had been leaning against the door. "Don't you people ever open these things?"

"If we did we'd be mobbed. It's probably a video demo and stills, or a screenplay or book proposal, that kind of thing." He suspected her of murdering Gloria, or they wouldn't be going through this. Wouldn't you know? The highest point of her career and she had Dalrymple, an ulcer, and Jesus Garcia to contend with.

"How do you know there isn't another *Gone With the Wind* in one of these things, or the next Mitch Hilsten working out in the buff?" the bag asked as she pushed the trolley into the elevator.

"If it is, they need to learn about marketing. And if they still need to learn, they aren't ready for us."

"Isn't that a bit pompous?"

"Look, you start your own agency and run it your way. We have eighty percent more talent than we can keep working now. Product is not our problem, and we cannot afford to hire someone to weed out all the unagented stuff thrown our way."

"Why not?"

"Because anybody capable of doing that has their own agency." Charlie pushed the trolley and the cop out into the first floor hall of the First Federal United Central Wilshire Bank of the Pacific. "And once we open these unsolicited envelopes we can be royally sued for stealing someone else's work and giving it to our contracted writers."

"I just opened this one. In fact we've opened many, in hopes someone was offering evidence anonymously."

"We've made it from the fifth floor back hall to the first level parking, and Larry was the only person who noticed us."

"Stop talking and look natural. Don't make any more eye contact than you need to, to see if you're being noticed."

A valet glanced at her to see if she wanted a car brought up, must have decided the cleaning cart wouldn't fit in one, and glanced away. He said something about the Oilers to the security guard, who laughed derisively, his eyes skimming over Charlie to something beyond her. She heard a car engine and stepped up her pace. If the guard had thought there was anything odd about her pushing a cleaning cart outside the building and in a dress and heels, he didn't let his expression show it.

The drive-in area for the building was covered by part of the second story. At the outside edge of that was reserved parking for bank VIPs and then a high protective concrete wall. Charlie pushed the trolley to the alley, rounded that end wall, passed the dumpster and the parking indentation for the first residence behind the bank building, and then the wall dividing it from Mrs. Humphrys' parking area and garage. She stopped and leaned over to look in the canvas bag. "Do you want me to throw you up in the bushes now?"

• • •

Having received permission to leave the trolley in the care of Dalrymple, who was studying the bushes, Charlie hurried back to the office, thinking one day could hold no more surprises for her and her stomach than this one had already. She was wrong.

Larry held up one of Gloria's phones as she stepped through the public door. "It's your mother."

"Oh shit."

"Thought you gave up swearing because of Libby."

"I'll take it at my desk."

"Libby says you're sick enough to vomit blood," Charlie's mother bellowed from Boulder. A smoker's voice like Mary Ann Leffler's. "Libby says you're going to a party with some jerk named Ed. How can you get to be over thirty and not learn any better than that?"

"Edwina, what do you two do, call each other every day after school?"

"She calls collect only when she needs me. You never call at all."

"Where are you? Are you home from the University already?" Charlie's mother was a professor of biology at the University of Colorado.

"Down with the flu. Didn't go in today."

"Well, see?" Charlie said. "You get sick, too."

"I'm *not* vomiting blood. I'm *not* at work. And I'm *not* going to party tonight."

The conversation went downhill from there, with Edwina ordering her daughter to stay away from coffee and booze until she'd seen Dr. Williams the next day, and left her with the usual guilt load.

She'd no more than slipped out of her pumps and queried Mom and Pop's homemade chicken noodle soup for forthcoming opinions than Maurice startled her by knocking on the doorjamb.

"Hi, sweetie, how're you feeling?"

"Oh Maurice." Charlie was soon in tears, snuggled against him on the office couch, telling him all about her stomach cancer. And she, a single mother. And Libby would have to go live with Edwina, who never understood a teenager sixteen years ago let alone now. "Teenagers have come a long ways since then. Maurice, did you ever throw up blood? When you thought you might have an ulcer?"

"I vomited something dark once I could have sworn was blood because I hadn't eaten anything dark. But it turned out I wasn't bleeding, so—Dr. Williams is good, Charlie, trust me and trust him. Just stay away from diet soda, chili peppers, raw veggies, coffee, and booze until after you've talked to him."

Was Maurice studying the flower arrangement on the table in front of them now? Would Charlie ever trust anybody again?

19

Maurice Lavender brought Ellen Maxwell to Richard's party that night, and they made a stunning couple. They looked like money, expensively preserved. Or perhaps they were talent. Heads turned trying to identify which. Ellen, of course, they knew they'd seen, but many couldn't place her.

It was Richard Morse, however, who stole the show, greeting his guests with Cyndi Seagal on his arm. Cyndi was the agency's hottest name at the moment, and Charlie decided he'd try to convince Ursa Major and the money to consider her for *Alpine Tunnel's* female lead. Cyndi had cropped black hair and large black eyes and the cutest nose doctors could build. She'd sprouted breasts since her last picture. They crowded up against each other in the slit of a snazzy white metallic number that ended just below her navel and accentuated her tininess elsewhere. She could look mischievous, helpless, angry, and sexually vulnerable. That pretty much summed up what she'd need for most of the work out there for female leads.

Charlie could not afford to sprout breasts and restricted her cleavage to the back of her dress, a shimmery emerald green thing she'd brought with her from New York. It left her spine exposed to the chill wind a change of weather had decided to inflict the moment it discerned what she would be wearing.

Everybody was there and nobody was there. What did Richard expect, calling up a dressy party this late and on a week night? Charlie recognized the *Hollywood Reporter* and *Variety* and maybe the *L.A. Times*, but what would there be to report? No network or syndicated gossip types that she could see. The only money and entertainment law there was that already committed to *Alpine Tunnel*, the only studio brass Ursa Major, the only stars other than tiny Cyndi—aging Congdon and Morse soap types or up-and-coming unknowns.

Was Richard Morse that desperate to cover up Mary Ann's disappearance? Did that mean he was behind it, and maybe Gloria's death as well? Panic can lead to bad moves, and this sure looked like desperation to Charlie. And desperation in Hollywood invited sharks, feeding frenzies, and a sudden retreat of the money fish. But Mary Ann wasn't even Congdon and Morse's client.

Charlie even had to work to keep from suspecting Edward Esterhazie of masterminding not only all her trouble at home (it wasn't Charlie's fault he belonged to the yacht club and had a live-in housekeeper) but the trouble with Gloria Tuschman and Mary Ann Leffler as well. Pretty soon she'd turn on him for giving her stomach cancer. Calm down, Charlie.

"Why are people looking at me so strangely?" he asked as they approached a table laden. "Am I dressed wrong?"

"Ed, you're impeccable. These people are just trying to figure out who you are and where you perch in the pecking order. Pretend you're home at the yacht club."

"Don't forget you promised to accompany me there Friday night."

"You sure Dorothy's going to go for this? Tell me she's not from Kansas."

"She's not from Kansas. Is that Ellen Maxwell over there? You do travel in exalted circles, Charlie. Next we'll be seeing Mitch Hilsten strut in the door with a babe to die for on each arm."

Charlie picked out some liver pâté, deviled eggs, oysters Rockefeller, creamed herring, lobster puffs, and crackers topped with creamy cheese. She avoided the low-cal things she usually went for while watching good old Ed unerringly choose them. More reason to resent him.

"Some of us must watch our diets," he said smugly.

Yeah well, some of us have stomach cancer.

Charlie ate slowly, testing the mood of her middle, washing it down with bottled water instead of champagne. Things felt pretty good. Maybe she was in remission.

"You okay, boss?" Larry whispered in her ear, then said, "Hi, you must be Ed. I'm Larry, the guy you always get on the phone when you need to get her at the office."

Charlie frantically scraped deviled egg off her front teeth with her tongue, while witnessing the most original choreography she'd ever seen at a cocktail party. Ed automatically balanced his champagne glass on his plate to free a hand to shake Larry's in answer to Larry's self-introduction, with Stewart Claypool intercepting it just as Larry said, "Oh, and this is Stewart Claypool, a good friend of Charlie's and mine."

Stew returned Ed's handshake, smiled a greeting, and passed in front of Larry to encircle Charlie with his other arm. "Any friend of Charlie's is great to greet." And in his John Wayne persona he added, "Hear the gremlins are gnawing at your gut, little lady. Don't let anybody tell you it's all in your head, got that?"

He and Larry quizzed Charlie about what she was eating and drinking and moved on.

"Something's eating your gut?"

"I'm not well, Ed," Charlie said bravely. "Libby thinks I have stomach cancer. Even Mrs. McDougal should get turned off by that. Hey, we might not have to do the yacht club thing, although I was sort of planning to expire there."

Ed stared at her over his champagne glass, probably still caught up on stomach cancer. He'd want to be the hero-provider, and that wouldn't work. Which put him out of the running, should he have wanted to be in it, and mellowed her mood toward him. She selected one last creamy cracker and set her glass on a passing tray.

"Don't worry, tonight I feel wonderful." And she did. Charlie gave Ed her thirty-five-millimeter smile. He drained his glass in a gulp.

You've been through a lot of mood changes in the last two hours, Charlie. What time of the month is it?

Oh shit.

They crossed the tiled floor and were heading for the patio and pool when Elaine Black popped up in front of them and in front of Dorian's back as he tried to sell—himself, an idea, a used car?—to an Oriental gentleman gripping a martini glass like a shield.

"Charlie," Elaine gushed, "you look stunning. I envy you so. I wish—"

"Elaine, this is Edward Esterhazie, a good friend," Charlie interrupted. "Ed, would you excuse us a second?" She practically lifted Dorian's wife out of her shoes to gain them a private word. "You don't happen to be carrying any plugs in that suitcase, do you? I think I'm in trouble." Elaine's purse resembled a diaper bag and totally negated her attempt to look businesslike in a dress that would have been suitable for the office about ten to fifteen years ago. For a party like this, never.

"Guess what? I'm going to work." Elaine bubbled in the hall outside the bathroom. "I'm so excited. And for myself, too." She rummaged through the bag. "Here, take two. I always carry lots of everything."

"Don't tell me," Charlie said. "Real estate."

"I just got my license, but how did you know?" Elaine was

small and thin with a distinctive overbite and blond hair darkening naturally to dishwater. Disappointment dragged the lean features downward in a preview of what the years would bring. "Dorian told you. I wanted to myself."

"No, he didn't, honest. I just guessed." When the economy is in the toilet, people go into real estate and novel writing. Or selling cosmetics or vitamins nobody wants even in good times. Desperate people. Charlie took another look at Dorian Black's wife. Maybe she was growing up. "Be careful," she told Elaine. "It's rough out there."

But when Charlie emerged from the bathroom, Elaine hadn't moved. "Charlie, do you think the police think Dorian killed Gloria? They've been hanging around, asking questions . . . you know. I mean, he can be a real asshole, but I know he didn't kill her. He said you were kind of unofficially looking into things for the agency. I mean, the police make a lot of mistakes and—"

Charlie guided Elaine around a corner and into a telephone niche papered with signed eight-by-ten glossies of aged stars when they were young and dewy. Mitch Hilsten was probably the youngest, and he had to be pushing forty by now.

"Charlie?"

Charlie turned her back on the sexiest gaze in the universe. "Elaine, did Dorian ever have anything to do with Gloria outside the office?"

"No, why would he?" Dorian's wife had good bones but no makeup sense. She accentuated her lack of color with dull lipstick and nearly beige eye shadow. Charlie watched a touch of color creep into pale cheeks now though, highlighting the cheekbones. Her eyes widened, and she became interesting. "Well, except for Halloween, but that—"

"Halloween." And I should be surprised? "Last Halloween? Dorian and Gloria Tuschman on Halloween?"

"Well it was both of us. And the kids. Only time we've ever been up there. It was kind of fun. They called it 'All Hallows' Eve' but it was neat. We all dressed in white—"

"What were you, the sacrifices?"

"No. They're white witches. At least I guess that's it. It's kind of a religion with them I think. Everybody wore white and danced around this bonfire in this orange grove in the moonlight. The kids loved it because it was spooky. But it was fun, too. And the food was good. Lots of people."

"Anybody else there from the agency?"

"Well, yeah. Everybody. Well, Richard wasn't there. He and Ann were breaking up in Acapulco. And you weren't there, were you? Irma Vance was, and Maurice. Uh ... Tracy. And Luella Ridgeway. Luella really got into it and wore a sort of white Grecian thing trimmed in gold."

Now that Charlie thought about it, she and Libby did get an invitation to a Halloween party at the Tuschmans, way last October. One she respectfully declined, needing no extra contact with the office witch. Gloria was already on Charlie's case about supposed psychic powers by then. "How about Larry?"

"Larry ... who—oh the—I mean, your secretary—Larry," Elaine caught herself in time. "I don't remember seeing him. But most of the people weren't anyone we've seen either before or since. You know. You could get into the spirit and act wacky because most of these people didn't mean anything to you. But it all doesn't mean Dorian would murder Gloria or anything."

"I hear Irma got very angry or embarrassed or something," Charlie fished.

"Dorian said he'd heard something about that too, but it happened after we left. She was fine while we were there, sort of aloof, you know how she is."

"Did he say what he'd heard about it?"

"She and Gloria got into it over something. I don't know what it was."

Ed was in deep conversation with Ellen Maxwell and Maurice Lavender when Charlie located him at poolside. He looked a lot more elegant and at ease here than Charlie would at the yacht club Friday night.

He slid an arm around her waist. "I thought you'd abandoned me."

"A little personal matter I had to clear up. I won't let you out of my sight the rest of the evening."

Maurice looked down his nose and out of the corner of his eye at the same time—which Charlie would have thought impossible if she'd seen it written. "Sweetie, you never told us you knew *the* Edward Esterhazie." Even Maurice's drawl was impressed. "What else haven't you told us?"

"I didn't know you knew him, why would I—"

"Well, it's the cement, dear," Ellen said, and everybody but Charlie snagged champagne off a passing tray. "Esterhazie Cement is blazoned on the side of just nearly every cement truck you see from San Diego to San Francisco. Wish I could get that kind of publicity, don't you, Maurice?"

Maurice merely winked approval at Charlie and led Ellen off.

"Cement," Charlie said to her date. "You made your money in cement. You never told me that."

"Actually, it's concrete. Every highway project you pass, to and from work or Vegas or Oregon has a damn good chance of its concrete trucks carrying the Esterhazie name on their cab doors. It's not a very ordinary name. I can't believe you didn't know."

"The things I seem not to notice would blow your mind to Zaire and back." The name Ed Esterhazie conjured up a self-employed handyman auto mechanic in rural Wisconsin. "Ed, do you think you could find me some more mineral water? I promise I'll stay right here."

Lieutenant David Dalrymple of the Beverly Hills P.D. came up to Charlie the moment Ed turned his back.

"Lieutenant, did you know about Roger and Gloria Tuschman's All Hallows' Eve party last October?"

"Not until yesterday. Mrs. Black mentioned it in passing and suddenly everyone else from the agency who attended is remembering that fact. You, I understand, were not invited?" His eyes had been skimming the faces on the patio and those coming and going through the two sets of doors leading inside. Now they settled on Charlie. Irritation peeked through the blandness perpetually masking his thoughts.

"I was invited. I just didn't want to go. And I totally forgot about it until Elaine Black mentioned it to me just now. I have never noticed the name Esterhazie on cement trucks before. And I learn tonight that my date for the party, Ed Esterhazie, made his fortune in cement, concrete actually."

"So what is it you're trying to say, Miss Greene?"

"That I better stick to agenting. That I'm no good at detecting because I don't notice half of what goes on around me. I'm no help to you."

"Then again, you may be noticing the half that other people aren't because you see things differently. And yours may be just the half we need."

20

How do you know Edward Esterhazie?" Richard Morse confronted Charlie, who was about to go looking for Ed and her mineral water. "You never told me. Charlie, I'm devastated."

Charlie was beginning to notice other people having a little trouble with consonants, and with standing still without rocking, and with dilating pupils. "Why do I never notice what I'm supposed to?"

"You didn't notice twenty percent of *Legionnaires' Disease* was Esterhazie money? We're talking cement here. Charlie, I'm disappointed in you."

"I never heard of *Legionnaires' Disease*. Well, I've heard of the disease, but—"

"You never heard of *Leg*—that was box office. Smash. Hit. I can't believe what I am hearing. And what's that Dalrymple doing here? Don't I pay enough in taxes I shouldn't have to put up with police gate crashers?"

"Take it easy, Richard." Charlie's boss could be a belligerent drunk. She tried to deflect his attention. "Who are the Oriental types?" She'd noticed three more.

"Japanese. They just bought Ursa Major."

"God, did I not notice that, too?"

"Won't be announced till tomorrow. You making any headway tonight? I'm counting on you, Charlie. Congdon and

Morse has got to get the cops off its back and itself back to business."

She wanted to ask how he could count on someone who devastated and disappointed him, but was growing weary of the smart-ass repartee. Probably just the time of the month.

The timing of the party had been a major blunder from the beginning, and she watched Richard Morse walk off with a disconsolate droop to his shoulder blades. Things were not going according to plan. The entertainment press here was probably quizzing guests on their reactions to the murder at the agency and the strange disappearance of Mary Ann Leffler instead of the fantastic possibilities of *Phantom of the Alpine Tunnel.* This kind of blunder was not like Richard.

He's desperate, Charlie. That should be telling you something. Just because you don't want to hear it, doesn't mean it isn't so.

Where would she and Libby be without him?

Wind rippled the surface of the pool and sent goosebumps climbing Charlie's exposed spine and puckered her nipples into hard little tingles. There were other agencies, and she was good at what she did. Besides, she could always go into real estate.

The four Japanese businessmen stood together in front of the lemon tree on the other side of the pool. It was lighted from under water, and the night was dark enough that she saw their hands holding drink glasses or gesturing out in front of their bodies more clearly than the faces attached above.

Edna Thurlow's daughter, Tessie, and grandson, Sonny, stood apart, appeared to have little to say to each other, looked like they'd rather be home in bed. Charlie didn't recognize most of the people in between. Until she saw Edward Cement-Mixer Esterhazie, a glass in both hands, leaning over tiny

Cyndi Seagal's no-longer tiny cleavage. They stood just inside the door, and Cyndi was doing her sexually vulnerable gig.

Sorry Dorothy, but Oz will never be the same.

Dr. Evan Podhurst was here. That did seem odd. He leaned sideways in a predictably awkward stance to hear Irma Vance, who gestured widely with the hand not holding her drink. Her blue full-length dress had long sleeves and a high neck. Sensible Irma did not shiver in the wind. The gesturing hands had big knuckles and crabbed fingers—witchlike.

You've got witches on the brain, Charlie.

Gloria might have decided she deserved part of Irma's winnings, too. Sounded far-fetched, but so had damn near everything since Gloria's murder what . . . a week ago Tuesday. Only nine days. And so much had happened—

"Hi, Charlie. That dress looks so great on you, I hate you." Linda Meyer, Dr. Podhurst's receptionist, stood at Charlie's elbow.

"You're here, too? What is this?"

"Mr. Morse needed extras for milling. Irma Vance even asked me to bring a 'companion.' But my boyfriend's out of town, and she didn't ask us until this morning. So Dr. Podhurst and I came together." Linda was cute in long curly hair just a shade darker than Charlie's and a sequined skirt a lot shorter than Charlie's. Like every other third person in L.A., Linda was being a receptionist only until she was discovered.

"I suppose Richard told Irma to promise you producers and directors and casting agents and stars and the moon."

"Hey, free food and drink—I'm not complaining."

"But how did he get Dr. Podhurst to come?"

"The doctor likes to be able to say he was at a Hollywood affair the other night. Some of the glamour might wear off on him. He could sure use it. He can say he spoke with Cyndi

Seagal and ... who's the old lady with Maurice? Does commercials for cornmeal and American Express."

"Ellen Maxwell. Linda, did you go to a party at the Tuschmans last Halloween?"

"Yeah, it was a real bash. Everybody was wiggin' out. You know, that's where I met Mary Ann Leffler? I'd read her newsletter, and after I met her I read *Shadowscapes*. First novel I ever read. Bet I've read it three times since, and every time I find something new. I wrote to her when she went back to Montana and asked her about the things in it I didn't understand? And she wrote back. Nice, nice lady. And some guy just asked me if I'd heard about her being missing."

"Mary Ann Leffler was at Gloria's All Hallows' Eve party?"

"Yeah, she was sort of the witch of honor. Gloria took it real serious, too. Me, I just figure the witch stuff's another excuse to party." Linda Meyer did a wiggly little dance step and shook out her hair, shoulders, tits, and ass. "You know?"

"So it wasn't the witch stuff that made you read her book three or four times in less than a year?"

"No, it was the people, the people in the story. I couldn't forget them. I couldn't keep from thinking about what was happening to them after the story ended. And how all of it came together—oh, I don't know. But I saw it like a movie. I laughed and I cried. And it was just a book. And I kept seeing myself as different women in the story and wondering if I'd do what they did when I got that old."

Charlie couldn't help asking, "So did you start reading lots of novels after that?"

"No, just that one. It's pretty exhausting. There's always the boyfriend and TV, working out, dance lessons, acting lessons. I just know nobody else can write like her. I sure hope you find her alive and up to writing more books for me."

Linda started to walk off, but Charlie caught her by the thin strap of a shoulder bag. "You hope *I* find her alive?"

"Well, I just heard Mr. Morse tell someone that he'd hired you to look into Mary Ann's disappearance and Gloria's murder. I didn't know you were a detective *and* an agent, Charlie. How do you find time for everything?"

"Listen, did you know about Gloria's funeral, or what passed for one? Were you even notified of the Memorial Séance and Dance?"

"No. But that's no surprise. I didn't make a very good witch. They were always saying stuff at their little ceremonies and cracking me up. And you know how jealous older women get. If Gloria had been alive, *she'd* have asked me to her funeral."

Charlie let Linda go this time, grinning over those last words. David Dalrymple popped up in front of her again to ask anxiously, "Are you getting anything? Vibes or telepathic thoughts? Auras? Anything?"

Charlie wouldn't know an aura if one goosed her, but she played along, "I'm working on it, Lieutenant. I need to know one thing. What was Gloria struck with? Well, okay, two things. How do you know she died up in the hall on the fifth floor?"

"One, a blunt object. Two, she would not have somehow led you to believe she was in the janitor's closet there. She can't escape that hall until you clear up her death. Simple?"

"She was wrong a lot when she was alive. She can't be wrong when she's dead? Lieutenant, Gloria doesn't even know she's been cremated." If Congdon and Morse's ex-receptionist really was a ghost, it hadn't improved her intelligence. "And she spoke through Marvin Grunion at the séance in her condo. Why aren't you after him to psych this out?"

"But she thought she was still at the agency on Wilshire. He was able to contact her through her material possessions then.

Perhaps because you were present. He's had no luck doing so since." He was talking to Charlie while his eyes scanned the people present.

"Have you found Mary Ann yet and whoever bugged my office?"

But before he could answer, Tweety pushed her face into Charlie's. "I'd like you to meet James."

Tracy'd had too much to drink. James looked hired. In L.A., dates or companions were important enough to pay for.

"I'm delighted to finally meet you, James. Tracy speaks of you constantly. Has for years."

"Charlie handles screenwriters for the agency," Tracy told her date, her tone bestowing on Charlie's position a great deal more prestige than it had yesterday afternoon at the office. "And this is Lieutenant—"

But David Dalrymple, still uncharacteristically nervous, slipped off between two Ursa Major execs who stood eyeing the gentlemen from Japan. Would the new ownership bode well or ill for the *Alpine Tunnel* project? Was Dalrymple so anxious because maybe the Beverly Hills P.D. was getting tired of his off-the-wall methods? Charlie sure was. Maybe if he kept refusing to answer her questions, she wouldn't tell him if she did discover something.

"Well, will you?" Tracy and the handsome rent-a-date looked expectantly at Charlie.

"I understand you were at Gloria's Halloween party last year," Charlie answered.

"So? I didn't know what it was till I got there. Not that I shouldn't have suspected, knowing Gloria." Tracy wore a black shapeless dress and huge gold earrings. "Us secretaries beneath your notice, Charlie? And therefore our friends? You didn't even answer James."

"Did you ask me a question, James?"

"He asked if you'd look at a screenplay he'd written. He's even got it out in his car."

"Uh, have him call Larry, okay?" And Charlie slipped away, too, but not before she heard Tracy begin to explain to James in detail why he would want nothing to do with Larry Mann even on the phone.

Keegan Monroe stood alone on the other side of the pool, a short distance from the four men representing the new owners of Ursa Major. They in dark suits, faces hidden by the pool lighting. He in formal Western dress, standing in such a way that the light at the corner of the pool caught his face and eyeglasses rather than his hands and drink glass. Charlie decided to join him and discover if this was the best vantage point. She didn't know about the Japanese, but Keegan Monroe was very likely to seek out such a place in this world to be quiet and to study it.

"Nice dress, nice body, I'll take the *Alpine Tunnel* project if offered enough. I've got *Shadowscapes* wrapped and with me."

"You're such a good boy. So, where's Mary Ann Leffler?"

"Under wa-a-ater-r-r in her ca-a-r-r."

"Very funny. Why didn't you just deliver the script to Carla at Goliath?"

"I thought she'd be here. Printed it out maybe half an hour before I left home. I thought everybody who was anybody would be here—according to Irma Vance. This party's half extras, Charlie."

Charlie watched Shelly Maypo step from the shadows at the side of the house with an empty tray balanced on his fingertips. He began filling it with empty glasses and plates left on ledges and tables and a stone planter that divided the patio. He moved slowly, not meeting people's eyes, attracting little attention to himself. He stopped just behind Lieutenant Dalrymple, who had returned to poolside to have a confab with Detective

Gordon. Charlie may not have convinced Richard to give her a raise, but she had convinced him to convince the caterer to put Shelly on the kitchen crew.

"Keegan, why did you and Mary Ann suddenly decide to cooperate on the script after all the trouble you two had been the day of the murder?"

"We told you—"

"Mary Ann told me she worried she could be suspected of the murder because the Tuschmans wanted part of the proceeds from *Shadowscapes* for assisting in her research, but what was your problem? I can't believe it was concern for Mary Ann Leffler. You're the one who thought I should look into things. Did the Tuschmans think you should share the wealth, too?"

The odor of pool chemicals mixed with that sweet tang of lemon tree to fill the void left by his silence. And lemon blossoms reminded her of orange blossoms, which reminded her of the grove behind the Tuschmans' condo complex. "Keegan, did you go to Gloria's All Hallows' Eve party last year?"

The nod of his head was nearly imperceptible.

"That's where you met Mary Ann, isn't it? Even before Carla got you two together on the screenplay." Why was it everyone wanted her to find answers only as long as they didn't have to reveal their own particular secrets? Somehow Mary Ann still seemed too down to earth to be a witch type. "Tell me about Mary Ann. She's a stranger to me."

According to Keegan, Mary Ann Leffler was simply an ordinary housewife who managed to rise above herself by means of her writing. "And as forceful and cranky as she appeared, she was a very insecure lady. Got herself tied up in knots because she couldn't think of the word on the tip of her tongue and got furious I could come up with it in a snap. She had mood swings, hot flashes, anxiety attacks—all the things my mother took hormones to avoid. I heard Lady Macbeth talking on the phone a couple of times, and she was driving her family nuts with all this, too."

Edwina took hormones and drove Charlie nuts anyway. "Why wouldn't Mary Ann take hormones?"

"Said they cause breast cancer. She might have eaten the wart off a newt or something, but she didn't trust doctors."

Keegan's mother had died of breast cancer some years ago. He and Charlie watched the people across the pool for a while.

"And she was really unsure of herself," he continued finally. "You'd think anybody that old who'd published a novel would have a better idea of who she was. All that putting down of L.A. and the industry she was doing at the Polo Lounge was mostly pretense and bluster. Truth is, she was scared to death of L.A., especially since the riots. She'd often pay cab fare rather than drive the rental car Goliath provided."

"You seem to think she's more dead than missing."

"She sure isn't out running around town alone."

"So where's the script?"

"Out in the car."

They walked around the side of the house the way Shelly had come, instead of through it, and to a gate in the hedge. A plainclothes guard nodded, noting their leaving. It seemed like ten percent of the population guarded fifty percent of it from the other forty. And it had been so before the riots. Mary Ann wasn't the only one afraid in the city. Charlie stopped her client before they reached the ground lights that flooded the drive. "Tell me about that party."

Keegan Monroe had been invited to the All Hallows' Eve party because he subscribed to Mary Ann's newsletter. "I get all kinds of weird stuff, Charlie, everything's grist for a writer. I mean, who's going to throw a better Halloween party than a bunch of witches? I even took Lou, she loved it." Lou was Louwan, Keegan's last live-in.

Nobody bobbed for apples, but there was a ritual circle-dancing around a bonfire and drinking from a chalice. The guests wore white, but no virgins were sacrificed that he saw. Just a dead cat.

Dead cat. A black cat? Was it already dead, or did. . . . They didn't kill a cat in front of Dorian's kids?"

"Actually, it was black and white. I don't remember how it got dead. Mary Ann was carrying it around doing some kind of mumbo jumbo stuff. It wasn't as bad as it sounds, Charlie. In fact, in the light of the next day, it just sounded silly. But that night it was easy to get caught up in it. Your Maurice Lavender was really coming on to Mary Ann."

"Maurice comes on to everybody. Keegan, was Roger or someone taking pictures of the party guests getting too caught up in it and maybe later charging money for the negatives?"

"Nothing like that, Charlie. I mean, not exactly."

"You sound haunted. What is it you're not telling me?" When he just stood there staring into the darkness she started on a new tack. "Elaine Black says she and her family had a great time at that party. Did you, Keegan?"

"There's so much of that night I don't remember. Lou didn't, either, but it didn't seem to bother her. She sort of shrugged it off. You're right, though, it's been haunting me. In my college days, I'd get drunk and lose a few hours and it didn't bother me, and when I broke my leg last year and they put me under, I lost time. I remember enjoying myself in the orange grove. But I'll bet there're three hours of that party I can't account for."

"Maybe you drank too much that night, too, maybe they threw something into the bonfire that made funny smoke, maybe there was a substance added to the communal drink in the chalice. Even something in the food. You'd think whoever owns that grove would start patrolling it with Dobermans."

"My guess is there was some good stuff hidden in nearly everything to make people happy to party on. And it's not like the loss of time kept me up nights. It just niggled back there somewhere and wouldn't go away, and whenever I'd call you and get Gloria first, it would come up front and start full-fledged nagging. But when I started working with Mary Ann, it became more like heavy bugging. And I kept asking her what happened that night, and she kept blowing it off. 'Don't worry about it, junior. You got bigger problems. Way you write, for starters.' You've met her, Charlie, you can imagine what she was like to work with. But I didn't kill her."

"Then you think Mary Ann's not only dead but murdered?"

"Don't you?"

They were protected from the wind here by an extension of the thick hedge, which literally towered over them. But a chill still fingered Charlie's exposed back. Not because of Keegan's description of a silly All Hallows' party—probably tame by southern California standards. No, what she found chilling was how accurately he mimicked Mary Ann Leffler, almost summoning her, conjuring her up. Charlie, too, thought the author must be dead because it was taking her so long to surface. Poor choice of words.

I am sorry, Mary Ann, and I know this sounds crass, because it is, but could you manage to not be in your car underwater? Anything but that.

Charlie!

Well, if she's dead anyway . . .

"Keegan, get me that screenplay, so I can get you some nice money, okay?"

Charlie convinced Ed to let her drive his Porsche home. He was feeling no pain, and she was. She also convinced him to let her stop by the office on Wilshire, not that far off the route, to drop off the *Shadowscapes* script, which, if accepted, could help pay her mortgage for a while and set Keegan up for another live-in and some novel-writing time, too.

She whirled the Porsche into one of the banker's private spaces. "Look, I'll just run this in. You wait here. It won't take a—"

"No way. I understand your need to impress me with the importance of your work ... career ... importance. And I want to give you this chance."

"Huh?"

He got out his side and she got out hers. "It's important for women to feel important. And I understand that."

"I'm just trying to make a living, Ed. You don't have to be condescending."

"And men insist upon trivializing what women do. No matter what it is. My ex-wife pointed that out to me. Fucking endlessly. And besides, you have stomach cancer, remember?"

"You guys be quiet in there?" a homeless man yelled from the other side of the concrete end wall. "I'm trying to get some sleep. Jeesh."

"Sorry," Ed yelled back and accompanied Charlie to the security door inside the parking area. She had a key card for this, too, and slid it into the slot lock on the door.

But this was, after all, a bank building, and a guard at a security desk just inside had them sign in and leave their driver's licenses with him to be returned when they signed out.

"Your boss told me he'd hired you to do some detective work on the side because of the murder of your receptionist," Ed said in the elevator on the way to the fifth floor. "You must be a very talented young woman." He put his hands out in front of him, palms outwards and cocked his head to one side. "Now I'm not being condescending, honest."

"And he told me twenty percent of the money behind *Legionnaires' Disease* was Esterhazie Cement."

"Concrete, Esterhazie Concrete. And more like five percent. I'll never do that again. It was a real bomb."

Secretly glad for his company in the empty, echoing suite of offices, Charlie locked the *Shadowscapes* script in her desk drawer. Ed insisted on seeing the murder scene. "Well okay, but it'll have to be fast. I have to work tomorrow."

He was a good listener, and Charlie found herself describing that part of the last nine days of her life that had been usurped by murder. He stopped the condescension and the even less appealing attempts to joke about it. He wasn't involved with anyone else involved in the case. And anyone who could make a fortune in cement probably had to have some brains.

At the window at the end of the VIP hall, she described standing there with Dalrymple, seeing Gloria spread out in the bush tops below. She didn't mention someone pretending to be Gloria whispering she was in a trash can.

One peep out of you now, Gloria Tuschman, and I'll get an exorcist in here first thing in the morning.

Gloria either behaved herself, or the imposter didn't work this late. How could anyone predict that Charlie would be in after midnight? She continued her tale all the way back out of the FFUCWB of P and onto the Santa Monica Freeway and was still at it when they hit the 405.

"Pull off at the next exit," Ed startled her by interrupting without warning. "Get over now. Get that signal going. Christ!"

Charlie glanced ahead, in the mirrors, to either side, and registered the background noise she'd been hearing and not listening to. "Oh boy."

"I'm counting on you, Charlie. This is the best Porsche I've ever owned. We have your lovely tush to consider and even mine. Not to mention a few dependents." Edward Esterhazie had gone heart-attack red even in the limited light of the dash. "Don't panic now. Easy does it."

Charlie sat up, tuned him out as he totally lost it, and tuned out the roaring that was upon them as well. She fought for the little car's access to ever closer right lanes, praying the metal monsters surrounding them had even an inkling of their existence and gave a damn if they did. She couldn't make the first exit, but she got them positioned for the next—her body, her face, her beautiful shimmery green dress, the roots of her hair, her hands, and probably her earrings drenched in nervous sweat.

But she got them off the 405 at two in the morning without a ding. "I declare you sober enough to be the designated driver. I hope you know a back way home." They both staggered a little as they exited the Porsche, met in the headlights, and took each other's seats.

They had unwittingly hit a semi rush hour and survived.

"You were wonderful, Charlie. You must think I'm a wuss." They sat there, seat belts buckled, engine growling, going nowhere—the day's groceries, booze, bikinis, building supplies, toxic wastes, and whatever racing by at the speed of light on the overpass next to them. "I've been a good boy all night. But I have to have a cigarette."

"It's your car. I'm sorry, Ed, I got so involved in telling you my story I didn't notice what was happening around me."

They wended their way back to Long Beach by side roads that only a native of longer than two years would have known about.

Charlie had time to finish her story. And when they pulled up in front of her condo, she asked, "Well? You're the first person I've really put this all together for. Who do you think murdered Gloria Tuschman?"

"If I say it's elementary, my dear Watson—"

"I'll slug you."

"At the risk of sounding condescending, and remember you did ask me, and on the basis of the information you have, which is clearly incomplete, I think it is tentatively obvious that two people were involved in the receptionist's murder, and that one of them was Mary Ann Leffler."

"Mary Ann—how do you figure that?"

"She had one motive we know of, the Tuschmans' demanding a share of her profits—"

"That strikes me as pretty weak."

"Me too, but murder has been committed for less reason. I think an even better one could surface with a full investigation of her relationship with Gloria and hubby. But the main giveaway is that Mary Ann is now presumably dead."

"Why would that make her a murderer?"

"Because she could identify her accomplice. And her accomplice has silenced her forever." He got out of the car and opened her door for her, walked her to the security gate, and then walked inside with her when it opened.

"Ed, I'd invite you in, but it's three in the morning."

"I need to retrieve my kid, remember?"

Charlie had forgotten, but even her embarrassed giggle was tired by now. "I'm not tracking. Murder's not my thing."

"Do you think it was wise to leave them alone together? This long, this late?"

"They couldn't know when we'd be coming home. And frankly, I was using Doug to ward off Jesus."

A road warrior on the screaming television lobbed something over a high fence into a lot crowded with eighteen-wheelers like those that nearly ate the Porsche. Charlie found the remote just as he grabbed his Uzi and the waist of the requisite female in jeopardy, and off they ran, he in sensible Army boots and she in heels more lethal than Charlie's.

When the set snapped off, she and Ed were left in booming silence and darkness complete but for the warm glow of radiation fading from the TV screen and the angry blinking of the red light on the answering machine. Charlie switched on the lamp next to it and they surveyed the scene of destruction in weary silence.

Papers, calculators, school books, pizza boxes, and paper Coke cups littered nearly every surface not covered by a motionless body. Lori huddled inelegantly in the easy chair, spit glistening on the rubber bands connecting her braces and holding her lower jaw on. Libby was curled in a fetal position on the couch. Doug sprawled on the floor with Tuxedo splayed on his stomach.

"Look dead, don't they?" Ed said and Tuxedo stretched and unrolled a long tongue in a wide yawn. "Seems to be the regular gang, though. Don't see any sign of loaves or fishes or sandals."

"Wonder what Lori's doing over on a school night?" Beverly Schantz was usually paranoid about that.

Ed managed to rouse his son, find the kid's eyeglasses, and aim him at the door. "Thanks for a most entertaining evening. I'm afraid the yacht club will be dull in comparison."

"Wait, who do you think helped Mary Ann kill Gloria and then killed Mary Ann?"

"It can't be anyone but your favorite client, Charlie. And, sadly, someone you are so obviously fond of—Keegan Monroe. I think all the witchcraft business is irrelevant except that it brought together that certain group of nuts. I'm sorry, and I hope you or the police prove me wrong. Then again, you're asking the great brain who let himself be conned into sinking a few mil into *Legionnaires' Disease.*"

When both Esterhazies were gone, Charlie rewound the tape on the answering machine and listened to Lori's mother plead and finally threaten in an attempt to convince someone to answer. "I know someone's home. I drove by and could see the TV was on. I have to know if Lori's there."

Tangling with supermom was the last thing Charlie could face right now—but she knew this particular gut-wrenching terror of the night as only another mother could and punched the number before she had time to talk herself out of it. Neither girl had moved an eyelash through it all, but the cat decided to be pissed about then and spat, taking a swipe at Charlie's hose and tearing off on one of its own idiotic versions of the Long Beach Grand Prix. "I'm going to donate you to the witches' association, you little—hello, Beverly, this is Charlie Greene returning your call. And yes, Lori's here, don't worry. I'll see that she gets to school in the morning."

Predictably, Beverly had not been asleep and answered on the first ring. "How could you wait so long? I've been calling all night and worried sick. It's after three in the morning."

"I just got home and found her here and the light blinking on the answering machine." The kids had apparently listened but chosen not to answer.

"Just got home? But—" something in Lori's mother's long-suffering sigh and longer pause suggested she was visualizing

Charlie swinging at singles bars and humping truck drivers. "Poor little Libby. Poor, poor—"

Charlie hung up and poor, poor little Libby pushed herself to a sitting position, squinting in the light of the lamp. "Mom? Lori's run away from home. I told her you wouldn't mind if she lives with us till she gets a job. Okay?"

22

Charlie stumbled into work very late the next day. Stumbled from lack of sleep. Very late because she'd been to see Dr. Williams first.

"So, is it terminal or what?" Larry sat at the front desk instead of in his cubicle where she needed him. He handed her a sheaf of phone slips.

"No results yet. I have to go in next week for more tests." Of what she couldn't imagine. The gremlins at the lab in the "medical arts" building where Dr. Williams tortured people had already taken juice and pulp from every orifice of her body and enough blood from her arm to feed a family of vampires for a week. It had been degrading, embarrassing, humiliating, uncomfortable, awful, and expensive. No wonder people had to be worried sick about their health to go to a doctor.

"Going to ream you out at both ends and X-ray what's left, right?" There was a certain lack of sympathy in Larry's ghoulish smile. What were her medical problems stacked against what he could be facing? But Charlie's blood would be tested for HIV, too. Dr. Williams claimed it was standard now.

For the first time in her career, Charlie would use up her and Libby's health deductible on herself and before the year was half over. The agency insurance plan carried a "healthy" deductible. She sure hoped Keegan's fix on the script would go over at Goliath. Keegan wouldn't murder anyone—Ed just didn't know him. Charlie was beginning to wish she really was psychic so she could simply stare at the murderer and identify him and get this all over with.

Keegan was one of her callbacks this morning, but before she started on the phone slips, Charlie poured herself a cup of coffee and had it halfway back to her office before she remembered she wasn't allowed it. Swearing, she poured it down the sink in the little utility niche. How was she supposed to work without coffee? She wasn't even allowed Diet Coke. She stalked back to her office, picked up the pink slips, put them down and called Bev Schantz instead, offering to take Lori in for a few days until she cooled off.

"I don't consider you an especially good influence for my daughter," Beverly said hesitantly, Lori's little brother screaming happy mayhem in the background, the family dog barking itself apart at the seams. "I can't imagine what's gotten into that girl. I never acted that way as a teenager."

I did. "The offer's open. Give it some thought."

"But there's no supervision at your house."

"I have no plans to be gone tonight. I do have plans for tomorrow evening."

"Well, we did, too. Her father and I had planned to have Lori sit with her brother—but now...." The old conundrum—who's to supervise the baby-sitter? "But *we* would have been home well before midnight."

"The decision's up to you. Maybe someday you could return the favor."

"We would be happy to take in poor Libby any—"

Charlie hung up on Beverly Schantz for the second time that day and raised the back of a second finger to the nodding palm fronds outside her window. She returned the New York calls of importance, ignored the rest of her messages for now—including one from Keegan—and informed Larry she was out of the office. Her priority now was reading the *Shadowscapes* script.

She was still immersed in it when Larry brought her a paper carton of Mom and Pop's homemade chicken noodle soup with the tiny aromatic green things, newly reheated in the office microwave.

Charlie had been unable to face breakfast that morning, having had to confront two teenage girls and force one to clean up the pizza barf the cat had left at two-foot intervals all over the tiny house.

"But UM, Tuxedo loves pepperoni and cheese."

"Does he love All Hallows' Eve? Scrape it up and flush it. Your cat, your puke."

"You puked the other night all over somebody's rocks and cactus and didn't stick around to clean it up."

Charlie had once scanned the novel *Shadowscapes*. The writing was powerful, but the story was so silly she couldn't get into it. She needed to know only enough to speak coherently about it in Hollywood-ese. Truth be known, reading or even thinking in depth was more alien in L.A. than in D.C., and the project was already sold. Charlie had only to connect one of her writers with the folks at Goliath when it was determined that, but for one small problem, everything was wonderful. The problem was simply the adaptation was totally unworkable. No big deal, just call in another writer.

So reading Keegan's take on the script—knowing him, he'd completely rewritten it his way—was the first time Charlie had concentrated on the story line. Fortified by the marvelous soup and licking real butter off her fingers from the fresh bread that accompanied it, she finally called him.

"Okay, my friend, how much is you and how much Mary

Ann, and who did the nude dancing scene? It's a great job, by the way, but that won't get you off the hook around here. I mean, there's black witches and there's white witches—you can't tell me Elaine and Dorian allowed their children to dance nude."

"But the script works by itself even if you never heard of the book, Mary Ann, or me—doesn't it?"

"You know it does. It's brilliant." Which didn't mean the hundreds of people that would turn it into celluloid could bring it off. But Keegan, using Mary Ann's incredible if warped imagination, had certainly done his share. "I'll messenger it over to Carla and start hounding Goliath for your money."

Charlie had no more than sent the screenplay off to Goliath when Sheldon Maypo called from downstairs wanting to know if he'd be allowed up. "Let's take a walk in the alley instead, Shelly. I'll meet you at the elevator."

"No kidding? Your office was bugged? That explains some of what I overheard last night, then." He pulled the bill of a baseball hat low over his sunglasses in the harsh light raging off white buildings and concrete as they strolled out from under the bank's overhang and into the sun. Shelly was a night person. He tossed a wadded up candy wrapper into the dumpster on the other side of the concrete end wall as they passed it. "Dalrymple was talking to his buddy with the tight crew cut and explaining he didn't think you were in any danger at the office, although the search would have tipped off the murderer you and the police knew what was afoot."

"So it's one of us, or someone connected with us, for sure."

"I wasn't clear from what I heard that they actually found a receiver or whatever, though."

"Why won't Dalrymple tell me anything? How can he expect me to help if I don't have any information?"

"That's what I wanted to talk to you about, Charlie. He was telling this guy—"

"Gordon. Detective Gordon."

"This Gordon wondered the same thing, see? Why ask you to help and then keep you in the dark? And Dippy Dalrymple says because he wants you to come to a psychic solution on your own to see if it matches the solution they build by laborious investigation. And that you are still on the list of suspects yourself, which says they aren't much closer than we are. And let's see, there was a third thing—oh yeah—if you come up with the same answer psychically that they get their way, it'll prove people like you can be helpful in police investigations. He thinks Gloria had some psychic talent herself, and this is the first time he's ever investigated the murder of one person like that with another one involved. Said it was the chance of a lifetime."

"What did Detective Gordon say to that?"

"Not a thing. Stunned silence, I expect. It's frightening there's someone like that in such a position of authority."

"Well the lieutenant did break down and tell me last night that Gloria died from a blow by a blunt instrument." She told Shelly about the witches' party in the orange grove. "Apparently, most of the suspects attended. You may be wrong about witchcraft having nothing to do with this. But I ran it all past that guy I was with last night, and he thinks it's irrelevant, too. Ed thinks Keegan Monroe and Mary Ann Leffler killed Gloria and then Keegan killed Mary Ann so she couldn't rat on him."

"I sure hope he's wrong about Monroe. Kid's one hell of a screenwriter. I did overhear a few other things."

"I want to know everything, Shelly."

"Your boss got stewed last night and wanted to know where the hell someone named Luella was."

"Luella Ridgeway, represents actors. Richard had ordered all the staff to be there and to bring dates to make it look like a bigger, more important party. You know, I don't remember seeing her last night. What else?"

"I talked to the little Vietnamese maid. She thinks Irma Vance did in Gloria and that Mary Ann Leffler is still alive, hiding out somewhere."

"Did she say why?"

"Part gut feeling, part observing people who come to the house, and part overhearing her boss's side of phone conversations. She heard him talking on the phone to Irma the night before Gloria's murder. Morse turned white as a sheet and hung up. He told the maid something like 'Damn that Gloria and her screwy friends. I could lose the agency.' Morse thinks this Luella who didn't come to his party and someone named Tweety did in Gloria because they had both asked him to fire Gloria."

"Who did Richard tell this to?"

"Me. I'm used to staying up all night. So when the caterers and clean-up crew and security people leave the grounds yawning their way into their vans and cars, good old Shelly's still on duty and spry beyond his years."

"In the house?"

"In the hedge. And your boss comes out carrying a small bottle and a big headache and parks himself next to the pool under the lemon tree. I think I'm invisible, but he sees me. Motions me over. We pass the bottle. The guy's practically in tears by now."

Charlie hadn't seen Richard today, but then she'd come in late and holed up with Keegan's screenplay. The only people she had seen were Larry and Irma. "He's drinking it straight?"

"Oh yeah. And talking. Tweety and Luella have explained to him how dangerous this Gloria is because she casts spells over people. She's going to ruin Congdon and Morse because she hates being an underling receptionist, having to answer to people like Luella and Tweety. He thinks Gloria might have some information that would embarrass the agency if it gets out, and if he fires her she'd see that it gets out. Poor Richard tells me being the boss sucks. Me, unemployed, and we're sitting under his lemon tree next to his pool."

Shelly stood looking up at the broken bushes so apparent from this side of the second block wall, the crushed red petals and leaves on the cement earth beneath had turned black, like old blood.

"What if Gloria climbed up into those bushes by herself?" Charlie asked.

"Maybe you are psychic. I was just wondering the same thing. I was also wondering if you're as safe at Congdon and Morse as Dalrymple seems to think."

23

Back on the fifth floor, Charlie confronted Larry at the front desk. "Are we the only ones here today? And Irma?"

"Maurice came in. But not until after lunch. Looks like everybody else had too much party."

"Luella's not in? I don't think she was even at the party last night."

"I didn't see her, but Stew and I didn't stay very late. Listen, Charlie, when Irma comes back, we need to talk."

"Not here," she half whispered, half mouthed.

"We can go in your office." He had a long yellow pencil stuck behind one ear, and when he shook his head in unison with hers, while making an exaggeratedly quizzical face, it fell to his shoulder and then to the floor.

Charlie used it to write across a memo pad that Dalrymple had found a bug in her office yesterday and that she was afraid to talk about anything important inside the agency suite in case there were more. She showed the note to Larry and handed him his pencil.

"That's why the police search yesterday," she whispered as an afterthought while tearing the note into ever tinier pieces.

Larry had grown so still he didn't look like he was breathing, didn't even blink. "When?" he said finally, still staring straight ahead at nothing. "Before or after our little talk?"

"After, but don't jump to conclusions. I don't think they

found anything." Charlie was still whispering even if he wasn't.

Larry Mann finally took a giant breath and noticed the pencil in his hand. He snapped it in two like a pretzel stick, flung it on Gloria's desk, and walked out of the office.

Charlie went after him and had almost let the door to the public hall close behind her when she realized she couldn't get in again with no one on the desk, because her plastic card key was in her purse in her office. She called after him, but Larry stepped into the elevator without glancing back.

"Damn. . . ." Irma must be out to a late lunch or on an office errand. Larry had referred to *when* she would come back. Charlie didn't know if Maurice was still in. He wouldn't answer the door buzzer even if he was. Charlie wouldn't have, either. The soft, but vastly annoying jingle chime announced a caller.

By the time Charlie made it around the U-shaped island of the front desk, two lines were blinking. She put one on hold and answered the other. It was Hal Licktman from ZIA—for her.

"What, they got the agents answering the phones there now?"

"Everybody's stepped out. I'm pinch hitting until Irma gets back. How did you know it was me?"

"That sexy, throaty voice is hard to miss, babe," Hal said. "But hey, I got news. We got a go for Tina Horton to write the pilot for 'Southwestern Exposure.' Shapiro himself called this morning."

"Already? And they're going to let Tina write it? At least the pilot? I don't believe this."

"I know what you mean. You think you finally got this business figured out and something like this happens. Enjoy the good stuff, I always say. Gives you something to remember when you're drowning in feces. Mary's already called Tina. Would you tell Maurice we are definitely interested in Ellen Maxwell for Thora Kay? I tried to get him earlier. And Charlie, don't get murdered over there, huh?"

Charlie let out a howl of triumph the second she was off the line. It echoed around the empty offices. Maurice didn't answer his phone. *Don't get murdered over there.* Good thing "female hysterics" was not in Charlie's resume. She jotted Maurice a note and answered the other line.

"Thank you for holding. This is Congdon and Morse."

"Charlie, they got you answering the phones now?"

"Edwina? What is this calling me at the office again? Are you still home sick?"

"Yes, I'm still home sick," Charlie's mother mimicked in that high whine that passed for sarcasm and that always made her daughter want to pick up something and throw it. "I called to find out what the doctor said this morning."

Charlie explained about the tests next week. That Dr. Williams was fairly certain her problem was not stomach cancer but said it could be anything from an ulcer to gall bladder to a "female disorder" to low-lying intestinal virus to simple indigestion exacerbated by stress. He'd also brought up the possibility of pregnancy, which she assured him was impossible and which she did not mention to Edwina.

"Well, I could have told you that. Not pregnant, are you?"

"No Edwina, I am not. Now if you'll excuse me I have work to do."

Charlie's mother signed off with, "Just take care of yourself, Charlemagne Catherine Greene. I barely survived raising you. I'm too old to raise Libby."

Charlie sat back in Gloria's chair, seething, wishing she knew how to switch over to the answering service.

She had never seen Congdon and Morse from quite this

angle. It could be day or it could be night. There were no windows. Rain was in the forecast for today. It could be raining right now, but from here you'd never know. Charlie didn't enjoy being in the agency alone. Irma would be back any minute.

She slipped out of her pumps and stared at the pencil halves a long while before her mind prodded her into paying attention. It was in the way they lay there that reminded her of the pencil stubs with the eraser ends Gloria used to punch computer or phone keys. They might have been thrown down in haste and anger just as Larry had thrown these.

Gloria could have been working with them and was suddenly afraid, furious, or sick. Hell, she could have had diarrhea and raced off to the ladies in the back hall.

Gloria may have been alone here as Charlie was now. Alone except for the murderer. Sure was a good thing "easily frightened" and "paranoid" were not part of Charlie's resume.

This place was not a bit quiet even when empty. Somewhere a blower whirred, circulating air filtered out of the pollution and temperature changes in the real world. The little refrigerator in the utility niche wheezed and gurgled in the hall behind her. There were creaks and rattles that seemed to come from within the walls.

Someone could have walked through the door that Charlie now faced and scared Gloria, who threw down her pencil stubs and ran off into the back hall to escape. Only to be chased and caught just before she reached the stairs.

Then the murderer hit her over the head with something blunt and stuffed her in the bag of the cleaning trolley in the janitor's closet. He wheeled her through the office, onto the elevator and down to the first floor, where he pushed her through a corner of the first level of parking and on across the covered drive-in area. They passed at least one, maybe two, parking valets and a security guard, not to mention various people coming and going from a busy commercial building. Then around the concrete end wall and up the alley past the private two-car parking space to Mrs. Humphrys' wall and flowering bushes. And then he or she threw Gloria's body up into the bushes. Heaved her. Stuffed her? Pushed her. How do you get a dead weight in that kind of position? Or did she climb up by herself? Why?

Did he, she, or they do it without being particularly noticed by people who are busy thinking about other things, people who are self-involved and who don't want to get involved? City people who keep their eyes averted and their profile low because bad things happen out there that need avoiding? People like Charlie Greene. Hey, if Tina Horton could get the go-ahead to write the pilot of a series pitched to a major network four days ago, anything was possible. Anything.

Who needed psychics and witches and paranormal stuff? Life was screwy enough the way it was.

But Charlie sure learned a lot about the agency and its people in a very few hours that day. Women who can afford them are always saying you have no secrets from your cleaning lady. Charlie was astonished to realize how much Gloria, as phone receptionist, must have known about them all.

Everyone who called wanted to know, first, what she was doing answering the phones, and Charlie told everybody that Larry had left on an errand for her, and everybody but Irma that she was just sitting in until Irma returned.

Luella Ridgeway wanted to speak to Tracy. "What do you mean she's not there? When will she be back?"

"She didn't come in today. Neither did you. What's up?"

A long silence and then a long sigh, "I don't know if I should tell you."

"You weren't at the party last night, either. Richard noticed."

"I'll bet he did. Charlie, I didn't go to the party because the Beverly Hills P.D. picked me up for questioning about Gloria's murder as I was leaving the agency last night. Would you have felt like going to a party after that kind of a session?"

You couldn't have done it. I like you. "Luella, you'd just got back from Minnesota. You hardly had time to plan anything, and how could you even think straight after what you'd been through?"

Charlie could hear the purposeless but companionable noise of a TV in the background. She would learn that afternoon just how different were the messages sent by pauses and inflections and audible breaths when the face and eyes were not there to convince you how they wished you to hear. You were not diverted by clothing or color or gestures or fake attitudes. Only the sounds of people thinking, reacting, planning what to say next.

A deep inhalation, the tinkle of ice against glass, a swallow. "I came back a few days early without telling anyone. But your buddy, Lieutenant Dalrymple, thought to check the airline schedules."

"He's not my buddy. He's driving me nuts. Why the big secret about being back early? You had that vacation time coming."

"I got back on Saturday, visited Gloria the Monday night before she was murdered. The homicide sweethearts already know this. What can it hurt if you do?"

"Luella, was Gloria blackmailing you, too?"

Tinkle, swallow, pause, inhale, surprise ... "Charlie, she couldn't have had anything on you. You're so worn out being a mommy you couldn't find time to—it wasn't blackmail ...

exactly." Luella must have decided she'd already said too much, because she hung up without a good-bye.

What had she meant it wasn't exactly blackmail? It either was or it wasn't. And hadn't Keegan said something similar at the party last night? Charlie had no time to mull it over, for Richard Morse came on the line wanting Luella. He did not sound especially chipper.

"She didn't come in at all today? And she didn't come to the party."

"She got picked up for questioning by the police as she was leaving work last night. It kind of threw her. They found out she'd returned from Minnesota on Saturday, visited the Tuschmans Monday night."

"Aw jeeze, that damn Gloria's even more trouble dead." Richard's mouth was so dry his swallow crackled. "If this doesn't stop we're going under, Charlie, I can feel it. Get a name as a bad luck hotel in this town and you're shunned. Superstitious bunch in this business." It was unlike Richard to be so pessimistic. His hangover must have been special.

"I have some news that'll cheer you up."

"What? They found Mary Ann Leffler alive and well? They found out who killed Gloria and we can all get back to work?"

"Not that good. But Keegan completed the *Shadowscapes* script, and it's magnificent. I've already sent it over to Goliath."

"Oh, that's good. Charlie, you know I haven't seen a mention of that party in any of the press today?"

"Probably waiting for the weekend gossip columns."

"You think so? Image is everything. We got to appear positive to the industry or we're all done, Charlie."

"I have some more good news, too. But I'm not going to tell you until you tell me what Gloria was doing that still seems to have everybody over a barrel around here."

"It was grounds for firing her, Charlie, not for murdering her. What's this other good news? I need all I can get."

"You don't talk. I don't talk. I'm sick of this, Richard. Get well, 'babe.'"

"Hey listen, Charlie, wait. Just don't let it go any farther, okay? Gloria was picking out certain of the unsolicited manila envelopes we get in the mail each day. She'd take 'em home and answer them as if she were more of an agent than a receptionist. Tell them they weren't ready for Hollywood yet and offer them a subscription to one of her husband's newsletters that would give them all the information they needed to study up and get ready for the big time at home in Georgia or Iowa before they hit L.A. They'd be way ahead of the pack when they got out here. In these newsletters Roger'd advertise books on the subjects of acting and screenwriting he'd written and printed himself in his little shop. Roger did videos for home study, and seminars, too. And he got an awful lot of inside information from Gloria. Problem was they used the agency's name and address."

"Jesus."

"Amen. I found out about it when Dan Congdon came across one of these newsletters in South Carolina where some local was auditioning for background. Handed him one to prove she was a pro."

"Your partner—he's in the industry?"

"He dicks around with it when he feels like it. But he got his thumb stuck up his ass about this one, I can tell you. I don't blame him. We could be ducking lawsuits, and the fraud guys could get interested. So don't blab. Remember who pays your mortgage. This could sink us."

"Does Dalrymple know this?"

"No, but he does know about the Tuschmans' witchcraft newsletters. So he's getting close. Christ, they knew gullible when they saw it and how to make a buck. Roger did books and videos on the witchshit, too. Now tell me your other good news before I asphyxiate on pathos and gall."

"Hal Licktman called from ZIA. They have a go from CBS for Tina to write the pilot for 'Southwestern Exposure' and are interested in Ellen for the lead. I think she's a shoo-in, Richard. She's a perfect match." What if Gloria had been on the front desk listening to this conversation? Would Roger's next newsletter tell his students all about a new pilot being written for CBS—hint that he talked to Tina Horton or that she'd been one of his students?

"Nothing happens that fast, Charlie. There's a catch here."

"Hal couldn't believe it, either. They got the call from Shapiro himself."

He managed a dry whistle. She could almost see the protruding eyes shutter halfway and the head nod as the mind tallied the take here. "Now that's going to make the trade papers and big. And we've got Ellen and Tina and Monroe. And you. Great job, kid. Now be good to your stomach and take the rest of the day off. I don't like you being there alone."

24

But as Charlie rose to leave, phone lights started blinking again, and she couldn't resist finding out who else would call in or if more wonderful news was about to arrive. Richard said good things came in threes.

Tracy Dewitt was on one line, and Charlie put her on hold. The other caller was a client of Dorian's. Charlie told him she didn't think Dorian would be in today but would have him call back tomorrow. She switched over to Tracy, who wanted to talk to Luella.

"Glad to see you have to work the front desk, find out what it's like, Charlie." Why had Charlie ever thought this woman pleasant and funny? Because she used to be, damn it. She had changed her stripes somewhere Charlie hadn't visited. "Is Luella home or what?"

"She just called in a few minutes ago for you, Tracy. Wanting to know why you weren't here."

"Least I was at the party last night. Richard's really pissed at her. Where's Irma? Or your tame fag?"

"Larry's on an errand for me. Irma will be back shortly. Maurice was in for awhile. And *we* all went to the party."

"Yeah, well you may have noticed I had a very heavy date last night. James just left about an hour ago." Even her yawn sounded smug.

Promised your rent-a-date you could get his stuff read here, didn't you, Tweety? Hope you got a discount. "Tracy, I'll read his damned screenplay on one condition only, and will not guarantee how soon or that I'll take him on. Understand? Have you seen the stacks of scripts we haven't been able to get to yet?"

"It's just a sample, Charlie. He'd be willing to work on anything to get a foot in the door. Without an agent he can't even get his calls returned. I mean, it's not fair." When Charlie didn't answer—"Okay, what's the condition?"

"That you tell me everything you know about Gloria using the agency to get inside information and promotion for Roger's newsletters and mail-order courses for wannabe actors and screenwriters, and why you and Luella wanted Richard to fire her."

Pause, breath, chewing something . . . "You know what Gloria told me once, Charlie? She said you were sensitive to psychic phenomena and attracted paranormal stuff without knowing it. She said it's a natural gift, and if you'd quit fighting it, you could learn to use it to your advantage. And if you don't cultivate it, you'll lose it. If you cultivate your gift, you could probably figure all this out yourself."

"Good-bye Tweety and good-bye James."

"No wait . . . it was just a suggestion." Tracy took another crunch and used the chewing time to think.

"Don't lie to me," Charlie made her voice low and spooky and threatening. When in Dipsville. . . . "I'll know."

"My uncle hit boiling when he came across one of Roger's show biz newsletters and blamed me for it, thinking I'd used the agency that way."

"Why you?"

"My mom mentioned in a letter a few months, maybe a year, ago that Uncle Dan was talking to some big deal writer who did vampires or something about maybe producing one of her books. You know, making it into a movie and—he's her brother, and she thinks he shits gold bricks."

"Anne Rice?"

"Kind of sounds like it. Anyway, nothing came of it, but I sent him one of Roger's witchcraft newsletters thinking maybe it'd give him some ideas. I mean if he was into crazy, why not? He must have kept it, because he noticed it had the same editors and address as the actor-wannabe newsletter and that one named the agency so . . . "

"Don't think you've won my cooperation yet," Charlie prodded.

"The name Tuschman means nothing to him, see? He doesn't even know about Gloria. She's just the receptionist. I mean, he never comes here. So he decides it's me. He makes a copy of the damn thing and sends it to me with a nasty letter. So I go to Luella with my problem. Well, I'm hardly going to get any sympathy from Himself-the-Dorian-jerk-off. Who else would I go to, you?"

"So you showed Luella the copy of the newsletter, and she showed it to Richard."

"And Gloria was murdered."

"But why did you and Luella go to him with some story about Gloria's casting spells over the agency?"

"She was. She had to be. Charlie, she knew things she couldn't have otherwise. Okay, maybe not casting spells. We were just trying to make a point, but some kind of magic—"

"You've worked the front desk enough to know how much information goes past here. It's hard to tell from the offices if someone out here is listening in on the calls." I've learned more this afternoon than I would have thought possible. But why the change in you, Tweety, and when did it happen? Charlie was willing to bet it happened since Gloria's murder. She used to enjoy Tracy Dewitt. David Dalrymple was right, murder was changing them all in subtle ways. "Tracy, were the Tuschmans blackmailing you?"

Tracy answered in a muffled voice and hung up. Charlie thought she'd said, "Not for money."

That last was tantalizing enough that she couldn't dismiss the beckoning of the little chimes and blinking lights and just walk out right away. If Charlie ever won big in Las Vegas, she'd lose it all before she left town for sure.

Elaine Black called wanting to speak to her husband. When Charlie informed her Dorian hadn't come in today she said, "Bastard," and hung up in Charlie's ear.

Irma called. "Where's Larry?"

"I sent him with Keegan Monroe's screenplay over to Goliath. Richard called in and said we should all just go home, but I don't know how to turn the phones over to the answering service. Are you coming back?"

"It's after five. If no one answers, the service will take over automatically." Irma had a lot in common with Dr. Podhurst. They could both make you feel like an imbecile in seconds. "And no, I'm not coming in. Get out of there now."

"Wait, Irma. Was Gloria blackmailing you, too?"

"You've been warned, Charlie." Congdon and Morse's executive secretary left Charlie with a dial tone.

Charlie groped around with her stockinged feet for her pumps. Edwina said she'd get claw feet from wearing them. The pointy toe of one had caught under a corner of Gloria's desk, and in trying to extract it with her foot Charlie snagged her hose and could feel the resultant run snake up her leg to and then over her knee. It was like a ribbon of relief.

She stared at the thrown pencil halves but thought of other things instead. Three other things at once. First, in one way or another, a lot of people had warned her of the dangers of being alone at the agency.

Second, something in her head was beginning to see a pattern to all the odd bits of information she'd collected while sitting in Gloria's chair. Not collecting psychically. Collecting rationally.

Third, this was a semicircular desk, U-shaped, and so was the little cave for the captive receptionist to scoot her lap, legs, and feet under.

Charlie knelt to grope first for her shoe with her fingers and then for the reason why there was a corner where none should be. A square, plastic-feeling thing with sharp edges, probably less than two and a half inches off the floor. Too dark in this receptionist hole to see, but she found a part of the thing's center that moved and then another. She jiggled, explored, and worried them with blind fingers until they pulled out far enough to come free.

Charlie pushed herself backward out of the hole and stood to look at what she held, hurried to fetch her purse, slipped the tapes into it, and headed for the door. Gloria had not only listened in to office business, she'd recorded it. Had she bugged Charlie's flowers, too?

The elevator was on its way up, and she was surprised when it stopped at the fifth floor. The door opened on a phalanx of men, all of whom she knew. But only one appeared happy to see her.

"Miss Greene, I was hoping to catch you before you left. Your phone lines have been busy." Lieutenant Dalrymple leaned over her, Dr. Evan Podhurst on his left, Larry Mann on his right. "We've found Mary Ann Leffler."

At the back and outer edges of the phalanx, Maurice Lavender looked old and ill. Dorian Black looked mussed. Murder was changing them all.

Charlie didn't want to hear about Mary Ann. She wasn't ready. She told Maurice about the call from ZIA and that Ellen was being considered for the part of Thora Kay. He revived enough to brush her hair with a kiss of breath. "My client thanks you, I thank you. I didn't expect word so soon, but I knew you would pull this off, you gorgeous creature."

"Well, Tina Horton wrote the thing," she reminded him.

But Maurice had his card out and was already trying to get into the agency to call Ellen. Then he would call ZIA and explain how full Miss Maxwell's schedule had become, the many scripts she'd already been asked to read and consider. And the dealing would begin.

"Elaine called for you. I told her you hadn't been in all day and she called you a bastard," Charlie informed Dorian. He hadn't quite gotten all the lipstick off his face.

He ignored Charlie and asked Dalrymple, "So where *is* the famous writer lady?"

"I remembered Irma probably wouldn't be coming back in and didn't feel right about leaving you here alone, Charlie," Larry whispered. "Glad to see you're okay."

Dr. Podhurst scowled at Larry and Charlie. "Yes, Lieutenant tell us. I hope she's all right."

"You know, don't you, Miss Greene?" Dalrymple asked.

"No, but I bet you're going to tell me."

"I'm going to go one better. I'm going to show you." He guided Charlie into the elevator and punched the button.

"Well, *is* she all right?" Podhurst persisted as the door began to close on the three men still grouped in the hallway.

"Hardly," came their answer, and the door shut them away. "Seems to be quite a sudden gathering on your floor, doesn't there? And your assistant implied you were alone inside."

"Lieutenant, I have to get home. My daughter may have a friend staying over who's run away, and her mother will never forgive me if I leave them unsupervised. I don't think I got more than three hours sleep last night, and I had to see a doctor first thing this morning. I don't feel well. Do we have to do this now?"

"I'm afraid so."

Charlie had an inkling of what Luella Ridgeway must have felt the day before. A black and white, with a uniform driving and Detective Gordon in the passenger seat, waited at the rear entrance. Dalrymple crawled in back beside Charlie, and they were off with screeching tires and sirens, playing havoc with the rush-hour congestion. Avoiding clogged freeways, they followed a tortuous route that soon had Charlie lost. But they angled generally north and west. The sun came filtered through a haze of looming moisture.

"Just got the call. Stopped to pick you up on the way." Detective Gordon leered pleasantly over his shoulder.

"Mary Ann's dead, isn't she?" What would Beverly Schantz say if they arrested Charlie? Or Richard Morse, or Mrs. Beesom, or Edwina Greene, or Libby? Even the driver watched Charlie in his rearview mirror.

"Yes," the lieutenant answered with little inflection and less sympathy. "Why were you alone at the agency this afternoon?"

"Apparently, after last night's party, Maurice, Irma, Larry and I were the only ones to show up. I sent Larry on an errand and thought Irma would be back any minute, so I started answering the phones. Maurice had left. I ended up doing it most of the afternoon."

"Why are you crying?" The man next to her thawed about thirty degrees.

"I'm not crying. What makes you think I'm crying?"

"Well, this for starters." And he brushed her cheek with fingers that came away wet.

Charlie glared back at the driver in the mirror. As fast as

they were going, if he didn't pay more attention to the road, they were all about to join Mary Ann Leffler. "I wear contacts, and sometimes the smog irritates my eyes."

He waited expectantly, zooming in on her through the lower, heavy-duty portion of his lenses. He must be able to see every pore on her nose. It was an enormously irritating habit of his that somehow forced her to blabber.

"I think I met Mary Ann only twice, and I didn't read her book very closely. Today I read the screenplay she and Keegan created from it and—Keegan's a great writer, you understand, and I know he moved a lot of it around to make it fit film—but some of the real off-the-wall wacky had to be her. I mean, he's very logical."

"So?" Gordon squinted over the seat back. That was about the extent of his repertoire—leering and squinting.

"The few times I talked to her she was either bitchy or worried, had her own agenda, wasn't ... wasn't particularly appealing, okay? I just wish I could have told Mary Ann how much I enjoyed her way of being humorous. I mean, she's in a class that doesn't need laugh tracks. She dared to be different, dared things I probably couldn't sell but would be so proud of if I did."

"What's the matter with laugh tracks?" Detective Gordon turned back to the terrifying situation facing them as the black and white screamed through a stop light, narrowly missing a terrified woman in a pickup caught in the crosswalk, and swung off onto a side road headed north that Charlie had traveled once before. When she and Keegan had dropped in on Gloria Tuschman's Memorial Séance and Dance.

Mary Ann Leffler had not been found dead in her car underwater—a fact Charlie gloatingly pointed out to a certain homicide cop.

Dalrymple's reaction was disappointing, if typical. "Yours is an untrained gift, after all. We can hardly expect you to be a hundred percent accurate, can we?"

Charlie took in huge lungfuls of quickly freshening air in order to tamp rising ire, and stalked back down the road. The road in the orange grove where two dead women and many of Charlie's live friends had danced around a bonfire last Halloween. "It may not be so much what you eat," Dr. Williams had warned, "but what is eating you. You have to learn to control stress."

Gloria and Mary Ann would never dance again. Loose-dirt roads were not meant for high heels. Charlie was not meant to view people when they were dead. Charlie was a literary agent, and literary agents were very good—but at other things.

"She did drown, however, Miss Greene," Dalrymple called after her. "I would appreciate it if you'd come back and have a look for yourself."

Charlie came up against a waiting ambulance blocking the one-lane road—sitting still, lights still whirling. And up against Detective Gordon and his freckles. Mary Ann drowned in an orange grove? The shallow irrigation ditches to either side of Charlie didn't look as if they'd seen water in months.

"She's not in a car," Charlie reminded Gordon as he took her arm and they started back. Mary Ann was in the middle of the road, in the middle of the grove, surrounded by lights, even though it wasn't dark yet. And surrounded by people taking pictures, scooping dirt into plastic bags, studying things with their noses almost touching the ground. And people holding onto a canvas waist-high barrier to keep a rising west wind from scattering loose dirt, prints, evidence.

Detective Gordon guided Charlie carefully around a barrier of yellow police tape that protected tire tracks in the road and deposited her beside David Dalrymple and Mary Ann Leffler. Dalrymple removed his sport coat and hung it over Charlie's shoulders. "Look, Miss Greene. Open your eyes. Tell me what you see."

Mary Ann had what looked like dried snot or spit caked around her mouth and nostrils, an ugly funny-colored splotch on her nose and forehead. Her eyes were open but rolled up so far that eyelids frozen halfway permitted no sign of pupil or iris or color. Like when Marvin the Shaman passed out at Gloria's séance and dance. Mary Ann's hands lay across her pelvis, their backs bruised. "She's not even wet."

Lightning, thunder, and the smell of ozone struck their little scene just then as if the witches had summoned up a sudden rain to solve that problem. Roger Tuschman and Marvin Grunion began to keen as the intensity of the wind grew. Police laboratory types scurried to erect a tent over Mary Ann and her evidence.

"What," Dalrymple shouted through the mounting noise of a tent refusing to be erected and a wind blowing orange petals into their hair and faces and onto Mary Ann, "what do you see, Miss Greene? Please, it's important."

Charlie didn't tell him about the tapes burning a hole in her purse. He was making her late home, and who knew what trouble was brewing there? It was all take and no give with this guy, and she was fed up. She stared defiantly back at his oddly opaque eyeglasses. The approaching clouds darkened the grove, and they backed away from the lights to avoid the men struggling with the tent in the wind. That and the way he held his head changed the lighting on his face to mysterious.

Charlie couldn't see his eyes, but she was sure he knew she was withholding something important. Several orange blossoms slid off his bald spot. She couldn't see her reflection in those glasses, either, but she did see Mary Ann in them. Mary Ann floating face down. Knees bent. Arms hanging. Forehead, nose, hands, knees, and toes brushing rocks as the water rocked her. It was no irrigation ditch.

"Miss Greene?"

"I have to get home. Now. Please. It's important, too."

"Lieutenant? Norton's here, and he's got something for you," Gordon called from across the road.

Dalrymple told Charlie to stay where she was and crossed over to them.

"Husband's alibi holds," said a voice she didn't recognize, probably Norton's. "Unless all eight people in that copy shop are lying for him. Nobody even saw him go to the crapper. Could have hired someone to kill his wife. Don't have anything on Morse and Greene yet, but it sounds like more than a few people at Congdon and Morse had reason to prefer Tuschman dead."

They spoke in low voices, and with the distance and the wind and the human commotion centering around poor Mary Ann, they certainly didn't expect their words to be overheard. What they didn't take into consideration was the direction of that wind and Charlie's acute hearing. Her family doctor once told her that her early pregnancy and resultant rejection by teen society, coupled with her tone deafness, must be partially responsible for it. Charlie had attended few rock concerts and rarely listened to loud music. Dalrymple, if he knew, would have chalked it up to some psychic ability that it was not.

What Charlie thought she'd seen in the reflection of his glasses had been imagination, pure and simple. No mystery there, either—and after the day she'd had, no wonder. But what she heard now, although not always complete, was real. Real evidence she was not supposed to have. Yes! Yes!

Charlie learned that Maurice had never gone to Cancun at all. Dalrymple said he'd suspected as much, because Maurice had not been tanned. Charlie, of course, hadn't noticed that. Charlie decided to notice everything from now on and beat David Dalrymple at his own game, the smug dweeb. Reliable witnesses saw Maurice visiting someone named Medora every day of that week, and that knowledge apparently was what could drive him to murder. Poor Maurice, you might know it would be a woman.

The tent was up and holding—sort of—and Charlie stood where she could see inside the flap just enough to notice someone scraping the funny dried mucus from Mary Ann's lips onto a glass slide and some more into a plastic sandwich bag. It was a pinkish color. Maybe Charlie wouldn't notice quite everything.

I hope from somewhere, you get to see the movie, Mary Ann. If it gets out of development.

Something about Irma, Charlie didn't quite hear—the words Scarborough House—and, "Not a bad motive for that shrink Podhurst down the hall, either. That leak could have come from his office."

But the clincher was that Luella Ridgeway had once "served time."

Larry Mann's "guy lover" may have been exposed to AIDS, and the county had tested Larry, warned him to inform any other lovers. "This Gloria might have threatened to spread the word, would have put a crimp in his social life. Those guys live for it."

Any of Tracy's dirty secrets had to be put on hold, unfortunately, when Charlie happened to notice Mary Ann's clothes. The dead author wore a thin cotton-knit jumpsuit. Kind of thing you see around the beach a lot. It was tight fitting, and the knees were torn. The tops and outer sides of her toes were discolored like her forehead, nose, and the backs of her hands. Like she'd floated face down and the lowest parts of her body were battered by rocks. Who had taken her shoes off?

Nothing on Dorian, the jerk? And Charlie couldn't believe what she'd heard about Luella. And what was Scarborough House? She wondered what they would dig up about Charlie Greene, whose biggest sin sat at home probably seething because there was no food in the house. But the fact that Libby had no father had never been a secret. Charlie usually told everybody right away, just to get it over with.

"Yeah, but does any of that explain the Leffler woman over there?" Detective Gordon said. "I still got my money on that Keegan Monroe. Anything new on him?"

If there was, Charlie was not meant to hear it. Besides all the background racket going on and the growing special effects dubbed by the weather mixer, Marvin Grunion and Roger Tuschman were shouting at each other.

"I knew it was somebody at the agency," Roger yelled and started for Charlie with blood in his eye. Charlie backed into the tent, nearly tripping over the man leaning over Mary Ann.

"Here, this is a crime scene, lady." The man pushed her aside. "You're contaminating a crime scene."

Marvin grabbed Roger's arms from behind and stopped him before he could knock the tent down in his fury. Grunion was soon replaced by two uniforms and Detective Gordon. They had him by both arms and around the neck, and still he struggled, as if possessed.

"It has to be her or why would you keep bringing her here? The bitch killed my wife and Mary Ann, too." A lightning flash reflected off Roger's gold loop earring, the tears on his cheeks. "If you're trying to get her to confess, I'll make her confess."

"Are you saying," Lieutenant Dalrymple drew Charlie out of the tent and into the fray, "that Miss Greene drove up here this afternoon and killed Mrs. Leffler when everyone thought she was at the agency?"

"She didn't die this after—" Roger Tuschman went suddenly very still in his captors' arms.

"No, she didn't, did she? And she didn't die here."

Marvin the Shaman still wore khaki work clothes and hiking boots and sprouting bristle hairs. "I told Roger to come clean about this, but he hasn't been right since Gloria—" He shrugged and swallowed hard, unable to finish.

"Where's her car?" Dalrymple asked.

"Rizzi Reservoir." Grunion nodded at the valley's ridge. "She called to me—"

"Shut up, Marv." Gloria's husband sagged now in the arms of his captors. "They won't believe anything we say."

"She kept sending me visions . . . images . . . of a place. I finally realized it was Rizzi. She kept saying she was in her car underwater."

Both Dalrymple and Gordon shot a glance at Charlie.

"But when we got there she wasn't in it. The window was open on the driver's side. She wasn't hard to find . . . floating nearby."

"But why did you bring her body here?"

"Roger thinks this part of the grove is a special place. That if

Mary Ann could tell us more about what happened to her and to Gloria, it would be here."

"Do you think this is a special place, Mr. Grunion?"

"Yes. But we weren't getting anything. I told Roger we had to call you."

The rain started suddenly, and Charlie was a lot wetter than Mary Ann by the time Dalrymple got her back along the line of emergency vehicles to a patrol car. One pair of pumps and one dry-clean-only dress ruined. The ladder in her hose that had started up one leg after snagging on the tape recorder under Gloria's desk had vast holes between rungs. She handed him his coat, which hadn't fared well, either.

He got in beside her to shelter from the rain. "I'd like your thoughts about this."

"My first thought is a question. Why don't the owners of this grove, who bother to put 'No Trespassing' signs on the gate, sue Roger and the witches?"

"Because he owns it. And a fair number of the condominiums in the complex behind us. He leases this land to a grower."

"On the proceeds of a copy shop in a broken down shopping center in Pasadena? And a receptionist's salary? You don't know the miserly Richard Morse." The business of defrauding Hollywood wannabes must really be lucrative.

"What else?"

"Mary Ann Leffler has been missing a week. She hasn't been dead that long. Unless she drowned in ice water in the North Atlantic. Where has she been all this time? And what was that dried pinkish stuff on her face? And was it an accident, suicide, or murder? She wasn't the suicidal type."

"I have no word as to the time of death as yet. The pinkish stuff is called edema, in this case dried mucus, which is often present in drowning cases. The rest I don't know."

"Remember when your expectations conned me into guessing she was in her car underwater? We were at the beach house in Malibu. That was six days ago. She obviously wasn't drowned then or in her car."

"No one conned you into anything. You were foretelling, Miss Greene. Too bad poor Mrs. Leffler was not there to hear you."

"You have an answer for everything. You don't think, you just spout your own beliefs and twist everything I say to fit them. And if she hasn't been dead all this time, where has she been? And where is this husband of Mary Ann's who was supposed to be in Canada fishing?"

"He and a large contingent of the family are staying at the beach house. They've been notified and are on their way up here." He stepped back out into the rain. "Would you like to stay and meet them?"

Charlie accepted a ride back to Wilshire and her Toyota instead, then headed for home in the rain, playing the tape she'd found under Gloria's desk and calling Libby on the way.

"Don't worry, Mom, Lori and I have dinner under control. Just come on home. How's your poor tummy?"

Something about the oily-smooth tone in her daughter's voice set Charlie's "tummy" off again. But she'd hit a lull in the choking traffic between full-bore rush hour and the evening go-out-to-dinner crowd and barely had time to digest what she heard on the illicit tapes before she was in Long Beach.

Most of the first tape was simply the give-and-take of office phone conversations, most from the day before the murder, including Charlie's call to Gloria from her car that morning. The second tape was of conversations around the reception desk only. And toward the end of it, Charlie could hear Gloria talking to Irma in the room, with Gloria's words clear and close and Irma's distant and incomplete, as if the executive secretary was standing far away from what was probably a "bug" hidden somewhere on the desk.

"Thought you were still in Vegas. How come you're back so early?"

"How dare you . . . that poor man . . . of his situation."

"I didn't threaten him, merely suggested he could be a little more polite and helpful is all. In fact, so could you. Don't think I don't know about Scarborough House and you still getting therapy for your problem from old Podhurst. Irma Vance, don't you give me that look. I'm warning you."

"Don't think . . . bring down . . . Mr. Morse, you . . ."

"I'm not trying to bring down the agency or ruin your precious Mr. Morse, only asking for a little respect and cooperation around here. Irma? Irma!" Gloria's voice faded as she left the desk. Then nothing except the ringing of unanswered phones. Just before the tape ran out, Charlie could hear Irma calling for Maurice very faintly and in a panicky voice quite unlike her. "Maurice, hurry, we need help!"

Keeping that tape would be "withholding of evidence." In the real world, did people go to prison for withholding evidence in a murder case?

Maybe Charlie could wipe all her prints off it and put it back under Gloria's desk when no one was looking.

Charlie sat cocooned in a dry fleecy sweatsuit, in the cozy breakfast nook in her snug home, eating beanie wienies and deli coleslaw. Across the table sat two bright-eyed, guileless teenage girls, transparently guilty. They had even turned off the damned radio when she came downstairs.

"How was your day, Mom?" Libby poured Charlie more milk and took a drink of her own, leaving a little mustache on her upper lip that Charlie used to think was cute.

You didn't notice my ruined hair, makeup, dress, hose, shoes, and mood. What can I tell you? "Pass the ketchup."

The girls exchanged winces and began mashing their beans in the Campbell's Pork and Beans sauce and stirring it into the ketchup juice. Libby mouthed to her friend, "On the rag."

Beanie wienies were filling, solid, inexpensive, comforting (and occasionally embarrassing the next day). And coming home to a warm dinner prepared by someone else after a stressful week . . . no wonder men got married. Charlie wasn't about to take on the download waiting to happen across the table until she'd savored for a bit, grabbed a moment. They might just as well learn how to handle the guilt burden now while they were young and strong.

But finally Charlie put her slippered feet up on the bench and leaned into the wall, hugged her warmed middle. "Well, let's have it."

They'd been Rollerblading on the sidewalks in the neighboring Naples area of Long Beach, to the south. A touristy community with high prices, quaint shopping, and signs exhibiting skateboards and Rollerblades in circles, graced with blood red diagonal slashes, placed high on poles cemented into every other seam of the sidewalks.

"Grandma's check arrived. Did it cover knee pads?"

"No, but I borrowed Lori's."

"Oh great, and Lori fell and sidewalk-burned her knees, and now what's-her-name is going to sue me, right?"

"If you're speaking of my mother," Lori scooted out of the booth and began to gather up the dirty dishes, "her name is Beverly. I always thought *your* mom had some sensitivity, Libby. Apparently, I was wrong."

"Well *my* mom has had horrible murders and things and a job to worry about and vomits blood, so how would you know?" Libby blinked and sat up. "That's right, you saw the doctor this morning. Do you have cancer?"

Charlie was curled up on the couch watching a tow truck on TV haul Mary Ann Leffler's rental car out of Rizzi Reservoir, when Maggie breezed in with a caramel custard thing and sympathy.

"Do you know the girls are playing gazelle out in the court-yard in the dark? Liable to break something."

"Practicing for cheerleader tryouts next week. But that's nothing. Cops picked them up Rollerblading in Naples this afternoon, one pair of knee pads between them. They get to explain it all to a judge on Monday."

"Yeah, I know." Maggie had met them at the gate when the police car brought them home. "They'll probably just get a light fine and some community service for a first offense. Picking up trash along the beach path or something. What'd the doctor have to say?"

Charlie explained it all again and grazed channels to find more news of Mary Ann.

There was the famous author's husband—tall, gray, weary—flanked protectively by a grown son and daughter. Nice family—handsome, decimated, shocked. They were leaving the grove through the gate with the "No Trespassing" signs. The family refused comment. The police refused to rule out foul play or to speculate on why Mary Ann's "friends" had brought her from Rizzi Reservoir to the grove.

"But the author, whose books were filled with the bizarre and often included droll depictions of modern witchcraft, is rumored to have been a practicing member of the psuedoreligion known as Wicca. And neighbors say that for years there have been strange 'goings on' going on at night in this orange grove behind a condominium complex just off Happy Valley Canyon Road."

"How could such a normal, nice-looking family have a witch for a mother?" Maggie said, bringing back a spoon from the kitchen for Charlie to eat her flan with.

"Oh, I don't know, I did. Libby's sure she does."

"Come on. Edwina just worries about you. Like you worry about Libby. Comes with the territory. And finish that, damn it. You know how long it takes to make those things?"

"It's wonderful, but I ate too many beanie wienies. I promise I'll eat the rest for breakfast. We're out of Cheerios, anyway. Thank God." Charlie flicked off the TV and took the custard cup to the refrigerator. "I'm supposed to go out for a walk about now to control my stress, but I think I'll go to bed and try to catch up on the night I lost last night. I need to get to work early." She explained about returning the tapes. "If I don't I'm liable to end up seeing a judge on Monday, too."

"Oh Charlie, you're not really trying to solve murders? You're a sick woman. And a mother. And you don't know how.

Why did I used to think you were so sensible?" But Maggie Stutzman agreed to take the girls to school in the morning on her way to work. Charlie would have had Libby walk, but she knew Lori's mother would come unhinged. Beverly Schantz insisted the neighborhoods around the school were too dangerous for young innocents. Charlie figured there wasn't any danger out there that couldn't walk right onto the school grounds with them. As long as they avoided Recreation Park, where the Vietnamese gangs held sway, they weren't in any more danger in that neighborhood than anywhere.

Charlie was up and on the road so early the next morning she beat the rush hour traffic. But the morning fog didn't end at the ramp onto the 405 as usual, and it was cold and clammy, and all she could think of was a cup of hot coffee. Still, she made it to the office before anyone else and, wiping them off with a rag she'd brought for the purpose, she replaced the tapes under Gloria's desk, then wiped off everything she thought she might have touched in the area. She searched through Irma Vance's desk until she found a list of addresses and used the rag again. Then, like a true criminal, she left the scene of the crime and threw the rag up into the dumpster on the other side of the end wall on the alley to destroy all evidence of what she'd done.

"I'm getting sick of this," a voice raged from the dumpster, and Charlie's rag came flying out again, and so did a plastic bag filled with trash and then a whole flotilla of loose paper and an empty vodka bottle and a constant stream of profanity. Charlie didn't stick around to watch the airborne garbage hurtle through what a commentator on the Toyota's radio had just referred to as the morning phlegm of the Pacific. She left the incriminating rag with all the rest of the jetsam and ran for her car.

Traffic was picking up and the fog getting patchy as she turned off the Hollywood Freeway into North Hollywood. She soon pulled over and got out her Thomas Guide to find she was only a few blocks away from Maurice's but on the wrong side of Riverside Drive.

Odd to realize now that she had never visited the homes of any of her cohorts at the agency except for Richard Morse's. Maurice, Larry, Richard, and Luella had come down to a party of Charlie's in Long Beach.

When she located the house, she was stunned at its modesty. She would have expected Maurice to live in a fifties version of a swinging bachelor's pad in which to entertain his lady friends. But she could see why he chose to visit this Medora woman on his vacation time instead of inviting her over for the week. The house was smaller than Charlie's, and shabby. A huge old car, all motor and trunk, sat on concrete blocks in the front yard across the street. The tiny lawn next to his was surrounded by a massive chain-link fence enclosing a medium-sized, tired-looking dog.

The houses were all small stuccos with flat roofs and patches and faded paint and metal window frames. Charlie checked Irma's list again. She drove around to the alley behind to get a look at the car in the carport. It was Maurice's car, and next to it he sat in a rusting metal lawn chair like you saw only in movies or at garage sales. It had a rug over it to protect his pants. He wore a black shirt with a purple tie and light lavender sport coat. He was dressed for work. And drinking a cup of coffee. And staring at Charlie.

She pulled in behind his gleaming last year's deluxe Oldsmobile. She didn't like this detecting, prying. Maurice Lavender was one of her favorite people in the world. He may be a lech, but he was comfortable. Like mashed potatoes and meat loaf.

He came to open her door. "Charlie, what are you doing here? Are you lost?" They didn't make men like Maurice anymore. He was like the Cary Grant of talent agents. He drew her out of the Toyota and to the foot-wide concrete sidewalk leading from his back door to his carport. Talk about a no-frills house. "Here sit, I'll bring out another chair. Can I get you a cup of coffee, sweetie? One cup won't hurt. And it's not that strong. I'll be right back. I'd invite you in, but we bachelors are terrible housekeepers."

Charlie sat in Maurice's chair, the rug still warm from his body, and stared at the chilly, greasy, gloomy morning. In a couple of hours it might well be hot and glaring, but how bad could your house be to make you want to have your morning coffee outside this early on this kind of morning?

Still, when the thick mug came with the rich, fragrant black liquid, the morning brightened even in this dismal place. She felt like a rat as Maurice settled in a chrome and plastic kitchen chair that had to be authentic old and cheap—not a costly reproduction from one of the shops on Robertson Boulevard.

"What's the matter, sweetie? Is it the coffee?" His voice was the soft, stroking kind. Unlike Irma Vance and Dr. Evan Podhurst, Maurice and his marvelous voice made you feel gifted and desirable.

"Oh no, it's wonderful. I've been craving it since visiting your . . . our Dr. Williams yesterday." And so of course she had to explain, one more time, what the good doctor had said and planned to do. "But that's not what I'm upset about. Maurice, I have to know."

"Yes?" He leaned forward with an expression that said her problem was the only one in the world worth considering all morning. "You can tell old Maurice. Anything."

Why do you live this way? "Maurice, who is Medora, and why didn't you go to Cancun like you said you did?"

• • •

Maurice guided Charlie firmly down the hall of Our Lady of the Only Way Nursing Home not three blocks from his tiny patched stucco. He'd walked her here through back alleys, saying it was too close to drive. Every time she tried to talk, he waved a hand at her and increased the pace. Once inside, the odor of institution breakfast and morning bedpans mingled with the cheery voices of nuns and nurses and aides and with the morning phlegm of the ill and aging. And the drone of generic morning television shows at every door they passed.

Maurice swung Charlie into a doorway and startled an aide eating off a tray and watching the television screen behind a slumped form in a wheelchair. Maurice grabbed the tray from the man, whose thinning hair was caught in a greasy ponytail at the back of his neck. His droopy mustache had pieces of scrambled egg in it. "Well, she never eats it. Just goes to waste."

"Another tray—and now, if you please. And she prefers toast and tea to eggs, and I want it back here fast and prepared right, or I'll have your job, bucky."

Charlie was impressed. The guy was out of there in seconds. The woman in the wheelchair hadn't stirred.

"You have to watch them," Maurice said, "drop in when they least expect it. I was here last night and she was lying in a lake of urine. They didn't expect me."

"Maurice, I—"

"Oh, I'm sorry. I haven't introduced you, have I, sweetie?" He swung the wheelchair and it's occupant around with a flourish. "Charlie, I would like you to meet Medora Lavender. Mother, this is Charlie Greene."

Medora gummed the toast Maurice dunked in the tea then slurped the tea from a cup he held to her lips, her hands curled into claws in her lap as if the fingers could no longer part. Her eyes glanced from Maurice to Charlie as if she didn't know either one of them, but when he wiped her chin and stood, bending to touch her forehead lightly with his lips, she closed her eyes and smiled, placing a crippled hand over his. Charlie almost choked.

"Can you find your way back to your car, Charlie? I'm afraid I'm going to have to speak to the sisters again. It's hard to find caring, capable people who can afford to work for the little they can pay. Sometimes the shiftless and ignorant are all that's out there. I'll see you at the office, sweetie."

Charlie just nodded and got the hell out of there. She wanted to cry so bad, everything backed up in her throat and she couldn't.

Luella Ridgeway's house was every bit as much of a surprise as Maurice's, but for the opposite reason. High in the Hollywood Hills with a spectacular view of the smog. Sunny redwood decks, pool, and Jacuzzi. Luella was putting on her earrings when she answered the door. "Oh Charlie, I thought you were the cleaning lady. Come on in ... is something wrong?"

"I've just come from Maurice's house." And Charlie lost it right there. It was the time of the month. It was having to go see doctors. It was being around murder. It was not being able to do the work she loved. In other words, Charlie was not the type of person who broke down this way.

Luella had Charlie on a comfortable sofa in front of the view with a box of tissues before Charlie could explain it all. The sun was out, the fog was gone. It was warm. It was like night and day from where she'd just come.

"Honey, have you eaten anything this morning?"

Don't be so nice. I came here to ask you nasty questions. "I had flan."

"Flan." Luella blinked fast like Tracy, thought a moment, and shrugged. "Right. Got eggs in it, I guess." She tried again. "So you visited Maurice . . . and—Maurice wouldn't hurt you, he's the sweetest, gentlest—"

"I know. He took me to see his mother. I feel like such a total shit. . . ."

"But Maurice's mother has to have been dead for years— you don't mean Medora? Charlie, get control of yourself. You didn't know about Medora? No, you might not. He doesn't advertise her much. Charlie, Medora is Maurice Lavender's wife, not his mother."

27

But he called her 'mother.' And, Luella, she's one of the oldest people I've ever seen."

"Their daughter died years ago, college age, I think—before I ever met him. Couples of that generation often call each other what their children call them. I expect that's what he meant by 'mother.'"

Medora Lavender had a mysterious and hereditary wasting disease that took her daughter at a much younger age than it had even started in Medora, but the shock of the daughter's death accelerated the process in the older woman. Several years younger than Maurice, Medora had aged mentally and physically beyond his ability to care for her and earn a living, too.

"It takes a good portion of everything he makes to keep her in that nursing home. And he's a good agent, charismatic, he makes money. But it's a no-win situation. It would be a blessing if she died in one way, but he's so devoted to her, I worry about him when it happens. God, would you stop that sniveling?" Luella removed her earrings and slid off the couch. "I'm going to make us some coffee."

Charlie couldn't stop sniveling long enough to explain she shouldn't have coffee. So she had some—more.

"You realize you've ruined your face for the day?" Luella handed Charlie a cup and blotted her cheeks with a tissue. "You see why Maurice couldn't advertise his devotion to an all but catatonic wife? He earns their living with charm, which he's always had in abundance. I would guess Ellen Maxwell doesn't know about Medora, Charlie. To so many of his clients, he's a safe, handsome escort *and* their *agent*. You know what talent's like—who do you know better at stroking without intimidating than Maurice Lavender?"

"This is so embarrassing." Charlie had always admired Luella, even if Luella had to share her assistant with Dorian the Jerk. "Oh my God!"

"What? Charlie, I missed getting to the office yesterday, and things are backed up and I have an early lunch meeting."

The orthodontist bill is due today. It's Friday. It was due yesterday. And tonight I have to go to the friggin' yacht club. "And here I sit in your beautiful home making you late to the office, and I already made an ass of myself bothering Maurice and Medora. And I have to ask you some questions."

"You're investigating." Luella sighed and leaned back against the white and gold brocade. "I saw about your Mary Ann Leffler on the news last night and worried you would. Charlie, you have absolutely no expertise in investigating crime."

"I know that, but they won't leave me alone. Lieutenant Dalrymple dragged me out there yesterday to view Mary Ann in the orange grove hoping I'd get a psychic revelation."

"You're not psychic."

"I know that, too. But Gloria claimed I was, and now I'm in the soup. And my life and stomach will never settle down until I do something about this problem. So I decided to try to solve Gloria's murder logically to get the Beverly Hills P.D. off my case."

"I don't believe this world." Luella's suit was a perfect-fitting olive and white plaid, over a snowy white blouse and collar—stunning against her tan. She spent time on that deck in the sun. Who wouldn't? Bright red shoes and jewelry. "And if it looks out of control from Hollywood, what must it look like from Peoria?"

"Maurice makes more than you do, doesn't he?" Charlie looked around, knowing she was being obvious, just wanting to get this over with.

"My first husband had money, and I did well in the divorce settlement. My second husband died and left me this house and some investments. But it doesn't make my job any less important to me, Charlie. My self-esteem is based not on what I have but on what I can do. I'm a damn good agent, and that's how I want to be remembered. All this is wonderful, and I don't deny it, but my work is what I get up for in the morning."

Charlie could certainly identify with that.

"Can't you just see me sitting here, playing bridge with the other widows? Being a pink lady at a local hospital? I want to feel important for my own working skills, not the time some organized charity would like to steal from me. I do volunteer, but it's after work, and they don't ask me to stuff envelopes, either."

"Why did you go see the Tuschmans the night before the murder?"

When she was in Minnesota helping her siblings put their father in a nursing home, Luella came across one of Roger's newsletters. "'The Hollywood Insider,' it was called. Claimed to have the latest news that could be found nowhere else and all the knowledge needed to break into show business."

In it was a piece of information that he could only have come by through the agency. "I didn't tell Gloria or even Tracy about Joe Marsdon's coming divorce from Lorna on 'All My Lovers,' Charlie. That kind of privileged information would earn money from the soap tabloids, but apparently Gloria got a hold of it and just passed it on to Roger. Lance Gregory is my client, and he shouldn't even have known about it. He told me because he was upset it could mean the end of his job."

Lance Gregory played Joe Marsdon on the afternoon soap "All My Lovers," and the only reason he knew about it was that he slept with a guy who also slept with the head writer.

"And Lance called you about it?"

"That must have been where Gloria picked it up. It wasn't in writing anywhere. I thought I'd lose my client and maybe my reputation because of the Tuschmans' little prank. They'd already used the agency name in one or more of these newsletters and got Tracy in trouble."

"And you and she went to Richard with it and tried to get Gloria fired. Why did you tell him Gloria was casting evil spells to get information for Roger's newsletters?"

"My, you have been a busy little thing, haven't you? You may not have noticed, but Richard is really very superstitious. We thought we'd get his attention that way."

Phy Duong, the cleaning lady arrived—young, Oriental, efficient, politely unimpressed.

"Oh Charlie, I wish I could stay and chat but I do have to get down to the agency." Luella slipped her earrings back on and punched her garage door opener. "Have I answered all your questions to suit you?"

"All but one." Charlie followed her into the garage, where a door lifted soundlessly and where there were two cars— Luella's Honda Accord and a sleek black Jaguar. One for work and one for the weekend. "The Tuschmans had something on you, didn't they? You confronted them that Sunday night with the inside information on your client that they'd stolen. But they confronted you back with something worse. They knew you'd spent time in prison."

Luella Ridgeway stopped and turned to look through Charlie, petite and perfect, one slender hand with professionally manicured nails—red to match her costume jewelry—resting on the car, outwardly everything Charlie would have liked to have been, maybe could have been if she hadn't screwed up at sixteen. "Why are you doing this to me, Charlie?"

I don't want to. Oh God, do I not want to. "The police know about it. Better you hear it from me."

Luella put the Honda between them and eyed Charlie over its top, the angry tapping of a shoe toe sounding hollow in this cavern that could have handled two more cars. "When I was a senior at the University of Minnesota, I was the public relations officer as well as treasurer of the student body government. I embezzled fifteen thousand dollars from the treasury. I figured the world owed me. At the time it seemed a perfectly natural thing to do. I had access, I had the opportunity to cook the books, and I was fed up with never having enough money. It was stupid. I have always admitted it. I admitted it then. It's a stupid age when you're likely to do stupid things, what can I say?"

"But you got caught."

"Charlie, it wasn't as if I'd raped someone. Or committed murder. But I spent fifteen months in prison and served five years probation, paid back every penny plus fines that amounted to a good deal more. Do you have any idea how hard it is to find work if you have both a college degree and a prison record? I went back to finish my degree in journalism and worked to pay restitution. I cleaned houses like the superior little ass inside. I pumped gas. Think I could get a decent job? So I married. I had no choice. But first I changed my name, paid for a new identity. Husband number one had money, and we had a good time. He moved me out here. He dabbled in the industry at first but got lucky, got interested, got busy. Turned me loose and I found what I wanted to do."

"Be an agent."

"Be an agent. He lost interest and came back, and now I was busy. We split. Simple. And I remarried well and continued working at what I loved, almost had myself convinced the big bad world had forgotten all about my mistake, had forgiven me that—and then Gloria and Roger came up with it. Charlie, killing Gloria wouldn't have helped hide my dirty secret. Roger would still know about it."

"But how did they find out?"

"I went to an 'All Hallows' Eve' party at their house last year and met your Mary Ann Leffler. She kept insisting she knew me but couldn't place me. Her sister had been in the student government at the university at about the time I was. That family had followed my trial and attendant troubles with understandable interest, and of course my picture appeared in the local newspaper along with the story. Mary Ann finally remembered where she'd seen me and wrote to tell Gloria from Montana."

Charlie would have liked to know more about that Halloween party from Luella's perspective, but hadn't the heart (or stomach) to go on. She walked around the Honda to give the woman a heartfelt hug. Luella stayed statue stiff. Charlie left before she could feel any worse. How did real investigators live with themselves?

Back at the agency, Charlie called Tina Horton to congratulate her and warned her not to do any work on the pilot until they saw the white of at least the deal memo. Other than eating the flan, it was the first pleasant thing she'd done all day, and she tried to sound up through it all. Then she called Shelly and asked him to meet her in an hour out back in the alley. "You know where."

Then she whispered in Larry's ear that she was taking him

to lunch so they could talk about what was bothering him in the privacy of a public restaurant.

Next, she visited Dr. Podhurst's office. Linda Meyer was reading a fashion magazine to the accompaniment of her boss's choppy drone and irritating throat-clearing coming from the open door of his office. Charlie gestured her surprise, and Linda got up to close his door.

"Don't worry, there's no patient in there. He's just dictating into his machine. You should have heard him before he got a hearing aid. I had to go shush him if a patient came in. Did you need to see him? He's got an appointment in ten minutes."

"No, don't bother him. I just wanted to ask you more about that party last Halloween. Did they actually sacrifice a black and white cat and dance naked in front of Dorian Black's children around that bonfire in the orange grove?"

Linda's giggle was so cute it reminded Charlie she used to giggle—way last week. "Oh, I know what you're up to Charlie, you're investigating. It's so exciting. I love to gossip. The cat was already dead. It was Gloria's what-do-you-call-it—?"

"Familiar?"

"Hey, right. Just hours before the party, it got hit by a car. Don't you remember Gloria carrying on about it for a month? No? Well, I've always thought you were beautiful but not very perceptive, you know? Hey, don't take offense, I mean, what do I know? Gloria said you were psychic, but Gloria said the weirdest stuff."

"So it was some kind of funeral rite for the cat."

"Bingo. And yes, everybody danced skin out, and it was so much fun. Have you ever tried it? The kids loved it. It wasn't just Dapper Dork's kids, either, but we'd all had some interesting social—let's say, party snacks? Kids were no problem. These weren't toddlers. I mean, it wasn't taking advantage of innocents or anything."

"Was there sex?"

"Well, not for the kids, and not for me. It was after the people with kids left, too, but if my boyfriend had been there, we'd have shown them how. I mean, I was greased. There was a couple there—the guy was sort of wimpy, but he dressed like a cowboy, and he wasn't taking his clothes off for anything. His girl was a real skinny Oriental thing. No breasts. I mean flat-out flat."

"This wimpy cowboy—did he ever take his clothes off?"

"No, his girl took them off him. She was damn near lactating. He finally got in the mood. He's not as wimpy as he looks. Gloria told me she sent them home in a cab, delivered their car later. Gloria was a flake. But she was responsible." The twinkle in Linda's eyes faded. "I heard about Mary Ann. I sure am sorry. Are you investigating her death, too?"

Charlie's next stop was the VIP hall. She didn't hear any voices claiming to be Gloria's. She didn't study the view outside the window. She studied the hall, the stairs, made three trips down to the outside door, peeked out, came back up.

When Charlie met Sheldon Maypo out by the bushes where Gloria's body had been found, she asked him if he still wanted to aid her investigations. "I know I shouldn't ask you to spend time on this, you with no job and I haven't sold your stuff. Yet."

He yawned and leaned back against the woody part of the bushes where getting Gloria down had done so much harm. He took off his baseball cap to run a hand over his white tufty hair and regarded his agent with a certain mischievous glee. "You say that every time you see me. Tell you what, I'll help you if you'll try harder with my 'stuff.' How's that?"

"Oh I will, Shelly. I promise. But I still feel guilty."

"Well, don't. I just landed a new security job. Start tonight."

"That's wonderful. Night jobs work so well for you. And you can write and eat, too. Where?"

"Right here. No thanks to you. But I have impressive references nonetheless."

Charlie had forgotten all about trying to wangle him a security job at the FFUCWB of P, or even looking into who might have some clout in the matter. One more reason to feel guilty. But that job would help out with what she had in mind for him to do next. "It may not solve Gloria's murder, Shelly," she said after telling him what she wanted. "But it could explain how she got up in the bushes."

Charlie thought she'd had all the surprises anyone would come across in one day already, until she took her assistant to lunch at Mom and Pop's to hear his secrets in private.

28

"Charlie, it's not bad news—what I wanted to tell you yesterday. It's good news. That is, if whoever bugged your office doesn't decide to fuck it up." Larry snapped a crisp potato chip between those gorgeous teeth and said around it, "I've got work."

"Of course you've got work. You work for me. Oh you mean—"

"Real work. Come on, Charlie, you always knew I'd leave when a break came. Don't look like that."

"It's just such a surprise." I don't need more surprises. "I'm happy for you, of course." You can't leave me. I need you. "What is it?"

"Beach-beer commercial. Hard hat. Coors." He raised a glass of Pepsi on ice to her in triumph.

He certainly had the body for beach shots and the jaw for hard-hat stereotyping. "Isn't beach and hard hat kind of a funny combination?"

"There's a pickup instead of a volleyball net, and they're roasting steaks instead of baking clams but—see, after a hard day of building roads or whatever, a bunch of guys go to the beach, swim, pop a cool one, throw around a football, jock it up."

"No girls? In a beer commercial?"

"Well, yeah, they come along and decide to join the party. But you know the best part? It's to air locally first."

Some producer sitting home with his feet up after a hard day punches his remote and there's this fantastic guy on this beer commercial, and he thinks to himself this fantastic guy would be perfect for the part of Fantastic Guy. Producer's on the phone in seconds telling his minion to find this guy and line him up for an audition. Actors.

Oh well, all Charlie's writers were going to hit the *New York Times* best-seller list or win an Oscar—most of them both. She looked down at the disgusting mess on her plate. Mom or Pop—they were both women—had said she had just the thing for an ulcer. The man at the next table was turning green merely watching Charlie eat it. But it was strangely soothing. A poached egg with a soft yolk on a piece of toast with hot milk poured over it, salt and pepper to taste. "So how long will it take to shoot it?"

"Three, four days, probably."

"And you're willing to give up a steady paycheck and medical insurance for a few days of work?" Why not? You'll be discovered in a week and a superstar in a year.

"What else can I do? I've used up my vacation time. Look, I don't want to be an assistant all my life, same as you don't want to be a housewife. Okay?"

"Okay, but what if I could convince the Vance into letting you have a week of unpaid leave for that time? Just in case new work doesn't come right away after the commercial's shot?"

"Fine by me if you can work it, but you're not going to get Irma to go for that. Might not be good for dear Richard's business."

"Let me see what I can do." Let me see if I can't just do a little blackmailing on my own.

Charlie cornered Irma Vance in the ladies off the VIP hall. Talk about taking unfair advantage. She stood outside the stall door and waited for the woman to stop peeing. "I want you to talk Richard into giving Larry a week's unpaid leave starting a week from next Monday."

Irma waited to flush and come out to wash her hands, meticulously of course, before bothering to answer. "And how do we expect me to do that, Charlie dear?"

"We expect you to figure out a way."

"And why should we do that? And since when have we demanded such favors in this office?"

"Since we found out about Scarborough House."

Irma's eyes met Charlie's in the mirror over the sink. Richard once said Irma's sharp stare could slice a man's balls thinner than home fries before he felt the blood in his shorts. Charlie didn't back away, but she had the urge to.

"You found the tapes. Yesterday afternoon when you were here alone. Yet they were here when I came in this morning. Why did you put them back?"

Charlie shrugged. "My turn to have secrets. About time, too."

"First Gloria. And now you. Where does it end? Mr. Morse already knows about Scarborough and so does Mr. Congdon. Besides, I can support myself now. What is it you expect to do with this information, Charlie?"

"I expect I'll think of something, Irma. And you'll never know when that particular gun's going to go off, will you? It'll be just like before Gloria died."

"I'll see what I can do. But little girls shouldn't play with fire, Charlie dear."

Maurice didn't even smile when Charlie passed him on her way back to the office. Luella made a point of avoiding her all afternoon.

Tracy passed Larry by and brought James's script right to Charlie's desk, said nothing, and left. If Dorian came in, Charlie didn't see him. Richard seemed to be bouncing back, though. Richard was like that. Edwina would have called him rubbery. Charlie preferred elastic. But the biggest surprise of the day was that the deal memo from ZIA arrived by messenger. Would Tina Horton begin work on the pilot at once?

"This does not happen in this town," Richard Morse said and drafted a leak to the trades. "Nothing so quick and easy. Then again, don't look a gift horse in the asshole, I always say."

He handed Irma the rough copy, but she didn't rush off to key it in. She stood there and cleared her throat. Then she tilted her head toward Charlie and coughed.

"What, Irma? You can speak. You are among friends. Oh that's right, I forgot. So Charlie, you're trolling for favors for your friends instead of yourself? That's not smart, baby, but it's your tush. What will you do without Larry the Kid for a whole week? And who will help out on the front desk? You? We're already shorthanded around here. Everybody's working two jobs the way it is."

"Relieve me of all detection responsibilities and I'll help out on the phones. Or you could hire a temporary."

"Jesus, remember the last time we hired a temp? Shut down the system. Lost business. And we should do it again so the Kid can take a trip or something? Charlie, I thought we were on the same side in this war. Maybe I was wrong."

"Not all temporary receptionists are as bad as the last one, Richard. And these are hard times, as you so often tell us. Extraordinary measures are needed at times like this. And I, in the last week, have laid 'Southwestern Exposure,' *Phantom of the Alpine Tunnel*, and *Shadowscapes* on your plate—and you still think you're going hungry. Maybe I need to look for another job."

With that Charlie Greene sashayed her terrified ass out of the boss's office and left the agency early to get ready for a stupid dinner at a stupid yacht club.

She left an office suite once full of colleagues and now full of enemies. An office that supported her and her bastard child and saved them both from depending on the bile of Edwina Greene. Charlie didn't burn bridges, she dissolved them. Maybe Libby was right, maybe she should latch onto a safe older male with money.

Incredibly, after all she'd been through and all she still faced at work, at the doctor's, at the Beverly Hills P.D., and at home, Charlie had a good time at the yacht club dinner in Long Beach that night.

She broke her word to Dr. Williams and had a couple of glasses of wine and a small beef fillet swimming in a naughty sauce with strange herbs, mushrooms, liqueurs, garlic, and probably cream and butter. It was Friday night, and after her week she was taking a well-deserved break from stress in her own way. She danced with Ed and she danced with strangers. She applauded as he and they presented each other with trophies for some regatta. She was assailed in the powder room by women wanting to know what it was like working in "the industry" and how they could get their niece, daughter, neighbor an audition or their book published. She was assailed outside it by men wanting to know about the murder at the agency and how they could get their son, nephew, friend an audition or their book published.

She even went out to look at Ed's boats. A smaller thing with a mast and sails he used for racing and a larger one with motors he used for travel. There were quite a few signs of Dorothy about on this one. They talked about murder, standing on the deck watching city lights twinkle just like people used to watch stars.

"Everybody has a motive, and damn few of them have alibis," she told him. "And I've pissed off all my friends at work and probably my enemies, told off the boss, and decided to solve Gloria's murder on my own and hope when I do the reason for Mary Ann's death will become clear. Ed, I think I've lost my mind."

"I hope you're not being set up for a dangerous situation, Charlie. I hope the Beverly Hills P.D. is prepared to offer you some protection, since they seem as open about involving you in the investigation process as your boss is. I hope this Lieutenant Dalrymple is not depending on your so-called psychic powers to protect you here. I hope Dorothy will start speaking to me again." He lit a cigarette and tossed the paper match overboard. "I'm sorry. I am trying to quit, but you are not helping at all."

"I'm not surprised Dorothy isn't going for this. I'd have thrown you to the sharks by now. Would it help if I spoke to her? Assured her that there's nothing happening here?"

"Frankly, Charlie Greene, I don't think it would be wise for her to meet you. That's a compliment, you know. I'll never understand how women think. They chart such hidden, tortuous routes to the simplest mental destinations, and then make such sudden, accurate darts into harbors on no map I'm familiar with." He threw the barely started cigarette into some poor fish's living room. "I always talk like this after a few drinks and the yacht club."

"You explained how harmless our relationship is and why we entered into it and she didn't buy it."

"Right." A Marine patrol boat glided out to the Queen's Gate in the breakwater. "Charlie, you are lovely. Lovely trouble."

Ed gripped the metal pole railing that topped the gunwale, and Charlie ran a finger up and down its cold surface, felt a big grin concerning something completely unrelated to him answer this poor man's confusion. She may just have discovered the blunt object that killed Gloria Tuschman.

Charlie woke up the next morning to find Lori gone, Libby home, and Jesus Garcia in her front yard.

"But UM, I don't want to go shopping on Rodeo Drive. Lori and I need to practice our cartwheels and handstands." Shimmery strands of platinum sailed across Charlie's peripheral vision as Libby threw her hair over her shoulder in outrage. "Thought you wanted me to be a cheerleader. I can't make the squad without practicing. Besides, I thought you were mad at me about having to go to court Monday."

"You don't want to go shopping on Rodeo Drive?" Charlie swung the gray Toyota onto the ramp to the 405 and headed them north. "You've been begging to ever since we moved to California."

"You wouldn't buy me anything anyway. It'd be too expensive."

"We might find a bargain." Personally, Charlie detested shopping. One more thing to eat up time she'd rather spend otherwise. But lately it had been a way to get her daughter away from friends and television and blasting music and into neutral territory where communications weren't so blocked. "I'll take you out to a nice lunch."

"And then won't let me eat half of it. When *I* run away from home it won't be anywhere you can call somebody's mother and check up on me, I promise you that." The dangerous flush of anger, near tears, and "it isn't fair" suffused the skin over Libby's cheekbones and all around those lovely eyes.

Charlie wondered how long before her daughter simply refused to get in the car when Charlie ordered it, and realized there wasn't a great deal Charlie could do about it. "Why did Lori suddenly change her mind and go home this morning?"

"Her mom was going to make waffles. Not the toaster kind. Real ones. With bacon in them, or berries on them, and homemade syrup. They've got this great old black waffle iron, a round one from her grandma's mother. Lori wakes up and that's all she can think about, talk about. Lori's a wimp."

"I don't know, sounds delicious. And maybe we can get back in time for you to get in some practice."

When they pulled onto Wilshire, Charlie explained she'd park in her reserved slot under the First Federal United Central Wilshire Bank of the Pacific because it would be free.

"You are so cheap you creak." Libby's disdain cut cruel slashes in Charlie's already wounded motherhood. "Look at this car, for instance."

"What's the matter with it? It was brand new last year . . . well, the year before." Did you notice the rusted hulk that delivered Jesus the stud?

"It's gray. It's depressing. It's obviously a year-end model they were selling off to tightwads cheap before the new cars came out. Who else would buy something the color of dead fish guts just because it's cheap?"

29

Charlie slid them into her slot under the FFUCWB of P in the smoothly purring car that didn't break down in traffic and leave her stranded to the terrors of the 405, that didn't eat up more of her income with costly repairs. Charlie was not fond of gray, either, but she had a cancerous attachment to this little number. It didn't turn on her, asked only for fuel and occasional tune-ups. She turned off the engine, which was so quiet you could barely tell the difference, and stroked the dashboard in a sudden fit of superstition.

She's just a dumb kid. Don't listen to her, okay? We need you, baby.

Charlie had her door open and was half out of the fish-gut colored Toyota when Libby said in what almost sounded like awe, "Is this where you work?"

"You know, I've meant to bring you here, honey, but one of us is always too busy. And you have to admit it's often you. Your social schedule is—would you like to run up and see the agency before we shop? I doubt if anyone will be there, but it might be fun to see ... if we don't spend much time at it."

Charlie took Libby's insolent shrug as affirmative and guided them both up to Congdon and Morse Representation, Inc. on the public elevator. She let them into the suite with its hushed rustlings, the soft whirring of the invisible blower circulating air, the gurgle of the refrigerator in the utility niche, the creaks and rattles in the walls, all the sounds you never heard during bustling business hours. Charlie took her daughter past the front desk to the inner hall, around the corner, through Larry's cubbyhole into her own office, explaining the use of each room along the way.

Libby hesitated in the doorway. Charlie passed her to stand by the window and watch a derelict, cradling a paper bag and crossing Wilshire, move obediently with the lights. He disappeared into the alley behind the Beverly Pavilion across the way.

She turned back to watch her daughter survey the work world of Charlie Greene the agent while her tormented middle levitated. Why should this kid's immature, fickle opinion carry that much importance in the scheme of things?

"Nice," was Libby's spoken judgment, her expression uncommitted. She ran her hand over the back of one of the chairs, checked out the view of Wilshire, and turned to scan Charlie's desk and computer station, and the loaded shelves behind them. "You obviously didn't have anything to do with the decorating."

"Just A. E.'s poster. The rest was here when I moved in." But they were both trying hard not to grin. "You remember Mr. Mous. He stayed with us in New York once when he came in for Edgars week. He's sort of short and bald, grouchy looking."

"And this was where Gloria the Witch sat." Libby perched in Gloria's chair when the tour took them back by the reception desk. She whirled it and her hair in a 360. "And now she's dead."

"Let's not get morbid. Come on, the world renowned Rodeo Drive awaits."

Libby wanted to see where Gloria was murdered.

Funny, Charlie liked showing off her office and prestige in

the work world, as good old Ed would have put it. But she was a lot less happy about sharing murder with this tall, graceful creature who had a razor blade for a tongue and who called her mom.

Charlie took her daughter out to the VIP hall, stood at the window, and pointed out where the body had lain in the bushes. At least she had the kid's attention.

"Charlie, I'm in the trash can. Help me."

"Mom, who said that?"

"I didn't hear anything. Come on, let's go shopping." Charlie grabbed Libby's arm and started them off down the hall.

"Don't do this to me." The girl-woman stopped short in front of the door to the janitor's closet, and the jolt nearly toppled Charlie. Not only was Libby taller and prettier than Charlie, all this cheerleading practice was making her stronger. Oh boy.

"I know what I heard. I heard a woman whisper. She sounded like lots of people in New York did. She said she was in the trash can, and she was talking to someone named Charlie. Mom, she sounded an awful lot like the crabby bitch who used to answer the phones here when I'd call to get you. And she was asking you to help her. I want to know what's happening. And I won't take another step until you tell me. I might not be a fancy career woman with an ulcer, but I have rights, too. Was I hearing a dead person whispering? Can they do that?"

Charlie had never heard her daughter string that many words together that coherently. "No, of course they can't. You know that."

"Then what was it?"

"I don't know. I just know it wasn't Gloria. Sometimes . . . just because we can't explain something we assume it's unexplainable, paranormal, some ditzy thing. But there's always a rational explanation, Libby. Sometimes we just can't see it because we're too close to the problem."

"That's pretty weak—even for you. This is your problem. I'm not close to it at all. But I heard what I heard, and I notice you can't get me out of here fast enough. Which means you're afraid. Like you were afraid of Jesus this morning, right?"

Right. "I just want to get some shopping done so we can get you home in time to practice with Lori."

But Libby shrugged off Charlie's hand and started back down the hall. She tried the door to Dr. Podhurst's office and found it locked, stopped at the window to stare at the where-the-body-was-found scene. Then offered a graceful silhouette against the darkened window as she started down the stairs, placing a hand on the metal pole railing that probably killed Gloria Tuschman. When had those fingers become as long and graceful as the rest of her? How could anyone be so awkward at fourteen and so all in place at fifteen?

Damn it, Libby, I forbid you to do this. "Libby, wait for me. What do you want to go down that way for?"

Charlie was in comfortable Keds instead of killer heels today but she could still hear her shoes hitting the stairs as she raced after her daughter.

Libby looked up from the landing below. When had she mastered that light touch with makeup? It was just right for her, highlighting the size and shape of her eyes and nose, blending out all but one or two of the zits around her mouth. With one fluid movement, this exasperating creature of Charlie's loins turned to descend to yet another floor.

Charlie caught up with her at the bottom of the stairs at the ground-level parking, and together they stepped out through the door that always opened from the inside but opened from the outside only with a private key.

Charlie headed for the Toyota. Libby headed for the alley.

"Shit." Charlie turned to follow, the burn in her stomach flaring up.

"Thought you gave up swearing," Libby's voice drifted dreamlike over her shoulder. She didn't stop until she stood before the white concrete-block wall with the green leaves and red blossoms that showed a lot more damage from murder down here than they did from the fifth floor window.

"How could anyone throw a dead body up there?" Libby asked.

"I think there were probably two people involved. Remember when Mrs. McDougal made you kids leave Doug's pool when she caught you and Doug swinging Lori by her wrists and ankles out over the water and letting go? I've a feeling that's something like what happened here."

Libby gave Charlie a skeptical look and walked around the wall to where the bushes grew to hide it from Mrs. Humphrys' off-alley parking and garage. Then she came back to stand at its end and look at both sides. "Sounds like you really are investigating."

"The world's not giving me much choice."

"You know who did it?"

"I've got some ideas about Gloria's death and even who might, in a panic, carry her out of the building. But it was so stupid." Was it a misguided attempt to draw suspicion away from the agency? "But I can't fit Mary Ann Leffler into the picture." I need to know where she was between the time she disappeared and the time she died.

"Mom, you and Ed have fun last night?"

Charlie felt the tenseness begin to seep out of her shoulders. Anything to get Libby's mind off murder. "Yeah, I did. He's a pretty mean dancer for a man his age." She did an imitation of Linda Meyer doing her quick bone shake-down at Richard's party the other night. "Even got to board the yacht."

"You know, I don't really think he's your type. I mean, I like him, but somehow I don't see the two of you as a match."

"Why not?" Reverse psychology really does work. I'll be damned. "He's got a gorgeous big house and a yacht and a racing boat. Lots of money. He's even good looking."

"He's too old for you. You'd be fine while I was home. But when I went off to college you'd be miserable. He sits around reading all the time, and when he falls asleep he snores."

"I thought you weren't going to college, were just going to get married and have babies."

"Well, either way, I'd be gone, wouldn't I? You wouldn't have anybody to have fun with."

"Libby, you're the one who started all this." Dorothy, there may be an Oz after all. "Let's go shopping, huh?"

But Libby walked listlessly through the first little shop. It was all leather with heavy-metal accessories. Charlie pretended interest, only to notice her daughter suddenly back out in the street waiting.

"I'm hungry."

Charlie took the fretful princess to the El Torito. To hell with her own stomach cancer. Again, over Coke and tacos and enchiladas, Libby maintained she didn't want to shop.

"Okay, after lunch we can go back home." Jesus will be gone by now. "I've got chores and shopping and reading to do. You can practice with Lori." Maybe we can talk on the way home, when you're fed and happy. We have to discuss what to do about the damned cat. Last day this week the animal shelter will be open.

"I don't want to go home."

"You don't want to go home." Charlie was picking out mostly guacamole, sour cream, beans, lettuce, tomato—staying off the salsa, but a wave of something in her abdomen got her attention.

"I want to investigate with you." Libby leaned across the table, dark eyes sparking. "Mo-om, don't you see? They're not going to expect you on a weekend. They're going to expect you to be home expecting me to take down my panties for the gardener. Right? We can catch them off guard." Libby crunched a taco shell so hard, her mother jumped. "Timing's perfect."

"They who?" Charlie pushed her plate away. "I mean, who's they?"

"Whoever killed Gloria and Mary Ann. You said it would take two to get Gloria up in the bushes—so it's they, right?"

"Where is it you suggest we investigate?"

"Well, if it's Mary Ann's death you can't figure out, why don't we start there? In the orange grove?"

"Because she drowned in Rizzi Reservoir and was taken to the grove afterwards."

"So let's go to Rizzi Reservoir."

Libby's insouciance was gone. Waves of adolescent energy slammed across the table. Oh boy.

"You keep saying 'Oh boy,'" Libby noted when they were once again back in the car. "Is that supposed to substitute for 'oh shit' or what?"

Charlie pretended to fight traffic and didn't answer. Why was she doing this? Giving in to a spoiled teen's every whim was asking for nothing but grief. Then again, they were communicating, and Libby wasn't getting into trouble, and maybe there would be a path to the kid's limited interest span from here. Maybe they could be friends someday. Maybe—

"Mom, why did the guys who found Mary Ann take her to the orange grove when she was already dead?"

"Well, first of all, they shouldn't have moved her. The police certainly prefer citizens not tamper with dead bodies and crime scenes." Odd that Charlie would even know two witches, let alone two dead ones whose bodies were moved after they got that way. "But they said they thought she could tell them something about how she died if she was in the place where she had played witch."

"Whoa ... like Gloria was trying to tell you something in the hallway there where you work, huh?"

Rizzi Reservoir looked different in real life than it had on TV news the night before. It was more your water-holding pond than your recreational spot.

The yellow crime scene tape was gone, but the area had seen a lot of unaccustomed traffic. The thin layer of coarse gravel that was provided for limited parking had been mashed into the linings of ruts after the recent rains. And Charlie and Libby Greene were not the only sightseers today. A middle-aged couple in black leather, silver studs, and helmets waddled back and forth across the remaining crime scene scenery, effectively destroying anything that might have been of interest to future voyeurs.

There was one other couple there, too. Gloria Tuschman's husband, Roger, and Marvin the Shaman Grunion.

"Libby, I think this might have been a bad idea. I think—"

But Libby was off to join the excitement and stomping of the crime scene. It was a pretty place—if you liked pretty places for loners—sort of a mountain valley with piney-type trees giving off piney smells, a few birds and bird calls, no freeway in sight.

Charlie decided to act natural rather than threatened until she could think of something better. She smiled and walked casually toward the two men. She could hardly pretend she didn't know them.

They both looked rumpled and decidedly seedy, as if they'd just stepped off a trans-Pacific flight.

"So, what have we here? Returning to the scene of the crime?" Gloria's husband stuck his face in Charlie's. "Tell me, how did you get Mary Ann to drive her car into the water like that? Or did you knock her out and then push it?"

Charlie swung her purse off her shoulder and wrapped the strap around her fist. She didn't answer him. She didn't back away, either. For God's sake, stay with those people, Libby.

"Control yourself, Roger," Marvin warned and forced his way between them just as the other man lunged.

Charlie watched Grunion's back absorb the shock and then straighten as Roger Tuschman's snarl dissolved into sobs. She stepped around them both to inspect the shaman's face.

He stroked the other man's hair, tears in his own eyes. "He really loved his wife, Mrs. Greene."

"Call me Charlie."

"Charlie, he won't be himself until they find out who killed her."

"I don't think she was exactly murdered," Charlie said, and Gloria's husband pushed away from the other man's arms to face her. "I think she was running from someone and fell in the back hall at the agency. I think she struck her head on the metal railing there, struck it in just the wrong way. I think it killed her, and the injury looked like a blow from a blunt instrument. If she'd been left there, it would probably have looked more like the accident it was. There might have been no charge of murder, maybe manslaughter or whatever. I think running in those high heels of hers may have caused the fall. That's bare tile back there, not carpet like in the offices and customer halls. It had been newly waxed the night before. I slid on it myself later that morning while looking for Gloria."

"Were you there?" Roger asked skeptically. "Did you see it? How else could you know?"

"Did Gloria's spirit tell you this?" Marvin asked almost at the same time.

"Gloria is dead and can't tell me anything. And no, I wasn't there."

"But who hauled her out to the alley and those bushes, and why?" Roger said, shaking off his friend's cautioning hand on his shoulder.

"I don't know who. But I suspect it was an attempt to shift suspicion from the agency. It was a stupid move and probably carried out in panic." And probably because everybody at Congdon and Morse has their identity tied up in their job. Except maybe Larry and Tracy.

"And because Gloria knew damaging secrets about everyone that could be used to destroy their professional positions. Because she had you, Roger, to broadcast them to the public if we didn't cooperate. But those secrets would come out in a police investigation anyway. Maybe whoever was responsible hoped it would look like anyone in the alley or elsewhere in the building could have killed her. Which was silly, because those who knew her would be looked at first and hardest."

"If you weren't there, you can't know any of this. But even if you're right, it's murder. Whoever chased my wife down that hallway and scared her so she fell and hit her head murdered her. And I think if that's what happened it would have to have been you, Charlie Greene," Roger said, never taking his eyes off Libby down by the water.

"Roger, Gloria said Charlie was psychic, remember? I feel that from her too. I doubt—"

"What do you know, Marv? You can't communicate with either Gloria or Mary Ann." Roger wore very little jewelry today. Just earrings and his wedding band. His face was swollen with grief far worse than either of the dead women's had been swollen by death. Her heart went out to him despite his threatening posture.

Charlie, this man's a blackmailer. For information, but he uses it to make money. Roger's identity is wrapped up in his work, too, and he lost a great conduit of information to feed his little empire of newsletters, books, mail-order seminars, and videos when he lost Gloria.

"So why did Mary Ann have to die, then?" Marvin asked Charlie, moving in front of Roger, maybe to interrupt the man's scrutiny of Libby. "If Gloria's death was an accident, was Mary Ann's too?"

"Mary Ann's death may have been planned. She'd been missing for over a week. Maybe she was kidnapped and then murdered."

"Oh, right." Roger looked away finally from Charlie's kid. "Mary Ann's death is premeditated while my wife's is an accident. People can drown by accident, too, you know. Or is it because Gloria died at *your* agency and Mary Ann died here, so far away from it?"

Charlie heard the Harley spit into life, rev, throw gravel when it took off, and Libby's footsteps coming up behind her. She saw Marvin's helpless shrug, saw Roger lunge past her frozen vision.

And all, it seemed, in an instant.

Then Roger stood before Charlie with Libby pasted to his front in a hostage position, the sharp edge of a pocket knife against her throat. "Funny how your deductive powers serve only your purposes, isn't it, Charlie Greene?"

Charlie drove the Toyota. Libby sat in back with Roger

Tuschman and the pocket knife. Marvin Grunion drove the old dusty blue pickup that had brought him and Roger to the reservoir. It tailgated her all the way to 1132 Honeah Place.

Marvin had pleaded with Roger not to do this. Charlie was disappointed when Marvin didn't turn off on a side road and race away to get help. Maybe he thought that would panic Roger into doing something even more drastic. Maybe Marvin had a cellular and had already punched 911. Maybe the police would be at the condo when they arrived.

Charlie's chick hadn't made a peep, and Charlie couldn't see her in the rearview mirror. When she started to turn her head, Roger snarled a warning.

"I don't understand why you're doing this," she mustered the courage to say, still numbed at how suddenly a normal day had turned on her. "We've done nothing to you."

"You killed my wife, bitch. Gloria practically said as much at the séance. Mary Ann dies, and who do the cops bring out to question at the scene? Just one suspect—you. We can't all be wrong." His voice dropped back to a snarl. "Marvin gets a 'feeling' about Rizzi Reservoir, and we go up there to see if there's any answers—and who comes along? You. I don't believe in coincidence, babe. Everything happens for a reason. And the reason Marv and I went to the reservoir today was to find justice for the murder of my wife. I think we found it."

If there was smog up here, Charlie couldn't detect any blurring of colors, which were stunningly bright even through her smear of tears. The two-lane road was black, the spring growth of weeds and trees bordering it, new-minted green. She had to slow for a gaggle of colorful cyclists, wanting to honk the Toyota's horn at them for help—the knife blade against her daughter's throat keeping her from it.

"If you hurt her, I'll kill you." Charlie thought she might have heard a slight whimper from the backseat.

Of course, no matter how glorious the day, no one at the apartment complex stood out around their back doors enjoying it at the particular moment Charlie, Libby, and their captor left the Toyota and entered 1132. No sign of police, either. Charlie could only hope someone would notice this outrage from a window and run to a phone and punch 911.

Libby was wide-eyed and pale. Never letting go of her, Roger exchanged the pocket knife for the far larger and more lethal ceremonial blade from the floor-to-ceiling shelves of fish-tank decor on the wall behind the dining room table where Marvin the Shaman had arranged and muttered over Gloria's effects the last time Charlie visited this place.

Holding the double-edged blade against Libby's long slender throat, Roger ordered them both into straight-backed chairs at the table in the dining room, and when Marvin arrived ordered him to bind Charlie to hers—chest, wrists, ankles—with strips of flat plastic ribbon rope. Charlie expected him to secretly cut her some slack. He had, after all, tried to talk his friend out of this. But the fake rope was so tight she felt the partial loss of blood flow to feet and hands within minutes.

Libby was soon bound the same way, but Roger added tape across her mouth. The two men went about silently closing Levelors against the beautiful day, where normal people went about their normal business, not knowing. Then they disappeared upstairs.

The room included a living room at the other end of the "L" that held the dining room, plus the small kitchen across the counter space. Charlie thought of screaming for the neighbors, but feared the two men would rush down to hurt Libby before help arrived. You had to be pretty brave to answer screams nowadays.

Libby's eyes questioned Charlie's, a lone tear dropping suddenly down a smooth cheek and across the tape that kept her silent.

"Hang in there, honey, I'm working on it."

Charlie must have imagined the incredulous look across the table. The same look Libby had displayed earlier that day when Charlie realized she'd never brought her daughter to the agency before.

When Marvin and Roger returned, they wore long, black, hot-looking robes. They set the large candelabrum in the center of the table and lit the one red and three white candles. Marvin's expression suggested he wasn't going to be any help after all. Roger set the lemon skewered with nails before Charlie, while Marvin lit a stick of incense that gave off an odor Charlie could equate only with that of vomit.

"Now I want you to tell me what brought you to Rizzi Reservoir on this particular day, Charlie Greene," he intoned. "And if you lie, your daughter will suffer for it before your eyes."

"I went to Rizzi Reservoir because Libby wanted to see where Mary Ann drowned."

"Wanted to see where her dear mother committed a crime?" Roger took over. "Why did you kill Mary Ann Leffler? What had she ever done to you?"

"I didn't kill her." Please Marvin, tell me you called 911 on the way here.

Roger leaned over Charlie so close she could smell his excited sweat through the putrid incense. "Why did you chase my wife down that hall then?"

"I didn't."

"How did you get her out to those bushes off the alley? You couldn't have done it alone. Who helped you?"

"I didn't do that, either."

Roger went to the kitchen, and after a while returned with a pewter plate. He passed it back and forth under Charlie's nose. There was something long and flat and sliced on it. He mumbled from deep in his throat and then lit a match to the juice on the plate. The fumes came right into Charlie's head before she had the sense to hold her breath.

She had an impromptu memory of her mother mellowing uncharacteristically after a shot of something while being prepped for surgery years ago. Edwina had turned her eyes in drunken love toward Charlie, who found the situation embarrassing. Charlie ached with wanting to embarrass Libby the same way, but drifted away before she could focus.

Charlie came back to a melodic ringing in her ears. She wanted to slide back into the peaceful sleep where she had been so comfortable, but a dancing flame directly in front of her divided into two dancing flames and then into four. Small flames. How did they do that?

"Who helped you carry Gloria Tuschman out to the bushes?" a voice echoed from on high, and something black blocked out the miraculous flames.

Charlie giggled. People should feel this good all the time. "They held her by the ankles and the wrists and swung her back and forth and flll-ung her up over the wall and into the bushes."

"Who did this?"

"I don't know them, but they're always out there. They're real easy to piss off, too." Charlie started laughing with no good idea why.

"Do you see Libby? Do you see what I'm going to do to her?"

"I see these cute little fires coming apart and coming together. Soooo—"

"Move the damn candles," another voice said.

"Now do you see her?"

"Nooooo."

"Take the tape off and let the kid talk to her mother."

"Tell your mother—"

"I have to pee and I'm pretty sure throw up, too." Libby's voice came from far away and in a panic. Probably too much pepperoni and cheese.

"Oh, shit. Take her to the can, Marv. Hurry, cleaning lady won't be in for a week."

"I don't think that woman killed anyone. But she might be able to tell us who did. She's psychic, all right."

"Take the kid up to the can, Marv."

Charlie wasn't feeling so euphoric suddenly. Her hands and feet had frozen into solid chunks. A weird sensation moved inside her.

"Jesus, Marv, get back down here! She's ... Oh, God. Oh, shit. Marv?"

Is that blood? What do we do? She going to die?"

"I'm not a doctor, Roger. Untie her. Rub her hands. Circulation's cut off."

"You rub her hands. You tied her up. Where's the kid?"

"Upstairs in the bathroom."

"You left her alone up there? What are you—crazy?"

"Even I can't be two places at once. Charlie, can you hear me? It's Marvin. Charlie?"

Charlie could hear them both. She couldn't seem to work up the energy to answer, though.

"Don't worry, Charlie," Marvin was whispering now, "I'll get help. I'm in enough trouble for moving Mary Ann from the reservoir. I'm not taking the blame for this, too. Not even for Roger. He's a crazy man. Lie still now, I'll be back."

"Hey, don't leave me alone with him, forgodsake," Charlie was pretty sure she said aloud. But she could feel the draft from the open doorway. She was laid out on the couch facing it. It was night out there.

Upstairs Roger stomped about, slamming doors, swearing in an increasingly unstable pitch. Charlie had about decided to get herself into a sitting position when he came thundering down the stairs. She closed her eyes and hoped she looked dead instead.

"Fucking tramp kid. She's gone, Marv. What she do? Fly? Jump from a second story window? Last time I listen to you, buddy. Marv? Marv!" His swearing degenerated to grunts and enraged snorts before he, too, ran out the door. But Roger slammed it behind him.

The odor of vomit was more than incense now. Charlie's head and heart pounded in syncopation. She struggled to find the proper muscles and inform them she wanted to sit up.

"Mom?" Libby whispered from the head of the stairs, and Charlie managed to sit up too fast.

"They're both gone for a minute. Hurry."

Libby came down the stairs running. "Let's make a run for the car and the cellular."

"Where's my purse? We'll need the keys."

"Right here." Libby bent down beside the shelves of occult paraphernalia.

Leaning on her child, Charlie found herself run-walked to the door on numbed feet. It opened easily from inside, and they were out in the night, Charlie sucking in cool orange-blossom air. They could hear Roger's demented screaming not far away. Libby shoved Charlie into the rider's side of the Toyota, slamming the door on her.

"Whadaya gonna do?" Charlie asked, her tongue getting lost in a general scary dizziness, when Libby climbed in behind the wheel and flipped the door locks.

"Help me find the keys, Mom, don't wig out on me now."

"Keys. Help her find the keys. Don't wig—" Charlie pawed through her purse with hands that had no feeling in places and were filled with painful tingles in others. She did feel the plastic teeth of the shark key chain her daughter had given her for Christmas and pulled out the private keys to her life. "Still wanna know what you're gonna do. You can't drive."

"Mom, don't start in being trouble, okay? We're in really deep shit here. And I'm the best we got. Which one's the car key?"

"One with the black rubber top thingy on it. Here comes Roger." Charlie wasn't sure which she feared most. Libby trying to drive or Gloria's deranged husband throwing himself across the Toyota's hood, as if that would stop it. "You even know how to start this thing? How to get it in reverse?"

But Libby already had it started and in reverse. Charlie hoped there was no one behind them, human or automobile. This was the first and only new car she'd ever owned, and it wouldn't be paid off until Martians landed in Manhattan. Kansas. The dependable little model that never broke down. But the cellular was dead. Probably because the cord to the receiver had been sliced through.

Charlie watched Roger's surprised look as the three of them set off across the parking lot. Two inside and one out. She tried to marshal her wits to save her child. She must do something heroine-like. "Where did you learn to drive a five-speed?"

"I only sort of did. Doug's dad's car. He'd leave it home when he went traveling, and when Mrs. McDougal would take the station wagon to go shopping, we'd practice on the—"

"Not the Porsche?" Charlie watched Roger slide off the hood as they passed under a lone streetlight at the entrance to Happy Valley Canyon Road. At least he went sideways so they didn't run him over.

"Well, you never leave this heap home for kids to learn on. And Lori's mom never leaves home, period. What are we supposed to do?" Libby pulled out onto the two-lane road.

"Libby, you're in the wrong lane." And in the wrong gear. And this should not be happening to you.

And the Toyota dropped dead. Left them sitting crosswise in the middle of a road with a blind curve in front of them and one in back. And not that far from their front and back, either.

"Told you this was a dreary pile of junk. If you weren't so cheap."

"This little number has never let me down. Not once. Just relax, try again." Before someone comes barreling around the corner and kills us. "You're working the clutch wrong. Don't flood the engine."

"Mo-om, shut the fuck up."

When Libby started using four-letter words in earnest and against Charlie, the grating shock value of those same tired expressions took on sudden added power. So Charlie decided to break the habit, be a better role model. It hadn't worked. Nothing worked. Not even her cellular.

"Not even my Toyota Corolla." Charlie started bawling.

"It's okay. You're just drugged up. And you barfed all over yourself. And you're sick anyway."

"I stink."

"Hey, you can't help it. I'll get us out of this. Just relax." And the kid had the engine running again, even eased the car over into the right lane before it jerked to a stop once more. "Now what did I do?"

"You were in third instead of first." What was the use? The whole world was against Charlie. "Where's that stupid Marvin? He was going to go for help."

"I don't know, but somebody's pulling up behind us in that dirty blue pickup, and I have the feeling it's Roger." Libby had the Toyota moving once again, and this time in first. "I can't see. . . ."

"Turn on the lights."

"How? Can't you do it? I don't want to worry you, but I don't think I have time, Mom."

The lights coming at them were almost as good, but Charlie leaned across to flick the left wand. The headlights showed the close-up of the coming collision in an overexposed shot. Charlie and her daughter groaned in unison.

At the same time Libby, in the sort of perfect reflex action only the young brain can produce without thinking, nearly put them in the trees on the other side of the road and in a 180. All this before Charlie could blink away her tears to see it happen. The oncoming car, too, must have escaped oblivion because the dirty blue pickup careened up the road behind them, unscathed.

Then they were off again, but something wasn't right. The Toyota began to smell almost as bad as Charlie. "Oh, boy."

"What's that smell?"

"You forgot to release the emergency brake. It's this cute little handle here between us." Charlie released it and the Toyota leapt into the air. "You're going to have to shift sometime. You can't stay in first."

"I just want to stop. But I can't remember how. And I can't let you down. You're all sick and I need to—"

"Honey, I'm feeling lots better." Actually, Charlie was feeling lots more frightened. "Now let up gradually with your right foot on that pedal, but keep an eye on the curves. We're going to make it, don't worry." We have to change drivers before the pickup turns around and catches up with us, is what we have to do. "Okay, now move that right foot over to the next pedal, and get that left one working the clutch and ease into that paved turnoff ahead. If you can't make that, no big deal, there'll be another soon."

Libby killed the engine again, but not before she had them pretty much off the road. She did it without hitting a tree, ditch, or embankment. Charlie pulled her stinking T-shirt off and flung it at the darkness at the side of the road while she and her daughter raced to exchange places.

"Mom?"

"I can't stand the smell. Neither can you. I'm wearing a bra."

"Just get us out of here. I sure hope you've sobered up."

Me too. "No problem."

Automatically scanning the lighted dials on the dash, Charlie changed her plans and swung the Toyota around, heading them back the way they'd come. She blinked her contacts back into place and squinted at the road ahead.

"You're taking us right back into trouble. Jeez, I thought you were sober."

"Libby, I don't know what's up there. Not much I think. We're running low on gas, and this way leads back to safety and to the police, I hope." Someone must have called them by now. "When I came to, it was night. What happened all that time I was out?"

"You kept talking crazy stuff. You seemed like you were awake a lot." Marvin had decided that if Charlie inhaled the proper mixture of exotic herbs, her natural psychic ability would overcome her right brain, and she'd be able to contact both Mary Ann and Gloria.

"Did I contact them?"

"You went on mostly about the funny things you were seeing and about why you and grandma don't get along and how you were afraid I'd turn out like you. You even started singing some embarrassing song, and you can't carry a tune when you're high, either. What were those herbs?"

"Sounds like nature's own psychedelics. Libby, they didn't do anything to you, did they? While I was out of it?"

"They were too busy getting high themselves and then getting mad at each other. And then getting mad at you because you wouldn't get to the point. You're starting to drive kind of funny."

"I know." The double center line wiggled like a snake, and a tree walked right into the middle of the road.

Libby reached over and jerked the wheel, and the tree

stepped aside. And bowed. "Pull over and rest a minute. Let's think about this, okay?"

"I'm afraid to stop. I'll just go real slow. How did you get away to hide upstairs?"

"The geek with the nose hairs stuck me in the bathroom and held the door open a little so I couldn't lock it." When Marvin rushed downstairs in answer to Roger's call, Libby ran into a bedroom. "I hid on a closet shelf behind some blankets and pillows. When that Roger guy came banging around looking for me, he checked out the closet floor and the wall behind the hanging stuff. Didn't even look up on the shelf. That closet smelled bad like Grandma's house. Mom . . . I think he wants you to pull over."

The flashing lights and the siren were the last things Charlie remembered before she found herself trying to walk in a straight line down the road in her bra. Libby was shouting at a police officer, "She's not drunk, you moron. We've been kidnapped. She's drugged."

Charlie lay flat on her back looking up at Maggie Stutzman's devilish smile, trying to remember why. "I knew you were faking it, Greene."

"How'd you get out here?"

"We're in Canoga Park Hospital, and you're going to be okay."

"Where's Libby?"

"Asleep over there in the chair. She's in a lot better shape than you are, but I can't get her to leave."

"My throat's so sore."

"That's because they stuck a tube thing down it to fix a little hole in your tummy. Not to worry."

• • •

David Dalrymple leaned over Charlie. "Feeling better, Miss Greene? Not to worry. We have Roger Tuschman under lock and key. We have some leads on Grunion. And there's a guard outside your door."

"But Marvin was going to go for help."

"Afraid he headed for LAX instead."

"But he tried to talk Roger out of taking us."

"Maybe Grunion's psychic powers told him he was getting in too deep with kidnapping."

"Did he go off to the airport in a dirty blue pickup?"

"Seventy-nine Ford, blue, well worn. Why?"

"We thought it was Roger. That's why he didn't come after us."

"We found Roger stoned in the grove, talking to his dead wife." Neighbors had called police when the commotion finally interfered with their dwindling leisure time.

"Where is Libby?"

"Gone home with Miss Stutzman for a much needed rest."

"Do you know where Mary Ann was the week before she died? Was she kidnapped?"

"Roger Tuschman claims she spent that time at his condo. That she drove up the night of the memorial séance after everyone had left, demanding he take her in and hide her. Apparently, she was delusional. She had to get away from personal demons. He claims her car was parked in the lot behind his condominium complex the whole week we were searching for it. But the night of her death he came home to find it gone. He says he helped her hide because he hoped she could help him contact the dead Mrs. Tuschman."

"But she was having problems with the Tuschmans. They wanted some of the money from *Shadowscapes*. If she wanted to go away, she could go home to her family."

"Again, according to Mr. Tuschman—Mary Ann Leffler suffered from mid-life symptoms that had left her family fed up. One of the reasons her husband was in Canada, in fact. She insisted they were the last people she'd go to for help."

"Keegan said she was afraid of L.A., too. Had anxiety attacks." And Libby said that closet smelled like her grandmother's house. Neither Tuschman smoked, but Mary Ann and Edwina were heavy smokers.

"Well, Miss Greene," Dr. Williams had replaced Dalrymple when she woke next, "I wish we hadn't needed to be so precipitous with your treatment, but it looks as if the cauterization was a success. You had a tiny perforation of the stomach lining, which we have sealed. You're young and healthy. If you keep your stress levels down and alter your life-style appropriately, you should be home free."

He patted Charlie's shoulder and was gone. Three minutes later she could barely remember what he looked like. Generic medicine, generic doctors.

32

Richard Morse, Irma Vance, and Maurice Lavender stood around Charlie's bed the next morning. Richard was saying, "So what's it going to be, Charlie? You want Maurice here put in jail and Medora Lavender left to her own devices in that nursing home? You want Irma in prison for just trying to save his tush and thwart a blackmailer? She's had her problems under control for years. They got great drugs for that stuff now. The Scarborough House thing is history. Hey, you're calling the shots, babe. You heard the tapes."

"Why didn't Lieutenant Dalrymple? If I could find them, his men could." Then again, they couldn't find Mary Ann's rental car parked in the Tuschmans' parking lot—if one could believe Roger. As much as she didn't want to, Charlie did.

Now the boss was saying, "But they didn't find them. Old Charlie did, though. If she could just keep Irma and Maurice out of jail for pulling a stupid but well-intentioned stunt—which on the face of it wasn't a bad idea. Irma had noticed some unsavory types hanging out in the alley, so some bum doing in Gloria wasn't that far-fetched. They thought they'd wiped all trace of Gloria off the railing."

"Richard, tapes or no, the Beverly Hills P.D. probably has both deaths about solved. They and the courts will decide who goes to jail and who doesn't. Besides, somebody was whispering up or down the stairwell and trying to sound like Gloria, someone who kept saying she was in the trash can."

"Who would pretend to be Gloria and do that? Not Irma or Maurice. Who else knew she was even dead till the next day?" He raised his hands toward the ceiling like a TV evangelist. "Wouldn't it be the mother of all ironies if Gloria herself managed to tip off the Beverly Hills P.D. that way? God, talk about your concept."

"But she wasn't even in a trash can."

"Hey, for goofy Gloria, that's close enough."

"We did not put Gloria in the bushes." Irma rubbed enlarged knuckles in an odd, nervous gesture Charlie had never seen before.

"You put her in the dumpster, which is more logical. Why do I have the feeling there were more than two of you? Did Mary Ann help?"

Maurice sat on Charlie's bed to hold her hand in one of his and stroke it with the other. It was the most natural thing, and yet he'd chased the office witch out into the hall in a rage so awful she fell and struck her head. And then he helped stuff her into the bag on the janitor's trolley and later in the day—in fact shortly before security and the police searched the entire building for her—helped carry her down the back stairs and out to the alley. Something didn't wash.

"Far as I know, Mary Ann was nowhere near the agency at the time," Maurice said.

"Okay, then who *was* the third culprit here? You and Irma may have stuffed Gloria into the bag, may have even gotten her body down the back stairs in that bag. I just wondered if you had help tossing her up into the dumpster?"

Maurice and Irma slid each other a hasty glance. Maurice's stroking paused. "And Maurice, you might have been the reason, but I think Irma was the one who scared Gloria." Always the gentleman. In one way your poor Medora is a lucky lady. "I heard the tapes, remember? Why didn't somebody destroy them?"

"When the cops didn't find them, Irma decided that was the safest place for them. Those guys were dropping in whenever they felt like it. That way nobody'd catch her trying to get rid of evidence," Richard said. "Simplicity always works best. These two just explained the whole thing to me on the way up here. First I knew the tapes existed."

"Are they covering for you, Richard?"

He pulled long fingers through short hair and then ran them down the back of his neck before he met her eyes. "I knew Gloria was getting information over the phone lines, didn't know she was taping it. Irma found the tape machine when she felt it with her foot while working the reception desk after Gloria died."

"Who was bugging my office, then?"

"Irma. Charlie, I had to know how things were coming with your snooping. I'm responsible for the whole agency. I knew Dalrymple would be talking to you about things he wouldn't let you share with me. I knew you were ornery enough not to share them anyway. I had to have that information. Think about it. Makes sense, babe."

"If Larry loses his job because of your stupid mistrust, I will never forgive you, Richard."

"No stress now, remember?" Maurice gently pushed her back into the pillows and patted her hand instead of stroking it.

"I like The Kid. Hell, I like Stew Claypool. But I admit if Larry's new career leads him elsewhere I'm gonna be relieved. He comes back from wiggling his buns on the beach and takes up his old job, I don't say anything to the agency insurance company unless they come say something to me. Best I can do."

Charlie still wasn't satisfied. "I have trouble believing Dalrymple's people didn't find Gloria's recording machine. Now you're telling me they didn't find Irma's? I know they searched her office."

"Yeah, but they didn't search my partner's. At least not very well." Richard allowed a slow, satisfied grin. He'd always resented Dalrymple's coming in and taking over.

"You hid the recorder in Mr. Congdon's office?"

"Right, but we accessed it through your wall. So there were no footprints in the dust in his office. Looked like nobody'd been in there to set it up, see? Irma's idea. Sharp lady, Irma." Richard nodded emphasis and then kept on nodding.

"Through my wall . . . there's no hole in my wall."

"I sort of cut one, Charlie dear. Behind that garish book-store poster you insisted upon installing. On the other side of it, in Mr. Congdon's office, there's an enclosed cupboard with shelves but no backing. The drywall could be cut, lifted out, and slid back in after the recording device was inside. No one had to disturb the dust on Mr. Congdon's floor. So the police assumed no one had been in the office, which was true, and they therefore did not make a very thorough search."

"But the hole's still there, right?"

"Let's say it's no longer apparent. If you insist upon point-ing it out to the police, I'm sure they'll find it." Irma's demeanor said that if the police made a big deal of this, Larry Mann and probably Charlie Greene could go whistling for work in this town, even if the executive secretary had to arrange it from a jail cell.

Richard turned to the door. "Just get well fast and wrap things for us, will ya? So we can all get back to work."

Irma gave Charlie a calculated look before she followed him.

Maurice lingered a moment as if not quite sure she should be left alone. "I'm sorry for all this, sweetie."

"Maurice, how could you let Irma talk you into moving Gloria?"

"Scarborough House housed only the most violent and dangerous of the mentally ill, Charlie. Irma's life was completely turned around by a new drug twenty years ago. Dr. Podhurst still administers it. She would have been a prime suspect if it was deemed a murder. And you know how much the agency means to her. Me, too. But Charlie, neither of us had anything to do with Mary Ann Leffler's drowning, I swear."

Sheldon Maypo was Charlie's next visitor. "Your hunch was right. I even managed to interview one of the culprits. They hadn't been questioned by the police yet, either. We're ahead of dippy Dalrymple, my dear, even though we're denied his sources of information. And without the use of psychic powers, too."

"I just can't factor Mary Ann into it. It seems like too much of a coincidence that the two deaths weren't connected."

"I'll keep snooping around, drop in earlier in the day, talk up more people."

"The thing is, I don't want it to be anybody I like, Shelly. I'm already sick that Maurice is involved. He might get some kind of a deal. But I think Irma's in big trouble. After all she's been through, she finally has some luck and wins big in Vegas, and then has to go to jail instead of enjoying it. And if Luella is involved I'll slit my wrists. And if it's Richard, well, that's the end of everything. Why couldn't it be Dorian the Jerk? Or even Tracy? And if it's Keegan. . . . I even fantasize that it was Roger and Marvin Grunion who killed Mary Ann because I don't like them."

"Promise me you'll never go into police work," Shelly chided her and took his leave.

Charlie was sent home that day, told to rest a week before returning to work. Right. Sure.

Doug Esterhazie dropped off a large, elegantly wrapped package practically the moment she arrived. It was from "Ed and Dorothy."

"Doug says it's really from Mrs. McDougal, which means it's food. Mom," Libby's hand stopped Charlie's still trying to untie a six inch wide ribbon. "Do you mind a lot?"

"God no, Mrs. McDougal is probably among the ten best cooks on earth."

"No, I mean about Dorothy. Here I got you and Ed together and he goes back to her. I feel bad. Now that I've thought about it I think you're better off, but still it was wrong to get your hopes up if—"

"Honey, I like Doug's dad." Charlie clasped the hand that had been over hers for a rare, intimate moment and even got in a squeeze before it withdrew. "He's a nice guy, but there was no . . . we didn't feel uh—"

"Sexual attraction?"

"Welllll yeah, for starters."

Charlie's condo mates all showed up to get the latest news on the murders and to pay for it with gifts and opinions.

Mrs. Beesom handed Charlie a tuna casserole. "It was those two warlocks that kidnapped you and Libby. They look like murderers."

Charlie so wished Mrs. Beesom could be right. But as Libby pointed out, "If they already knew, why would they tie us to chairs and ask mom all those questions?"

"Maurice might be able to plea bargain his way out of an actual prison term if he agrees to testify against Irma," Maggie offered on the death of Gloria when she brought over a fruit basket.

"The D.A. will say it's murder instead of an accident. Whoever chased the witch down the hall will be accused of murder, the other one an accomplice," Jeremy predicted. "Probably settle for manslaughter or something."

David Dalrymple gave her until the next afternoon. He brought Detective Gordon. They settled out on Charlie's patio with tall glasses of iced tea.

Marvin Grunion had been traced to San Francisco and arrested for kidnapping and for selling illicit drugs to the Tuschmans' coven. They'd charged Roger with kidnapping as well.

"But not for the murder of Mary Ann Leffler," Charlie said.

"Not for the murder of Mary Ann Leffler."

"Made some arrests on the Tuschman case though," Detective Gordon said with satisfaction, ignoring the sharp look from Dalrymple.

"Maurice and Irma, right? Lieutenant, that was an accident, and a stupid attempt at a cover up—surely you can see that."

"I'd like to have your version of what happened to Gloria Tuschman that morning, Charlie, before my colleague and I go into any more detail. Please?" This was the first time she could remember him using her first name.

Charlie told him about the Tuschmans profiting from insider information at the agency. "It got so lucrative Gloria threatened to expose personal secrets to the tabloids as a way to throw her weight around and force the staff to cooperate. That morning Irma came back early from Vegas, unannounced, to find Gloria using poor Medora Lavender's existence to persuade Maurice. He probably has the highest-quality insider info in the agency, next to Richard Morse. Irma is a formidable lady, and her fury over what Gloria was doing scared the witch into throwing down the pencil stubs and taking off for the back hall. Gloria knew about Scarborough House and Irma's violent past, remember. Gloria may have fled to the ladies to lock herself in a stall, I don't know. Eventually she had to come out, and there was Irma. They haggled and Irma probably fired Gloria on the spot. Gloria ran for the back stairs and slipped on the newly waxed floor, and hit her head on the metal railing in a freak accident. Leaving Irma with a body instead of the simpler problem of replacing a receptionist."

"Why didn't she fire Gloria earlier? The woman had made enough trouble before this."

"It wasn't that easy. Gloria had something on Irma, too. Richard Morse knew about Scarborough House, but that didn't mean Irma wanted the rest of the world to."

"So Gloria fell and died in a bizarre accident?"

"Right, then Irma rushed back to get help from Maurice, and they decided it would look like murder, especially with Irma's history. The dirt on everyone else would surface with an investigation, too. Maurice is such a gentleman he couldn't let Irma take the blame, so they hatched this incredible plot to move the body. First they hid it in the utility closet and left the building. It would look like Maurice was out on business, and Irma wasn't even due in that day. Then later, when the coast was clear, they trundled Gloria out to the alley to make it look as if the death was not agency-related."

"Miss Vance and Mr. Lavender, fifty-five and sixty, toss a dead body up over a high concrete wall with such force it sinks into the bushes on the other side?"

"They toss Gloria into the dumpster off the alley next to the end wall of the bank parking. Two homeless men in the dumpster resent Gloria's arrival, so they haul her out and toss her up over the next wall and into the bushes. They're younger and stronger. People who live on the streets often sleep in the alleys, scrounge meals from the dumpsters behind buildings that have restaurants, but prefer to sleep in those behind office buildings with better-smelling trash. And on a street like Wilshire, they don't want to be too obvious, so they tend to lie low when they can or risk being relocated by the Beverly Hills P.D. or private security forces. And at that time of day that dumpster would have been emptied, so they wouldn't be disturbed, and it would be in the shade. Good place to sleep or do some serious drinking without being seen."

"And how could a woman who wears the kind of shoes you do and who so rarely investigates that neighborhood possibly discover all this?"

"I have a friend on the security staff snooping for me, and he even interviewed one of the homeless men involved, and occasionally I do step outside and see guys, mostly, rifling through alley garbage for food. And just recently I tossed something into the dumpster in question and somebody inside tossed it out again and started heaving other things, too. And the night of Richard's party my date and I stopped in at the agency on the way home and we were shushed by a guy trying to sleep on the other side of the wall. And that," Charlie said triumphantly, "is where I got the idea. No hocus-pocus, just good old following through with logic."

"Why would these vagrants risk becoming involved in a murder, as vulnerable as they are to suspicion by civilian and police alike? And you still haven't explained how Mr. Lavender and Irma Vance could have tossed the body up into the dumpster, not to mention move her five floors down to the alley level."

"Shelly, my informant, says those alleys are a jungle, and the bums get territorial. Most of the good alley shelters are taken, and the current residents don't encourage newcomers. Too many vagrants in one place invites eviction. Both had left once they'd sobered up and realized there'd be cops around soon, but one guy came back because he couldn't find another place. And I think a third person helped Irma and Maurice with the body, but I don't know who."

"We do," Detective Gordon said.

33

Dr. Evan Podhurst had confessed to helping Irma and Maurice hide Gloria in the janitor's closet, and later in the day he and Maurice hauled her down in the bag from the cleaning trolley while Irma went ahead to let them know when the coast was clear.

"You know, that's possible," Charlie said. "I went up and down those back stairs several times the other day and didn't see a soul. They must have really been surprised when Gloria turned up in the bushes. Why did Dr. Podhurst help them? You'd think he'd have some sense, if they didn't."

"Two reasons. He claims to have heard a sound from his office and opened the door onto the private hall just in time to see Gloria slip and fall. He also claims that Irma Vance was just stepping out of the ladies' room at the time. He had treated her in Scarborough house some twenty years ago and was still responsible for her drug therapy. Scarborough handled only the most difficult patients—"

"Yeah, and it's been closed for years, so those kind of nuts are on the streets now," Gordon added. "Think about it."

"Ms. Vance's terror of being accused of murder, and the certainty that Gloria's death would not even be considered as an accident convinced the other two to attempt a cover-up."

"Why in hell would Morse hire someone like her?" Gordon wanted to know. "He knew about Scarborough House."

"That's just like him," Charlie said. "He likes to think he

runs a tight ship, but when it comes down to it, it's Irma who takes care of most of the problems you have to deal with, and usually you figure it isn't worth it to bring one up. Now I know why. But Podhurst didn't have his new hearing aid yet the day Gloria died. How could he hear something going on in the hall that morning?"

"He says he often heard sounds such as people speaking but couldn't make out what they were saying. His hearing loss caused him to search out sources of sounds he could not identify to reassure himself they were real and not a sign of something dangerous hidden in his mind. Which, given his profession, isn't as far-fetched as one might at first think."

"Where was Linda Meyer, his receptionist, all this time?"

"In the outer office, typing dictation with earphones on."

"But Mary Ann wasn't a threat to anyone. Why did she have to die?"

"We were hoping to hear your ideas on that."

"I don't have any."

"Oh, I think you do. Charlie," David Dalrymple's voice softened, and he'd used her first name again. "Whatever you think of your powers of deduction, which are impressive and imaginative, you have another power that's kicking in to help out when you forget to fend it off. How else could you have known Mr. Lavender and Miss Vance were involved at all in Gloria Tuschman's death before they came to the hospital yesterday?"

"Oh, didn't I tell you? Damn, I forgot." Gotcha now, Dalrymple. "I assumed you knew about the tapes under Gloria's desk."

Over the protests of everyone she knew, Charlie was at work the next day.

She missed seeing gorgeous Larry in his cubbyhole. He and

Stew had sent flowers to the hospital, but Larry was doing *real work* today. She checked the wall behind A.E.'s poster and found the outlines of Irma's hole. Somebody had done a good repair job. She sat behind her desk, put her feet up. Charlie loved this place and the excitement of the work. Would she kill to keep it?

Someone had left a callback slip on her desk from Carla Ponti at Goliath. Charlie punched the number, dreading that Mary Ann's death would have cooled Goliath's ardor for the *Shadowscapes* project. They'd probably use the economy as an excuse. They always did.

"Charlie, the script is wonderful. This one's definitely a green light. It's going to be bigger than *Witches of Eastwick*. We're so impressed. And it's good to hear you're back at work. I heard about the kidnapping. Are you and your daughter all right?"

"We're fine, thanks, Carla. Um ... you don't have any problem about Mary Ann's murder influencing the project?"

"Oh, God no, it's instant publicity if we move fast enough so everyone doesn't forget the details. In fact, I just got out of a meeting where they were throwing around the idea of a spin-off about her death. You know, witch writer comes to Hollywood, gets murdered by a coven of rival witches or something. Any writers you might suggest to work it up for us? You've been coming up with winners lately."

Charlie's spirits rose for a minute. She straightened up in her chair and nodded at Luella Ridgeway, who'd stepped in the door, and gestured for her to take a seat. "Well, yeah I have several," Charlie told her, feeling like a working agent again instead of a sick-at-heart detective. "Let me send you over some samples."

Luella had gone to stand in front of the window instead of sitting. She turned from watching the street below when

Charlie put down the phone. "Charlie, I've come to apologize for blaming you for doing what you had to do. Someday, years from now, I will probably discover how we have all benefited from your strange need to confess the truth to everyone you meet and tell the police every last thing you know or even suspect about the rest of us."

Actually, Luella couldn't be more wrong, Charlie thought as she headed the Toyota out of the alley and up Wilshire only minutes later.

But when she arrived, Dalrymple's unmarked car and a black and white already sat on the leveled parking area below the house in Coldwater Canyon. Charlie almost turned around, but decided that wouldn't change anything.

Keegan Monroe wore a pair of faded jeans and his tinted glasses, no shirt or shoes. He hadn't shaved in several days. He made a sound low in his throat when he saw her, but that was the only greeting.

He and the homicide lieutenant sat in Keegan's kitchen drinking coffee. Like friends.

"I'm sorry, Charlie," her client said. "I just wanted her okay on the script. I thought she could swim."

"I would have expected you to have been here long ago." Dalrymple pulled out a chair at Keegan's table for Charlie. "When did you know?"

Always, never. He was the only one with a motive. He never called or came to the hospital to see me. She reached across the table to take both of Keegan's hands in hers. They were clammy. "Better not say any more until you've talked to a lawyer. You've called someone?"

"Yeah. But Charlie, when I left, Mary Ann was swimming back to shore, I swear it."

Mary Ann had been hiding out at Roger Tuschman's because, according to Roger, she couldn't face working on the script with Keegan that night as she'd promised. He was younger, faster with words, accustomed to working under intense deadlines without breaking for sleep at night, working through a project without giving a thought to anyone else's schedule.

Mary Ann had spent her working life fitting her work around the lives and schedules of husband and children. The last child no sooner left home than the husband retired and the grandchildren showed up at times scheduled by their lives and not hers. She wasn't that aware of the difference until she began working intensely with a younger single man who had never known those constraints and who was also very talented.

"She fled rather than face working with Mr. Monroe that night. Writing must be more competitive than I would have thought to arouse that kind of sentiment," David Dalrymple told Charlie as they once again sat on the stone steps between terraces outside Keegan's house. Charlie's client and two uniformed officers had driven off in the black and white.

"Mary Ann *had* been invited to that exotic memorial service," Dalrymple continued, "but I think she chose not to go, fearing she could be a suspect in Gloria's murder because of her dispute with the Tuschmans. She'd hoped to distance herself from them at that point. But when it came down to it, she headed for a familiar place and familiar face. She feared the city."

Mary Ann had seemed like such a tough lady. Charlie had figured almost everybody wrong. Good thing she wasn't in law enforcement, or the psychic business, either. Manipulative, coercive Roger Tuschman really had adored his grating wife.

Flabby, grizzled Marvin the Shaman had never intended to get help to rescue Charlie and Libby from mad Roger.

Maurice, the lover and womanizer, was in reality devoted to the shell of a wife. Irma, of the razor-sharp brain, was an ex–mental patient. Luella, Charlie's role model, had a prison record. And Dorian Black, whom she could barely tolerate and considered a sleaze, apparently had a clean record. Charlie was no judge of character, that was certain. And then there was Keegan Monroe . . . one of her favorite people in the world.

Keegan had tracked Mary Ann down to the place where he first met her on a Halloween night, to get her literary blessing on a copy of the *Shadowscapes* screenplay already turned in to Charlie. "Your client says he needed her reassurance."

And he told me at Richard's party he thought Mary Ann was dead, and yet he went looking for her. But Charlie said aloud, "Didn't you check Roger's place when Mary Ann went missing?"

"We were looking for a body underwater in a car by that time."

"Oh, boy."

When Keegan found her, the night before Charlie saw her body in the orange grove, the novelist was depressed, bored, and housebound. And she'd run out of vodka. Again, according to Roger—she was anxious and a little ashamed of her erratic behavior and didn't know how to explain it to her family. They had already shown some impatience with her unpredictability symptoms, and she put off coming out in the open, not knowing how to explain her disappearance without looking foolish.

"In other words she was at sixes and sevens by the time Mr. Monroe located her. She told him she had to get out of the tiny condo and consented to read the screenplay if he would buy vodka and meet her up at the reservoir, which she had visited with the Tuschmans on an earlier trip to California. The two had the place to themselves, but Mary Ann made fun of the script and of Keegan's writing. He replied in kind. The bruising of two eggshell-tender egos and a bottle of vodka—and murder, involving two essentially decent people—was done. And two brilliant careers wasted."

"Did he push the car into the water with her in it?"

"He may well get off with manslaughter," Dalrymple backpedaled, "if a jury believes his story."

Keegan's story was that Mary Ann, furious and drunk, jumped into her car on the gently sloping beach and released the emergency brake, holding her door open to yell obscenities back at him. She belatedly tried to start the car but wasn't paying attention to her clutch work or her steering, and by the time she began turning the car around, it was too late. It lurched into the water like the Toyota, with Libby at the wheel, had jerked into an oncoming lane between two blind curves just the other night.

"Your client claims his first thought was of your foretelling this very thing at the beach house in Malibu, Charlie. His second was that the door was still swinging open, and Mrs. Leffler had gotten out before she actually hit the water and so could save herself. He drove off in an equally inebriated state without making sure she was safe. He knew she could swim. He swore she was doing just that and was on her way to shore as he turned his car around to leave. She might have had too much alcohol in her body to get it there. The reservoir falls off quickly. He made it home without being pulled over and says he didn't know she was dead until he watched the wrecker pull her car out of Rizzi Reservoir on the evening news the next day."

"Do you believe him?"

"Frankly, his story is complex and fantastic enough to be true. Then again, the man's a writer."

You're learning. "More to the point, Keegan's persuasive in an honest rather than a slick way, and he's impressive verbally.

He could clean up on a jury. He's pitched to the pros. Irma, Maurice, and Dr. Podhurst, on the other hand, are going to look very strange in court."

"The courts will, I'm sure, impose penalties, possible prison sentences, and probable probationary terms in the death of Gloria Tuschman. But the department has decided not to bring murder charges in that death. There's no excuse for the cover-up of an accidental death that way—"

"When did you decide on accidental . . . for sure?"

"We suspected the possibility when we connected the stair railing to the blunt object that killed Mrs. Tuschman and the fact the floor in that hall had been waxed the day before. And we have located your security guard, Mr. Maypo, and both the body movers from the dumpster. But from the beginning, and overriding all, was your sense that Gloria thought she was still in a waste receptacle in that back hall and not in the alley and, later, your sense that it was indeed an accident."

"You trust my 'sense' that much, huh?"

"Gloria did, didn't she?"

"Oh, boy."

34

Charlie took a Saturday afternoon off from the household grind to go to the athletic field at Wilson High and watch Libby practice with her junior cheerleading squad, something inside her relieved that there was more to her life than her work. Without it, she'd still have her tiny family to justify her existence.

Yeah, but who'd pay for it?

That evening, while they were folding laundry, Libby surprised her mother with, "Mom, if you're not psychic, how did you figure out all that stuff about how Gloria died and that Mary Ann would drown?"

"I didn't." And Charlie explained, it seemed for the trillionth time, how each of her conclusions was based on fact, or at least logic, and not psychic fantasy. "And I just said Mary Ann was underwater in her car to get them off my case so I could get back to the agency. Haven't you ever blurted out something and wondered where it came from?"

"No." Libby added another piece of folded nothing to her pile. It was getting harder to tell the underwear from the bathing suits.

"Well, you're young. Besides, I was wrong. She wasn't inside her car."

"Okay, then why was Gloria asking you for help when she was dead in that creepy hallway?"

"I'll admit that's a stickler. But there's a rational explanation for everything, Libby."

"I know." Libby somehow slipped her sandals under her butt and raised herself to a standing position in one graceful movement. "We just can't always figure out what it is."

Libby glided between piles of folded laundry to fondly muss Charlie's hair. "*You* are seriously anal."

Libby headed for the front door.

"Where're you going?" We have to have a talk about the cat. "Do you have a baby-sitting job?"

"No, Mom, it's Saturday night. Everybody but you goes out on Saturday night. I'll put my stuff away tomorrow. Hey, if I can't make my medieval curfew, I'll call you, okay?"

"But we have to talk about the cat," Charlie told the closing door.

Charlie was on her feet before she knew why, before she registered the familiar sound outside. A sound like the death throes of a dinosaur.

She was through the door and had let the security grate close and lock her out of her own home before she recognized the rusting hulk of Jesus Garcia's challenge to birth control lurch off down the street.

Tuxedo watched Charlie's inelegant reaction from the comfort of an inside windowsill. As if in commentary, he gracefully pointed the toes of a rear foot toward the ceiling and washed that portion of his anatomy at the very base of his tail.

FOR THE BEST IN PAPERBACKS, LOOK FOR THE

In every corner of the world, on every subject under the sun, Penguin represents quality and variety—the very best in publishing today.

For complete information about books available from Penguin—including Pelicans, Puffins, Peregrines, and Penguin Classics—and how to order them, write to us at the appropriate address below. Please note that for copyright reasons the selection of books varies from country to country.

In the United Kingdom: For a complete list of books available from Penguin in the U.K., please write to *Dept E.P., Penguin Books Ltd, Harmondsworth, Middlesex, UB7 0DA.*

In the United States: For a complete list of books available from Penguin in the U.S., please write to *Consumer Sales, Penguin USA, P.O. Box 999—Dept. 17109, Bergenfield, New Jersey 07621-0120.* VISA and MasterCard holders call 1-800-253-6476 to order all Penguin titles.

In Canada: For a complete list of books available from Penguin in Canada, please write to *Penguin Books Canada Ltd, 10 Alcorn Avenue, Suite 300, Toronto, Ontario, Canada M4V 3B2.*

In Australia: For a complete list of books available from Penguin in Australia, please write to the *Marketing Department, Penguin Books Ltd, P.O. Box 257, Ringwood, Victoria 3134.*

In New Zealand: For a complete list of books available from Penguin in New Zealand, please write to the *Marketing Department, Penguin Books (NZ) Ltd, Private Bag, Takapuna, Auckland 9.*

In India: For a complete list of books available from Penguin, please write to *Penguin Overseas Ltd, 706 Eros Apartments, 56 Nehru Place, New Delhi, 110019.*

In Holland: For a complete list of books available from Penguin in Holland, please write to *Penguin Books Nederland B.V., Postbus 195, NL-1380AD Weesp, Netherlands.*

In Germany: For a complete list of books available from Penguin, please write to *Penguin Books Ltd, Friedrichstrasse 10-12, D-6000 Frankfurt Main 1, Federal Republic of Germany.*

In Spain: For a complete list of books available from Penguin in Spain, please write to *Longman, Penguin España, Calle San Nicolas 15, E-28013 Madrid, Spain.*

In Japan: For a complete list of books available from Penguin in Japan, please write to *Longman Penguin Japan Co Ltd, Yamaguchi Building, 2-12-9 Kanda Jimbocho, Chiyoda-Ku, Tokyo 101, Japan.*

FOR THE BEST IN MYSTERY, LOOK FOR THE

□ **THE PENGUIN COMPLETE FATHER BROWN**
G.K. Chesterton

Here, in one volume, are forty-nine sensational cases investigated by the high priest of detective fiction, Father Brown, whose cherubic face and unworldly simplicity disguise an uncanny understanding of the criminal mind.
718 pages ISBN: 0-14-009766-X

□ **BRIARPATCH**
Ross Thomas

This Edgar Award-winning thriller is the story of Benjamin Dill, who returns to the Sunbelt city of his youth to attend his sister's funeral—and find her killer.
384 pages ISBN: 0-14-010581-6

□ **APPLEBY AND THE OSPREYS**
Michael Innes

When Lord Osprey is murdered in Clusters, his ancestral home, with an Oriental dagger, it falls to Sir John Appleby and Lord Osprey's faithful butler, Bagot, to pick out the clever killer from an assortment of the lord's eccentric house guests. 184 pages ISBN: 0-14-011092-5

□ **GOLD BY GEMINI**
Jonathan Gash

Lovejoy, the antiques dealer whom the *Chicago Sun-Times* calls "one of the most likable rogues in mystery history," searches for Roman gold coins and greedy bird-killers on the Isle of Man.
224 pages ISBN: 0-451-82185-8

□ **REILLY: ACE OF SPIES**
Robin Bruce Lockhart

This is the incredible true story of superspy Sidney Reilly, said to be the inspiration for James Bond. Robin Bruce Lockhart's book tells the thrilling story of the British Secret Service agent's shadowy Russian past and near-legendary exploits in espionage and in love.
192 pages ISBN: 0-14-006895-3

□ **STRANGERS ON A TRAIN**
Patricia Highsmith

Almost against his will, Guy Haines is trapped in a nightmare of shared guilt when he agrees to kill the father of the man who will kill Guy's wife. The basis for the unforgettable Hitchcock thriller.
256 pages ISBN: 0-14-003796-9

□ **THE THIN WOMAN**
Dorothy Cannell

An interior designer who is also a passionate eater, her rented companion who writes trashy novels, and a rich dead uncle with a conditional will are the principals in this delicious thriller. 242 pages ISBN: 0-14-007947-5